Book One

Deadly Reflection

Deadly Triad

Book One

Deadly Reflection

By

Nancy Kay

Deadly Triad

Deadly Revenge
Deadly Encounter

Desert Breeze Publishing, Inc.
27305 W. Live Oak Rd #424
Castaic, CA 91384

http://www.DesertBreezePublishing.com

Copyright © 2011 by Nancy Kay
ISBN 10: 1-61252-984-4
ISBN 13: 978-1-61252-984-4

Published in the United States of America
eBook Publish Date: July 1, 2011
Print Publish Date: September 1, 2012

Editor-In-Chief: Gail R. Delaney
Editor: Melanie Noto
Marketing Director: Jenifer Ranieri
Cover Artist: Jenifer Ranieri
Photography Credit: Joseph V. Schneider

Cover Art Copyright by Desert Breeze Publishing, Inc © 2011

Dedication

Among those who have enabled me to fulfill my dream of writing are fellow writers, stalwart friends, and loving family. They encouraged the seeds planted in my brain to take root. Yet the one who nurtured and pulled the weeds of doubt is my dear husband.

My Joe weathered neglect of both him and our humble home while providing the proper blend of criticism and encouragement to help me move forward and reach for my heart's desire. With gourmet skills he fed me; with wise intuition, he guided me.

With much love, I dedicate this first book to the man who made it possible.

Chapter One

Not bothering to shave, Nick McGraw pulled on shorts and yanked on a tee shirt. Once outside the cabin, he stretched his tight muscles and took a deep breath. The sharp-edged nip in the air would help clear out mental cobwebs.

He jogged beside Pine Shadow Lake, dredging up memories of kick-ass sunsets and of nights spent huddled by crackling campfires swapping scary tales with his buddies.

Old childhood haunts, *great* memories.

He'd come to Pine Bluffs for a vacation, traveling four hundred miles to escape an insane pace and a never-ending caseload.

"Damn it."

He smacked the whining mosquito flat against his bare arm. Too frigging bad locking up criminals wasn't as easy as swatting bugs. Damn well should be. If that were the case, thoughts about leaving Philadelphia PD wouldn't be bouncing around in his head like a damn rubber ball.

Nick couldn't remember the last time he'd had a decent night's sleep. Last night had been heaven. No sirens, no calls jolting him awake and sending him to another grisly crime scene. He'd planned to sleep in, to lounge away the morning in bed. But years of habit had won out.

Where the hell had the past fifteen years gone? The decision to move away from Pine Bluffs hadn't been his choice. The decision to return was. In Nick's mind, the sleepy little town provided the perfect spot to unwind and figure out where his life was heading.

Pine Bluffs, Pennsylvania, on the opposite end of the state from Philly. Opposite end of the chart for crime.

For the next two weeks, he planned to avoid anything having to do with law enforcement. This was *his* time. A long overdue vacation, and... what the hell?

Nick skidded to a stop.

Several sharp cries, followed by a high-pitched female shriek, made tension slam into his gut like a fist. From somewhere close by came the frantic sound of someone, or something, crashing through thick underbrush.

To his right was the lake, and on his left a steep slope led to swampland and the adjoining bog. The ruckus grew fainter and fainter, moving rapidly away, until only rustling leaves overhead and the eerie, distant call of a red-tailed hawk broke the silence.

Perspiration trickled down Nick's spine, and a steady breeze molded his tee shirt to his damp skin. Swirling up from the bog were smells he'd almost forgotten.

Moisture laden peat, thick as plush carpet, and an underlying hint of decay.

Then the wind shifted, and an all too familiar stench permeated the air around him. The hair on the back of Nick's neck rose and out of habit, he reached for his Walther PPK.

"Son of a bitch," he muttered, coming up empty-handed. He swiped at another friggin' mosquito. His off-duty weapon was locked up back at the cabin.

Gentle waves lapped the shore. Sunlight speared through a bank of clouds and danced on the lake's surface. Things appeared normal. Yet judging from what he'd heard, someone might be in trouble. Someone female.

Nick reached for his cell phone, then hesitated. Dragging Tom McGraw out for no good reason wouldn't sit well with Pine Bluffs' Chief of Police. And his cousin TJ, new to the force, would laugh his young ass off if it turned out a sluggish box turtle had scared the shit out of some silly girl.

Taking a deep breath, Nick closed his eyes and assessed the facts. Off duty, on vacation, sworn to protect and serve. He had no choice. Opening his eyes, he eased from the path and worked his way down the slick incline, testing each step like a cat stalking prey.

*****

After hurtling down an incline behind sixty-plus pounds of canine energy, Cassi Burke stopped with a bone-rattling jolt. She sat in an oozing quagmire, eye level with Rufus' plumed tail.

"Look at me," she snapped. "I'm covered with gunk, my shoes are gone, and I feel like I've been whipped."

Rufus stood statue-still, nose quivering, ignoring her. What in the world had possessed him? He'd pulled her from the path, paying no attention to her frantic cries, and dragged her through tangled underbrush into rank, murky darkness.

She unwound the leather lead and flexed her aching hand. Stinging cuts covered her bare arms and legs. Just great.

"I need a companion, not a damn sled dog." Cassi eased to her feet. What she needed was time to rewind, and for the plane carrying her parents to have soared instead of nose diving into the sea.

Tears stung her eyes.

Rufus was her *only* companion now. She wasn't ready to accept, or believe, the woman who'd come forward after the accident claiming to be her aunt. And she hoped coming to this quaint town from the suburbs of Pittsburgh in order to meet this long lost relative had not been a big fat mistake.

She swiped a hand across her eyes, crouched low, and peered into the surrounding shadows.

What is that smell?

Rufus lurched away, disappearing into the gloom.

"That's it." She scrambled after him. As she pushed through dense foliage, the swampy ground gave beneath her feet and seeped between her toes. Finally, frustrated and spitting mad, she caught sight of the retriever's golden coat.

"Rufus, come here."

He spared her the flick of one ear. He'd heard her, but he made no move to obey. Instead, he crept forward, heading straight for a pile of sticks, leaves, and God knows what else. *Something* reeked to high heaven, and the hum of insects droned in her ears.

She seized the trailing leash. Too late. Rufus reached his goal, and amidst noisy snuffling and frantic pawing, he chomped down and tugged, using his weight, jerking hard until his prize pulled free.

"What the..." Cassi moved closer.

The dog averted his head.

"Rufus give me that," she whispered fiercely, yanking on his collar. Thick, foul-smelling globs flew in all directions. Nausea welled up inside her, and her knees buckled. She murmured, stunned, "Oh, my God."

The cutting edge of a knife protruded from Rufus' mouth.

"Oh, God. Rufus drop it. Drop it!"

Rufus hunkered down, clenching the knife's handle between his teeth.

Cassi dropped the leash, twisting and swiping at the gore sliding down her bare legs. Off balance, she smacked down hard.

She scooted backwards, stifling the urge to scream her head off.

"I'm all right, I'm all right," she repeated, willing her skittering pulse to settle. Shuddering, she wiped her sticky palms on her shorts.

Focusing on Rufus, she lured him close. "It's okay, fella. Come here, baby."

Gingerly, she pried the wet handle, covered with dog drool, from his mouth. Indescribable slime coated the blade. First, she gaped at the knife. Then her eyes shot to the congealing smears on her legs and every instinct screamed, 'Get the hell out of there! Drop the damn thing and run!'

But she didn't. After coming this far, like Rufus, she wanted to know what lay beneath that smelly heap of debris.

Get a grip, Cassandra.

She swallowed, hard, and rose onto her knees. With his ears perked and his eyes on the knife in her hand, Rufus leaned against her. She bent forward, and using the blade's tip, poked the rubble. Hand quivering, holding her breath, she lifted the top layer. One disgusting clump came free. She flung it away, choking and gasping. Determined, she tightened her grip and with a flurry of bravado, flicked away leaves, sticks, and dirt.

No. Oh, no.

Horrified, she stared at a pale, hairy, human torso covered with gaping wounds. Her stomach heaved. She recoiled, rapid heartbeats thundering in her ears.

"Police! Hold it right there. Drop the knife and don't move."

Cassi whipped around. Looming several feet away, cloaked in shadows, stood a man. Her eyes went from him to the mutilated body, then back. She ignored his harsh command and scrambled to her feet.

He strode closer, forcing her gaze up a tower of muscle. Dark stubble roughened his jaw line and, glinting in the dim forest, his hard, angry eyes locked with hers.

This was a policeman?

What kind of cop slunk around a swamp, hovering near dead bodies? The shoe did not fit.

"I said, put down the knife. Now!" The man wiped sweat from his brow, moved closer, and reached for her.

Cassi raised her hand, forgetting she still clutched the knife. He froze, muscles bunched like a jungle cat ready to pounce. Going light headed, she gulped in air and cast a furtive glimpse around. Except for the droning insects, hushed silence surrounded them.

She was alone, and at his mercy.

Almost.

Rufus pressed against her legs, emitting sounds somewhere between whines and growls.

Cassi dropped the knife.

"Get 'em!" she shouted, giving Rufus a hefty shove. Resisting, the stumbling dog crashed into the man.

"Damn it!" he yelled, as Rufus' big puppy feet tangled with his long legs. He skidded, arms windmilling, and landed flat on his ass.

"Son of a bitch."

Rufus took off running.

Cassi seized the moment and followed. If this was a cop, she'd face the consequences later. Right now, she just wanted to escape and get out this swamp.

But her bare feet slipped and she sprawled, full out, on the greasy slope. The man's hand closed on her ankle. He uttered an unintelligible growl and hauled her back, cursing and dodging her feet as she kicked and punched blindly.

"Stop it!" he ordered. "I'm a cop, damn it."

He lurched forward and flipped her over, flattening her beneath him. Grasping her arms, he pinned them to the ground.

She wriggled and twisted, soon deciding that bucking against his hard body was futile. Unable to escape his unrelenting grip, she screamed, point blank, into his startled face.

"Hold still," he panted. "And quit that bloody screaming."

Cassi went limp and squeezed her eyes nearly shut. "Please, please," she pleaded. "Don't kill me."

"Don't *kill* you?" he muttered. "What the hell?"

Chest heaving, he pulled out a cell phone and punched in a number. "TJ," he said after a moment, "grab Uncle Tom and haul ass out to Piney Bog. You've got a damn homicide out here, and I'm sittin' on a prime suspect."

Cassi's eyes shot open. "Who *are* you?"

He pocketed the phone, not saying a word. With fluid ease, he stood and pulled her to her feet. Immobile in his vice-like hold, her fight gone, she stared up at him.

Smears of mud covered her arms and legs. Her ruined clothes clung to her like wet rags. Beneath his bold assessment, she cringed, knowing that her erect nipples were clearly outlined and poked against her soaking wet, mud-stained tee shirt.

He lifted his gaze and leaned close, until they were nose to nose. "My name is Nick McGraw," he growled. "You can bet your cute little ass I *am* a cop. And don't even think about moving until the local police get here."

Dumbfounded, she stared into his furious eyes. This was unbelievable, bizarre. Could things get much worse? Cassi trembled and attempted a deep, calming breath, only to have the ever-present stench fill her nostrils. When she clapped a hand over her mouth, the man jerked back. Then he held her as she leaned over and lost her breakfast at his feet.

*****

Cassi looked down at her dirty, wet shirt. Compared to Officer TJ McGraw in his crisp uniform, she could pass for a mud wrestler. He'd accompanied her to the Pine Bluffs Police Station after doing a cursory search. He'd confiscated her car keys, her driver's license, and her watch. She'd received moist wipes and bottled water at the scene, and on the way to the station had been promised a shower and dry clothes. So far, she'd gotten neither.

The day had become a nightmare.

A rough-textured blanket the police had provided failed to stop her teeth-rattling shudders. She lifted the hem of her filthy shirt and sniffed. Her throat contracted, and she gagged. She'd never forget that smell.

Huddled on a hard, straight-backed chair, she listened to muffled voices through a closed door, straining to understand.

"Holy shit, TJ, where did you learn to do a search?"

She recognized *that* voice. He'd scared her witless, appearing out of nowhere, yelling at her.

"Look, Nick," TJ shot back, "just because you're a big city detective, doesn't mean you can butt into my investigation."

Her head spun. Two McGraws? Officer TJ McGraw, the one who'd brought her in, had just confirmed that the scary man was not only another McGraw, but a cop, too.

Their encounter flashed through her mind. Up 'til now there'd been no mention of an arrest, but she'd been found with a dead body and had assaulted the policeman who'd found her.

Well, shit. Just lock the cell and toss away the key.

"In case you didn't notice," TJ continued, "she wasn't wearing much. I could see right through that shirt, and those shorts fit her like a second skin. You know how careful male officers have to be." Lowering his voice, he added, "But, man, what a body."

Cassi pulled the scratchy blanket tighter.

"Yeah, well... I found that *great body* crouched over a corpse with a knife in her hand," Nick pointed out. "And you're worried about touching her tits? I'd sure as hell have searched every inch of that body."

Now Cassi loosened the blanket. Heat crept up her neck and chased away the chill. His remark had been just plain crude, but the image of that tall, dark, dangerous-looking man searching her body made her *hot*.

Their voices faded, and a distant door closed.

Alone, Cassi waited in a small room with dingy yellow walls and recessed fluorescent lights. She rubbed her bare wrist and glanced around. A clock hung on the wall to her left. The second hand hovered just shy of the number ten and jerked in place. She stared, vaguely aware of the clock's steady whirring, mesmerized by its frozen hands.

Cassandra Burke wanted the ghastly day to end, and she wished to God she'd never left Fox Chapel, Pennsylvania.

*****

After closing his office door behind them, TJ gave Nick a once over. "You look like hell."

Nick glanced down at the streaks of dried mud covering his khaki shorts. "Shit, look at my clothes." He felt the seat of his pants. "That damn crazy dog of hers crashed into me, and I landed on my ass."

Twisting to get a better look, TJ scoffed. "Yep, that 'LL Bean' ass looks a little damp."

Frowning, Nick scrutinized himself, looking for more damage. Then he spied his spattered boots. "Guess I didn't move fast enough when she tossed her cookies, either."

He caught TJ's amused expression and shot him a dirty look. "What the hell do you find so funny?"

TJ chuckled. "You have to ask?" He swept his hand toward a chair. "Have a seat, cousin."

Nick eased onto the chair, grimacing as his wet pants molded to his butt. "What's your next move?"

"I'll call Rob Evans, the department photographer." TJ grabbed the phone, punching in numbers as he talked. "We'll comb the area Dad has already secured and have Rob get shots of the body and crime scene from all angles. Then we'll measure for cross reference and... Hey, Rob." TJ shifted his attention to the call.

Nick leaned back and folded his arms. He was impressed. He liked the way TJ took charge. More time had passed than he cared to admit since he'd last seen his young cousin. His career demands had made visits home almost non-existent.

Who would have thought TJ would end up in Pine Bluffs, Pennsylvania, working with his dad? The sight of him with Uncle Tom, both wearing the same uniform, had taken Nick by surprise. They looked alike, right down to their close-cropped hair. To see them side by side when they moved and talked was spooky.

His cousin had always been called TJ, short for Thomas Jacob. Good thing, Nick decided. Although most of the time people called TJ's dad *Chief,* having two Tom McGraws on the force could have been confusing.

Nick resembled them. McGraw men were tall and lean, but thanks to Mom's side of the family, his hair had deep auburn tones instead of Uncle Tom and TJ's eye-catching red.

TJ concluded his call. He made some notations, tossed down his pen, and turned to Nick. "As soon as Marcy gets here, Rob and I will head back to the scene."

Nick arched his eyebrows. "Marcy? That wouldn't be--"

Someone rapped several times on the office door.

"Enter," TJ said.

In burst a bright-eyed female police officer. There was no mistaking that familiar face and brimming energy.

"TJ, what's going on around here? I've never, ever been called in to work overtime. Is it true? We have a dead body in the bog?" Marcy glanced at Nick. She did a double take. "Nicky? Nicholas McGraw, is that you?"

He nodded.

Her eyes skimmed over him. Upon reaching his boot-clad feet, she wrinkled her nose. "You look a little rough there, Nicky. What brings you back to Pine Bluffs? Last I heard you were a big city detective in Philadelphia, right?"

She took a step back. "What happened to your clothes? You look, and smell, like you've been rollin' in the bog."

Nick smiled. Some things never changed. Marcy Williams still switched subjects and ran sentences end-to-end with amazing speed.

"Hello, Marcy," Nick said. "You're right. I'm a detective for Philly PD. I'm here on vacation, and yes, I managed to fall down in the bog, thanks to the very reason you'll be working overtime." He eyed her up and down. "You look good in uniform. What happened to being a teacher and saving the world's youth?"

While attending grade school with Marcy, Nick had been aware she planned to be a teacher someday. During summer vacations, she'd set up makeshift classrooms and coax him, along with any other willing bodies, to be her students.

Those sessions had usually ended in mayhem. But sometimes, on hot summer afternoons, they'd sprawl beneath the weeping willow in Marcy's backyard, listening as she read to them. The memory flashed vivid and sweet through his mind.

Somewhere along the way, Marcy's plans had changed.

"I made it to the student teaching stage," Marcy stated. "Then I realized schools weren't what they used to be. I wanted to discipline kids, make them listen and learn. The powers that be wanted to coddle them, to make sure nobody infringed on their 'rights'."

"So you became a cop?" Nick asked.

"I became a cop." She grinned from ear to ear. "I came back to Pine Bluffs, Chief McGraw got the process rolling, and here I am." She planted her hands on her well-rounded hips. "I'm the youth officer for the department."

He chuckled. Marcy would no doubt have an impact on the youngsters of Pine Bluffs. Before he could comment, she added, "Oh, and my last name is *Evans* now. My husband, Rob, is our resident photographer. We have two boys, ages five and seven, who know the difference between 'rights' and 'privileges'."

He digested all she'd said, and for some reason, was pleased that his childhood friend was happy with her life.

TJ broke in. "Can we continue this reunion later? Dad's waiting, and so is our suspect. She's soaking wet and needs dry clothes. A brief preliminary has been done. Can you handle it from here, Marce?"

"No problem, just fill me in and you can take off. Who is she, and have we charged her?"

"Her name is Cassandra Burke. *Miss* Cassandra Burke. And no, she has not been charged." He handed her a slim manila file. "Here's what we have. First, I want her made comfortable. After that, we find out what she has to say. Unless hard evidence turns up, we have a narrow window in which to question her. She hasn't asked to make any calls, so see where she wants to go with that. I want this done by the book."

He turned to Nick. "Will you write me up a statement? Tell me what you saw at the scene. Any details you can provide will help."

Nick pushed up from his chair. "I'll get right on it and have it to you by tomorrow at the latest."

"Good. Gotta run." TJ gathered his notes and left the room.

Marcy glanced up from reading the initial report. "Nick, how did you manage to get involved?"

He thought about it. "Before noon, I went for a run, and on my way back to the cabin I heard something."

"Something?"

"Yeah. Shouts, a couple of startled yelps."

"Like someone calling for help?"

"At first, I wasn't sure." Nick picked up a pen from TJ's desk and clicked it. "I tried to pinpoint a direction. That's when I noticed the smell."

"Hard to miss." She wrinkled her nose. "With the path so close to the bog, on warm days the air can be rank."

"No." He stopped clicking and flipped the pen onto the desk. "This was different. I've worked homicide, Marce. This smell sent a clear message."

Slowly, Marcy closed the file. "I'll look forward to reading your report." She glanced at her watch. "Now, I have to get moving or TJ will have my butt."

As they prepared to leave TJ's office, she turned and faced him. "Off the record, Nick, do you think she killed him?"

At first, figuring his opinion was best kept to himself, Nick didn't respond. He wasn't sure how long Marcy had been on the job or what she'd encountered so far. On the other hand, being hardnosed wouldn't help her. Other than firsthand experience, cops learned from one another.

"Forget I asked," Marcy said and started to turn away.

"Facts are what matter," he said, "not what we think."

His words stopped her. She swung around. "Go on."

Not wanting to point her in any one direction, Nick measured each word. "First, the man was dead, and he'd been dead a while. Trust me on that one." His wink brought a tiny smile to Marcy's lips. "Second, Cassandra Burke had a knife in her hand."

"Your statement will confirm that?"

"Yes. I'm an eyewitness. Now, number three is a combination of one and two. Together they'll create questions and give investigators a direction."

Marcy appeared thoughtful. "Maybe she'd known him, or knows who murdered him."

Nick grinned. "Good points, Officer Evans. See how the facts made you think?" He reached over and tugged on a lock of her hair. "Off the record, do *I* think she's a killer? Based on what I saw, not a snowball's chance in hell."

Head tilted, Marcy studied him. She opened the door, turned, and smiled.

"I'll talk to you later, Nicky," she said, and left.

Nick McGraw left the station, eager to return to his cabin and clean up. Aside from reconnecting with family and friends, his first day of vacation had sure as hell turned to crap.

*****

"Miss Burke, I'm Officer Marcy Evans. I have some dry clothes for you, and there's a shower down the hall where you can clean up and change."

Hunched beneath her protective blanket, Cassi eyed the female officer standing before her.

"I will remain with you while you do that," the woman concluded. "Do you have any questions?"

While loosening the blanket, Cassi met Officer Evans' dark eyes. "Yes. Yes I do. Am I being charged? And where is Rufus?"

"Rufus?" Looking puzzled, the officer flipped open the file. She looked inside, then raked an impatient hand through her dark, curly hair.

Cassi sat up straighter and dropped the scratchy cover. "I'm afraid he's lost. He's only a pup. I just got him from the shelter, and he'll be scared."

"Rufus is a dog?" Officer Evans cleared her throat. "Miss Burke. We have a corpse in the bog, an off-duty police detective, whom you allegedly attacked, and you're worried about your puppy?"

"I didn't stab that man," Cassi declared. "And maybe I shouldn't have sicced Rufus on Mr. Macho, but he just showed up and started yelling. How was I to know he wasn't the killer?"

The officer slowly raised one brow.

"Sure, he said he was a cop, but they're supposed to carry badges, and... and guns. No policeman *I* know wears shorts and skin tight tee shirts."

Officer Evan still didn't react.

Cassi's head threatened to explode. She slid to the edge of her chair. "Rufus is sweet-natured. He's loveable, not a guard dog. Instead of protecting me, he ran and knocked down--"

"Mr. Macho?" Marcy glanced up, then back at the file.

Cassi narrowed her eyes. "I think his name is McGraw, and he practically flattened me when I tried to get away. Then the police arrived. Lights flashed, sirens screamed, and Rufus just kept running. I can only hope he found his way back to Aunt Ada's."

The woman's dark tousled head shot up. "Ada? You mean Ada Blaine?"

"Yes." Now maybe she'd listen. But tears threatened, and Cassi almost crumbled when she admitted, "I just found out she's my aunt."

Marcy Evans closed the file and placed it aside. She retrieved a nearby box of tissues, and after handing them to Cassi, lifted the crumpled blanket and folded it.

"Let's get you cleaned up and into some dry clothes," she said gently. "Then you can call your aunt."

Cassi's brave defense evaporated. Her legs wobbled as Officer Evans helped her to her feet. How was she going to tell Aunt Ada, who had suddenly become her lifeline, she was a murder suspect on the verge of being arrested?

Chapter Two

The path skirting the bog from downtown Pine Bluffs was as busy as a thruway. Dismayed, TJ shook his head. He and Rob Evans threaded their way past kids on bikes and young mothers pushing strollers. He pressed ahead, cursing small town grapevine gossip. The air was repulsive and thick with flies, neither of which deterred the sightseers.

Unbelievable.

Up ahead, his dad blocked the way. Known as a stern but approachable chief of police, he now had to stop this flow of gawkers from trampling a crime scene.

TJ's dad held up his hand. "Okay, folks. I'm going to have to ask each and every one of you to turn around and head back into town."

Juggling sophisticated camera equipment, Rob collided with TJ. Carrying an inexpensive point-and-shoot model had been simpler, but the department's new 35mm, single-lens reflex offered greater flexibility.

A boy on his bike shot around them and skidded to a stop. "Is it true, Chief McGraw?" The kid's voice cracked. "Is there a dead body in the bog?"

In an attempt to hear Tom McGraw's answer, people surged forward. They spilled from the path, ignoring TJ's and Rob's struggles, adding to the problem.

"Listen up, all of you!" Chief McGraw demanded, eyes piercing the crowd. "We have a serious situation here, and we can't do our jobs with you people tromping all over the place. These woods will be pitch-black soon." He paused. Now he had their attention. "You don't want to be out here strolling around when that happens." He crossed his arms, not budging.

TJ ducked his head and hid a grin. He recognized his Dad's steely, no nonsense tone. The subtle hint might work.

Spying them, the chief motioned him and Rob forward.

"They're giving you looks, Dad," TJ remarked aside.

"Too bad. We're not dealing with someone having too many beers at the corner bar or an argument in the check-out at Sanders Market. We have a dead body here."

The pervading odor in the air left no doubt.

"Amen to that." TJ swallowed hard.

He was well aware that within moments of death, all bodily functions failed. The pungent smell was familiar to seasoned homicide cops, and TJ had been exposed during hands-on training. But the experience would be a first for many of Pine Bluffs' officers. One they wouldn't soon forget.

Despite the obvious decay, only an autopsy would determine the approximate time of death.

TJ ducked beneath the bright yellow tape marking the crime scene. He paused to help Rob with his gear. He gave brief instructions before moving to officers Chuck Long and Jake Montroy. They'd secured the scene, thank God. Nick, Miss Burke, and her damn dog had already contaminated the area enough.

Step by methodical step, Long, Montroy, and TJ set up a grid, working the site until light began to fade. They spent hours prying up clumps of peat, looking for anything that could lead them to a killer. But they found nothing.

Montroy handed TJ a chilled bottle of water. He gulped down half before pausing for a breath. Damn. He'd hoped to find something, anything.

His dad approached. "Nice job, son. You may be the youngest man in the department, but you've earned the men's respect."

With his degree, TJ damn well better know how to run an investigation, but praise from his Dad carried more impact than any piece of paper.

"Thanks, we're almost through here." He finished off the water. "I'll get your initial notes back at the station."

Training made TJ rigid about the importance of detailed notes. His mantra being, *If you don't write it down, it didn't happen.* Likewise, he was rigid about collecting evidence, and he approved of how the officers had measured the area, taken numerous photos, and prepared to remove the body from the scene. All while being plagued by a cloud of hovering insects.

"Hell of a situation," TJ swatted at the ever-present pests. "Almost lost my lunch."

"Since you have things under control, I'm heading back to town. His dad offered a grim smile. Did you get ID?"

"We have the knife and a damp looking wallet." TJ lifted two paper evidence bags. He had already double checked the evidence bags to be sure they were sealed and bore labels listing their contents, case numbers, date, time, and initials of the officer who'd collected the evidence. "They're going straight to the crime lab. I doubt we'll get any prints from the knife, but the wallet should give us a name and address."

"It's a start," his dad said.

"What we don't have," TJ noted, handing the evidence bags to Jake Montroy, "is this unfortunate guy's shirt."

His dad took a deep breath and nodded. "Yeah, I noticed. Hard to miss that little detail."

"Once they clean him up for an autopsy, we'll know more." TJ scanned the scene. Matching the shirt to the victim would be easy. All they had to do was find the damn thing. "I'll keep you posted, Dad."

The coroner indicated his work was done. Assistants from the county morgue moved in to place the victim in a body bag. They struggled as the gurney bounced over rough ground to the site, and donned plastic gloves to place the victim in a body bag. Debris from the bog, combined with the after-effects of death, intensified the odors wafting from the scene. And lifting the corpse caused a sickening, suction-like gurgle. After plopping the bag onto the gurney, the assistants moved their gruesome cargo to a waiting, nondescript van.

TJ peeled off his gloves, turned them inside out, and dropped them into a bag. Chuck and Jake followed suit.

"Thanks, guys," TJ said. "Check in as soon as you know something."

Evidence in hand, Jake left for the crime lab. TJ walked Chuck to his car.

"Follow the coroner to the morgue," he instructed. "I doubt they'll do an autopsy before tomorrow, but see if you can check out the victim's clothes. Maybe something of interest will turn up."

"Are we done here?" Chuck asked.

TJ nodded.

"We'll sweep the area one more time tomorrow. I'll assign an around-the-clock team to keep people away until then, though I think Dad's comment about being here after dark will give folks second thoughts." He shrugged. "It'll be a stretch of manpower, but we'll manage."

Chuck departed, and TJ returned to the scene. Trickles of murky water had begun to fill the indentation left by the body. At the sound of footsteps, he glanced up. Lon Peters approached. He looked a little worn.

TJ offered him a lopsided grin. "Quite a day, eh, Lonnie?"

"No shit." Lon pointed down the path. "I blocked the entrance with a big *Keep Out* sign. We'll need more than a sign, though, to keep the curious out of here."

"I'll see who Dad can shake loose from routine patrol." TJ dragged a hand over his face. "There should be at least two men at a time out here until we're done investigating."

Both men turned to stare at the murder scene.

"I'm sure by tomorrow Mother Nature will have reclaimed this little piece of her territory," TJ observed. "And unless our only suspect can be solidly linked to the crime, or something turns up with the body, we're screwed."

*****

Ada Blaine burst into Pine Bluffs PD. She headed straight for the officer on duty and flattened both hands on Frank Infantino's desk with a slap.

For hours, she'd been edgy, wondering why it had taken Cassi so long to walk the dog. Then she'd gotten the call. Not bothering to change clothes, she'd rushed to the station. Frank was used to seeing her in worn utility trousers and oversized denim shirts. He was used to her being warm and friendly, too. At that moment, however, Ada didn't feel warm or friendly. She was mad as a hornet.

"My niece, Cassandra, is here. I want to see her. Now."

Frank sat back in his chair, looking startled and peering up at her as she leaned over his desk.

"Mrs. Blaine, please step back," he asked politely. He stood and cleared his throat. "Will you please have a seat? Officer Evans is with your niece. I'll let them know you're here."

He waited.

Ada straightened, ignoring his invitation to sit. Arms crossed, she glared at the young police officer.

"Okay," Frank mumbled. After a long, tense moment, he conceded and left the room.

*****

"What's up, Frank?" Marcy asked.

Cassi looked up as another officer entered the room.

He glanced at her before addressing Marcy. "Ada Blaine is here. She's demanding to see her niece."

His words took a moment to register. Cassi was wiped out. Showering and dressing had been daunting while a complete stranger watched, although Officer Evans had been considerate throughout the process. Her cuts and scratches stung, and she'd had nothing to eat since breakfast -- which she'd tossed. They'd offered her food and soft drinks, but she'd declined, choosing to sip water instead. The twisting knot in her belly, combined with her raw throat, would not tolerate anything but water. The day had become a crazy cocktail, and *now* Aunt Ada had been added to the mix.

Marcy excused herself. After she left the room, Cassi slumped in her chair.

Ada Blaine claimed to be a blood relative. Claimed to be family. She'd had family, damn it. A wonderful mom, a funny, quirky dad. *They* were her family.

She'd been adopted, but it had never mattered. She'd been theirs, and they'd loved her.

They'd waited so long for their dream vacation, planning, saving every spare penny.

Then, that stupid phone call had changed everything. Their dream had ended before it began, and a cold, mater-of-fact voice had informed her that "no one survived the crash."

Cassi covered her face and sobbed. Once again, her world was falling apart. The registered letter from Ada Blaine claimed she was the sister of Cassi's long-deceased biological mother. Could she trust the sister of a mother who had abandoned her?

She wiped her eyes on the sleeve of her borrowed shirt. She could call Lanie, but right now if Lanie -- her club manager and possibly former best friend -- were here, Cassi would kick her ass. Lanie had insisted she connect with this new-found aunt, assuring Cassi she could run the business during her absence. So, Cassi had loaded Rufus into her Honda CRV and headed north to Pine Bluffs.

Now Rufus was missing, and she was about to be interrogated for murder. Under the circumstances, facing an aunt she hardly knew terrified her.

Could this day get any worse?

Chapter Three

Hands shoved into his pockets, Nick left Pine Bluffs PD behind. His long anticipated vacation was headed downhill on skids. After driving clear across the state, the detective wanted some down time, a respite from law enforcement.

And what happens? He lands smack in the middle of a gigantic mess. *Shit!*

The whole state of affairs just plain pissed him off. All he'd wanted was to take a simple, solitary jog by the lake.

But there she'd been, crouched over a dead body with a knife clutched in her hand. No way around that kind of *in your face* problem. In the process of detaining her for TJ, she'd fought like a wild animal. He'd had to physically pin her down.

That move had created a whole new set of problems.

Miss Cassandra Burke now kept popping into his mind, setting off x-rated mental reruns of her struggling beneath him in that transparent, wet tee shirt.

TJ's observation had been right on.

What a body.

Why in the hell did it have to belong to a murder suspect?

A killer headache threatened, and his swamp-logged, puked-upon boots squished with each step as Nick stalked up the drive to Tom and Mary McGraw's rental cabin. His aunt and uncle's rustic log structure was his to use while he was in town. Bless them.

He climbed the steps, crossed the plank porch, and pried off his hiking boots. Cleaning them could wait. On the way to the shower, he stripped.

The compact bathroom was unadorned but functional. Minutes after stepping into the dated moss green bathtub, a powerful hot spray rained down on him, making up for the cramped quarters and butt-ugly decor. After the shower, rejuvenated, he pulled on comfortable jeans and a fresh tee shirt, and grabbed a cold beer.

The screen door creaked as he stepped outside. After settling into a high-backed rocker, Nick pondered the day.

He tried to focus and separate Miss Burke's curvy body from known facts. Something didn't fit. The whole situation was cockeyed. When he examined details, his well-honed instincts screamed *wrong suspect,* and Nick gave himself a mental kick in the ass.

Less than a year ago, those same instincts *had* failed him. He'd almost blown a major case. As a result, several good officers had narrowly escaped with their lives. The incident -- one of the reasons he'd returned to Pine Bluffs -- still haunted him.

Damn if he'd repeat that colossal mistake.

Movement near the wood line caught his eye. The four-legged culprit responsible for his sore butt walked into the clearing and sat, panting hard. Nick put his beer down and stood, moving slowly to avoid spooking the silly pooch.

"Here, Rufus. Come here, boy."

Rufus' jaw snapped shut. He leaped to his feet, quivering and poised to run. Nick opened the door and slipped into the cabin. He returned gripping a leftover sandwich.

After sniffing the air, Rufus perked his ears. The sharp tang of bologna and cheese proved irresistible. Within moments, Rufus was gulping down chunks of food. When he finished, using his tongue to get every crumb, he raised his hopeful eyes to Nick.

"You're quite a guy." Rubbing the dog's velvety ears, Nick picked up the trailing leash. Rufus waved his feathery tail and bumped against him, depositing wet smears on his clean jeans.

"Shit," Nick muttered, then he softened. The poor pup must have been terrified. "Come on, fella."

Inside the cabin, Nick unsnapped the leash and filled a pan with water. Rufus lapped until the pan scooted across the floor, empty. After wolfing down another hastily made bologna sandwich, the dog turned in small circles and dropped onto a rug with a muffled 'woof'. His tail gave a half-hearted thump. Emitting a deep sigh, he closed his eyes.

Moving about the kitchen, Nick refilled the water bowl and stowed the leftover meat and cheese in the refrigerator. All while the exhausted dog slept, his sides rising and falling rhythmically.

An hour passed, during which Nick comprised a detailed account of his take on the incident. Sorting through a stack of folders -- casework he should have left behind -- Nick located an empty one and tucked the report inside for TJ.

He glanced at his watch. Whether he wanted to or not, he kept getting dragged into his cousin's case. After one last check on the sleeping dog, he slipped out the door.

Darkness closed in around him, and a deep woods chorus struck up as Nick headed back toward town. He missed the chirping, trilling background that had once lulled him to sleep on balmy fall nights. Along with the smoky, musky scent of autumn leaves, the familiar sounds stirred great memories.

He jogged the last stretch into town and approached the police station. Cars lined the street and groups of curious onlookers milled about.

Damn circus.

After giving a brisk nod to some familiar faces, Nick took the front steps two at a time and stepped inside, closing the door behind him. He stopped and scanned the room in disbelief.

Holy shit.

The place looked like an auction house on Saturday night. Officer Infantino manned the desk. His dark eyes radiated fatigue as he listened, phone wedged to his ear, and scribbled rapid notes.

Nick approached. "Is that an emergency?"

Frank mouthed an exaggerated, 'No.'

Resting one hand on Infantino's shoulder, Nick advised, "Let the emergency system work, Frank. Tonight the calls will be from nosey civilians, people seeing shadows, or hungry media. Tomorrow will be worse. Get some extra help to field calls, and free up the men for more important duties."

Ending the call, Frank squared his shoulders and stood.

"Excuse me." The hum of voices continued. Frank cleared his throat. "Pardon me."

No visible response.

"Hey!"

Every eye in the room zoomed to the rumpled-looking cop.

Stifling a grin, Nick stepped aside. Everyone now had a clear view of the bristling officer.

"Who is here on police related business?" Frank demanded, his weary gaze sweeping the silent room. "Need to report a crime? Take a seat. Incidents will be handled in order of importance. If you don't have a good reason to be here, please leave. This is a police station, not town hall."

Amidst shuffling feet and muttering, the room slowly emptied. Only two individuals remained, and they arrowed straight to a bench along the wall.

"Thank you." Frank's voice was calmer.

"Where's your dispatcher?" Nick asked.

"She has the day off, and I can't reach her. She isn't due to report until second shift tomorrow."

Eying Frank's advanced five-o'clock shadow, he asked, "When was your shift up?"

"Four hours ago. I haven't had a day like this since I've been on the job." Frank grabbed the phone and punched in a number. He waited, frowning and rubbing two fingers between his bloodshot eyes. "Hi, it's Infantino. Will you pick up calls? I need a break to organize things and get a handle on this situation."

After a pause, he smiled. "Thanks. I owe you."

Frank hung up and turned to Nick. "Emergency dispatch will handle calls for a while. I'm going to hit the head before I call out for food. Thanks, by the way. I'm so darned tired. Asking dispatch for help didn't occur to me. We're not staffed for this kind of sh--" He glanced at Molly Hirtzel and Ed Galbraith, who were waiting patiently. "Uh... stuff."

"No problem." Nick clapped him on the back. "Happens to the best of us."

Frank turned his attention to the glum expressions of the man and woman on the bench. "Mr. Galbraith, Miss Hirtzel, do either of you need help immediately?"

In unison, their two heads moved from left to right.

Then Molly Hirtzel darted a look at the man sitting beside her and cleared her throat.

"No, Officer Infantino. I know the 'head' is the men's room. And neither Mr. Galbraith's vandalized fence, nor my crushed flower beds, are more important than your... umm... personal needs."

Color flushed Molly's cheeks, and she tucked a strand of loose hair behind one ear. Ed Galbraith pursed his lips and drew his bushy eyebrows together, but didn't say one word.

Frank left the reception area and disappeared down a hallway. After making sure calls were being forwarded as requested, Nick followed. Footsteps echoing, he glanced into several unoccupied offices where desks appeared as boxy shadows. Drawn by light spilling from within, he stopped outside Chief McGraw's office. The chief had his nose buried in a file.

He looked up when Nick paused in the doorway.

"Evening, Uncle Tom." Nick studied the older man. He still appeared fit, with a minimal amount of gray hair, but tonight his uncle's eyes looked weary. Nick leaned against the door frame and shoved his hands into his pockets. "Have you eaten?"

"Not yet. Mary's holding dinner. We'll all be pulling some OT the next few days." He leaned back, lacing his strong fingers behind his head. "Frank stopped on his way past. Said you gave him a hand out front."

"Hope I didn't step on any toes."

"Your concern is appreciated. Infantino is a little green, but he's coming along. I'm sure you didn't jump down his throat like some damn know-it-all. Let's head out front so I can keep an eye on things while Frank takes a break."

On their way, Nick noticed light beneath the door where the enticing Miss Burke was being questioned. Too bad Pine Bluffs PD didn't have two-way viewing. He would have liked to have watched TJ question the lady.

*****

Cassi's stomach dropped like a rock when Ada Blaine stormed into the room. Without so much as a glance at the two officers, she crossed to Cassi, knelt, and wrapped her in a warm hug.

At first shocked and unsure, Cassi didn't respond. Officer Evans dragged another chair over beside Cassi's.

"I'm staying with you," Ada said. Keeping one arm firmly around Cassi, she sat and faced the two officers. "I'm staying with her."

She turned back to Cassi. "Are you all right?"

Cassi could only nod. Exhausted, she leaned against her aunt and lifted her gaze to the waiting officer.

Over the next couple of hours, Cassi answered endless questions interspaced with frequent breaks.

More than once, Ada expressed her displeasure. Her fierce defense and protectiveness surprised Cassi, making her almost ashamed she'd doubted the woman.

Finally, Officer McGraw pulled a chair close to the table, placed one foot on the time-worn seat, and balanced a clipboard on his knee. "I want to go over your previous information one more time. Is that all right with you, Miss Burke?"

"TJ, let's get this nonsense over with." Ada's outburst made Cassi jump. Her aunt's arm tightened around her.

Cassi cleared her throat.

"I'm fine. Really," she added, when Ada looked over and titled her head.

Cassi sipped from the water bottle clutched in her hand and returned TJ McGraw's steady gaze. "Yes, Officer, I'm okay with answering your questions."

He gave a curt nod and referred to his notes. "You own a fitness club in the community of Fox Chapel, Pennsylvania. Is that correct?"

"Yes." Cassi took a deep breath. They'd been over this ground. Did he think she was lying? With renewed confidence and a need to regain her self esteem, she added, "I have a degree in exercise science, and I'm a licensed dietician."

Ada chimed in, "She finished at the top of her class in college."

For a moment, Cassi forgot about the questions and turned to her aunt. How did she know?

"How long have you been in town?" Officer McGraw interrupted.

Cassi managed to give her aunt a weak smile, and then turned back to the officer. "I arrived late yesterday."

"What brought you here?"

"I came to--"

"She came to visit me," Ada snapped. "She's never been here before."

Officer McGraw glanced from Ada to Cassi, and then looked back at his notes. He rolled his shoulders and tilted his head from side to side. Releasing a long, slow breath, he set the clipboard aside and tossed his pen onto the table.

Was he finished? Cassi's throat felt raw, and she lifted the water to her parched lips.

He swung around. "You never visited your aunt before. Why not?"

"Because I didn't know she existed." Cassi's voice cracked. The water bottle slipped from her hand and hit the floor with a thud. Tears welled in her eyes, and she choked on a sob.

Ada shot up. Her foot hit the dropped bottle and sent it spinning across the room, leaving a trail of water in its wake. "I think it's time for me to call my attorney."

Officer Evans shot a look at McGraw, who clamped his mouth shut.

"Well?" Ada prompted. "Cat got your tongue, young man?"

Just then, someone wrapped on the door several times. McGraw gave Ada a hard look, then turned and strode to the door. After a brief conversation with someone in the hallway, he excused himself and left the room, closing the door behind him.

*****

TJ followed Officer Long into a nearby office. Hours had passed since he'd sent Chuck to the morgue. He'd instructed him to find out what he could and then swing by the lab for anything they might've turned up. He hoped Long possessed information that would help him make a decision. Thus far, TJ had conducted the interview by the book, but they were on borrowed time. He had to either charge Cassandra Burke or let her go.

Ada Blaine's mother hen response surprised him. She could have stopped him from questioning her niece sooner, but she'd known TJ since he was a boy, so maybe she had taken that into account and was being generous with Pine Bluffs PD.

Instinct told him to look for a seasoned killer. The young woman waiting with her *pillar of the community* aunt didn't fit the mold. But facts couldn't be ignored. Cassandra Burke had been caught at the scene, and she'd had the murder weapon in her hand. *Alleged* murder weapon, he corrected.

But what if she was lying? What if she'd been in town for three days, and not two?

He'd tread on thin ice with too damned many *ifs*.

Exhaustion muddled his thoughts. He led Chuck into the empty office and flipped on the light, hoping like hell the man had some concrete information. Depending on what he learned, he'd either read the woman her rights and arrest her or let her go.

Long looked tired. His red-rimmed eyes sported dark circles beneath them.

"I have a report from the coroner." He opened a folder and flipped through several pages. "They did the autopsy late this afternoon. The bog was a dump site. He was murdered, but not in Piney Bog. His name is Robert Morelli."

"Morelli," TJ mused. He rubbed at tension plaguing his neck. "How long had he been dead?"

"Approximately twelve hours, give or take an hour either way. The listed cause of death is multiple stab wounds to the chest." Chuck handed over the file bearing the report.

TJ flipped through several pages, mentally tucking away certain details. Then with the closed folder in hand, he returned to the room containing Cassandra and her aunt.

After closing the door, TJ asked point blank, "Miss Burke, do you know a man named Robert Morelli?"

"No." Cassandra reached for Ada Blaine's hand. "No, I don't."

"You're free to go. I'd like to know where you'll be staying in case I have more questions."

Ada helped Cassandra to her feet. "She'll be with me for a couple weeks, and you know where I live."

"Yes ma'am," TJ replied, then stepped aside as Ada swept her niece out the door. He followed them to the front desk, strangely relieved he didn't have to arrest Miss Burke, but pissed that he still had an unsolved murder on his hands.

*****

Nick perched on the edge of Frank's desk to talk and kill some time. At the sound of footsteps, he looked up. Cassandra emerged from the hallway and stopped. His eyes trailed over her. When he met her unwavering gaze, she stiffened her spine and crossed her arms.

TJ approached the desk.

"I'm releasing Miss Burke to her aunt, Frank. I believe we have some of her personal items." He turned back to Cassandra. "Everything will be returned except your clothes. They're evidence. They'll be returned when the investigation is complete."

Judging by her abrupt nod and the stubborn set of her jaw, Cassandra didn't like the idea they'd be keeping her clothes.

Frank returned with an envelope. He slit the seal, and after removing an attached form, slid her watch, her driver's license, and a single key onto the desk.

"Please confirm that I've returned the items listed to you," he said, placing the form in front of her.

Squaring her shoulders, Cassandra stepped forward. She glanced at the items and snatched up a pen. Her hand shook as she signed her name.

Ada scooped Cassandra's belongings from the desk and dropped them into her shoulder bag. She drilled TJ with a steely look. "You can call or stop by tomorrow if you need to check and see if Cassandra made a get-away during the night."

Nick raised his brows. He looked to see if TJ flinched.

"I'll do that, Ada." TJ looked right back. "We *will* find out who's responsible for that man's death."

Ada steered her niece toward the door.

Nick's gaze slid down Cassandra's ramrod stiff back and settled on the soft curve of her hip. "Not enough evidence to charge her, huh?"

"They surprised the hell out of me and did the autopsy already." TJ held up the report. "But nothing jives."

"Hmm. How'd the interview go?"

"She admitted picking up the knife. Her answers were consistent. According to her statement, she's been here for two days, counting today. Lividity tells us the body was moved after death. Taking the body's weight and temperature into account, they determined the victim's been dead at most fourteen hours, probably closer to eleven or twelve."

"She'd have had to kill him her first night in town, and then moved the body," Nick surmised. "Connecting her might be a bit of a stretch, don't ya think?"

"Maybe," TJ admitted. "Though she insists she doesn't know the victim, was adamant about it. She did notice the smell. Says she thought maybe it was a dead animal. Claims her dog found the knife and she took it away from him, and that was when she discovered it was a dead human."

"That puts her prints on the weapon."

"You're right. Maybe the position of the prints will support her statement, if it's true. But maybes aren't enough for an arrest."

After saying goodnight to Frank, the pair moved toward the door.

"I trust Ada," TJ continued. "If she says her niece will stay put, she will."

"Damn." Nick exclaimed, hurrying forward. "I forgot to tell Miss Burke I found her dog."

"Hold it, Nick. Where's the dog?"

"At the cabin. He showed up tired, hungry, and thirsty a couple of hours ago. Probably still sleeping off the bologna sandwiches I fed him."

"Could you hang on to him 'til tomorrow?" TJ followed Nick through the door. "I'll drop you off on my way home. I want to take a look at him."

"The dog?"

"Yeah, the dog. I'll notify Miss Burke in the morning. I need to see all the players in this little event. The more I know, the better." He poked Nick with his elbow. "Besides, from the way you've been ogling her, I figure you'd like her to drop by and thank you personally for rescuing her pooch."

Nick paused, narrowed his eyes at his smart-ass cousin, and then followed him out into the cool autumn night.

Chapter Four

Cassi rubbed her eyes. They burned as if sand had been tossed in her face. Last night when at last she'd crawled into bed, she'd been exhausted; her mind, numb. Awakening this morning had been like climbing from a deep well.

Her eyes flew open.

Rufus!

Where could he be? Was he safe, hungry?

Frightened?

Before she'd fallen asleep, Ada had placed a quilt over her, lowered the lights, and assured her that everyone in town would be on the lookout for her lost dog. She'd clung to that small thread of hope.

Her suspicions about Ada seemed trivial after the woman had stormed to her rescue last night. Without hesitation, she'd come to Cassi and stood by her. Ada Blaine's brisk efficiency and natural warmth restored Cassi's trust. Something she'd feared she'd lost after her parents' deaths.

With a yawn that threatened to unhinge her jaw, she settled against the old oak headboard. Her muscles protested, and she rested a moment, smoothing the quilt over her legs and gazing around.

Shuttered windows topped with colorful valances lined two of the walls. They weren't frilly colorful, but were in strong, earthy tones of red and gold, like a forest in autumn.

Above the shutters a marine blue sky peeked through fast moving clouds. Distant birds rode high currents. If she could only freeze the morning's calm beauty.

Several taps on the door jolted her back.

"Yes, come in."

The door opened, and Ada entered.

"Good morning." Steam rose from the tray she carried, creating a tiny trail as she crossed the room. On it were a small tea pot, a cup, and a fragrant muffin. She placed the tray on a stand by the bed. "I have good news. Rufus has been found, and he's fine."

Cassi pressed a hand to her heart and sighed.

"Did you sleep well?" Ada patted her shoulder.

"I did." Cassi swung her legs over the edge of the bed. The news about Rufus gave her a spurt of energy, and the aroma from the tray made her mouth water.

"Sometimes the body shuts down in order to survive. Self-preservation is a strong emotion." Ada pulled up a chair. "Help yourself. We missed dinner last night. I figured you'd need something as soon as you woke up."

Between bites of muffin and sips of richly creamed tea, they rehashed the previous day. Ada laughed when Cassi relayed her mad dash through the bog, but her description of how Rufus had discovered the body sobered them both, as did reliving the session at the police station.

"I suppose I was a little hard on TJ McGraw," Ada remarked. "I've known him and Nick, the hunky one you met in the bog, since they were kids."

Cassi choked on her muffin.

"Hunky? You surprise me." She took a sip of tea. "Scary would better describe that man. I never heard him sneak up behind me. Neither did Rufus. Tall, dark, and dangerous, and he slinks around like a cat."

Ada laughed. "I may be a generation ahead of you, honey, but I'm not blind. TJ and Nick are two handsome men."

"They're cousins, right?"

"Yes. Tom McGraw is Nick's uncle. He's been chief of police for years. I think he was surprised, and pleasantly so, when TJ returned to Pine Bluffs after college."

"Why was he surprised? From what I saw, they look like a close tight-knit family."

"Oh, they are. Don't get me wrong, TJ's a real asset to the Pine Bluffs department. I think maybe we all had the impression he wanted to get away from a small town and work for a larger department, like Nick."

Ada crossed the room and folded back the shutters. Light poured in. "With a criminal justice degree, TJ brought in new ideas to cope with changing times. We need to be ready when the world starts seeping into our little community."

She slid up the window, and a fragrant breeze swept through the room. The boldly colored curtains fluttered like fall leaves. "Looks like what turned up yesterday could be the start of those changes."

"Uh... Aunt Ada?" Cassi tested the unfamiliar title. She cast a worried glance at her aunt as she moved about making the bed. "Do they believe I killed that man? Should I call an attorney?"

"I talked to TJ this morning," Ada said. "He was pretty tight-lipped, though he did say the man's not from around here. They're trying to track down someone who knew him."

"Did TJ tell you about Rufus?"

"Yes. Your dog's at one of his mom's rental cabins, not far from here."

"His mom has cabins?"

"Tom and Mary own several along the shoreline."

Cassi slipped on her robe. "Who has Rufus?"

"TJ didn't say. Just gave me an address and said you could get him any time today."

"That's a relief. I'll go get him as soon as I shower and dress. Oh, and thanks for breakfast."

"You're welcome." Ada smiled, picking up the tray. "I've got late summer berries to harvest, and herbs to be cut, dried, and frozen. I'll have lunch ready when you get back with Rufus.

"Don't you have to hang herbs to dry?"

Ada laughed. "Heavens, no. Haven't you ever heard of a microwave? I'm an old fashioned girl, Cassandra. But I like new tricks, especially ones that save time."

She left the room and closed the door behind her.

Cassi studied the closed door. How interesting it was going to be getting to know this sage, earthy woman who had just stepped into her life.

A short time later, she gathered her keys and prepared to leave.

Her aunt reappeared. "Lock your car doors. The cabin is a short drive, but for now, I want you to be careful."

The thought had crossed Cassi's mind. Her keys jingled when she gave them a little toss. It was darned nice to have somebody care enough to remind her.

Streaks of sunlight streamed through the banks of clouds as she left her aunt's cottage. Coolness lingered, but she was comfortable in worn jeans and a long sleeved tee shirt.

Ada's directions steered her along the lakeshore. As she drove along, an occasional roofline or stone chimney appeared between the trees. A short distance from downtown, she came upon two squatty stone pillars. She turned between them and followed a winding, narrow drive through the trees.

At the end of the driveway, she broke into a sunny clearing and approached a solitary, rough-sided cabin. An inviting porch skirted the building's front, graced by a rainbow assortment of mums. Tall maple trees in various stages of color created a postcard-worthy backdrop.

A charcoal gray Honda Ridgeline parked alongside the cabin told her someone must be around, yet the clearing seemed deserted. Not one sign of life.

A tremor passed over her.

Quit being such a wimp. The directions were clear, and the description fits.

She parked behind the truck, took two calming breaths, and emerged from her CRV.

*****

Cassandra looked taller than Nick recalled, but he'd never forget the impact of her thick-lashed eyes. Reminded him of rich chocolate. Snug denim hugged her endless legs, and when she stopped to push up her sleeves, her tee shirt molded to her body, drawing his attention to her lush curves.

Muscles drew tight low in his belly.

Several sharp barks erupted behind him.

"You know who's here, don't you fella?" He opened the door, and a blur of gold shot by.

Cassandra knelt to meet the four legged tornado. Rufus crashed into her, and she landed on the porch floor with a thump. He covered her face with wet, sloppy kisses, forcing her to shut her eyes tight.

"Rufus. Oh, Rufus... You're okay. I missed you, boy," she crooned, then dissolved into rolling laughter.

Nick waited in the doorway, thoroughly enjoying the way Cassandra's unrestrained hair tumbled free. The silken waterfall cascaded about her shoulders. For a brief moment, he imagined those honey colored, tangled waves spread out invitingly on a pillow.

His pillow.

Down boy, he chided himself. He stepped forward, grasped her hand, and pulled her to her feet.

"Thanks," she said with a gasp. She shoved her tousled hair from her eyes, and froze. "Oh... hello." Her voice cracked.

She just stood there, looking stunned and clutching his hand. Then she snatched hers away. Her eyes darkened. She straightened and adjusted her disheveled clothes.

"So you're the one who found my dog."

"Are you taking back your 'thanks' now that you see who you're dealing with?" Nick teased, liking her bravado.

She gave him a hard look, then her gaze slid away and focused on Rufus. "No, my thanks are sincere. I was worried about my dog. Finding him with you surprised me."

He studied her. What a strange combination of defiance and manners. She obviously remembered -- and resented -- how he'd manhandled her the day before, yet she was grateful because he'd rescued her dog. Her ingrained manners overrode her displeasure, or at least pushed it aside.

"Come inside," he suggested. "I'll get his leash."

He turned and walked into the cabin. Rufus trotted happily behind him, and after a long moment, Cassandra followed. As of that morning, no hard evidence had turned up linking her to the victim, Robert Morelli. Though TJ had made a point to inform Nick that she was still a *person of interest.*

Nick wanted to draw his own conclusions. He also wanted to settle things between them and learn more about her. His fingers brushed hers when he handed her Rufus' leash. Again, she jerked her hand away.

Unable to help himself, Nick grinned. "Still don't believe I'm a policeman?"

"I kind of figured it out at the police station," she answered. "Plus, Ada Blaine explained that you're a detective in Philadelphia." She crossed her arms and gave him a stony look. "Regardless, I think you over reacted yesterday."

"I'm not going to apologize for tackling you. You tried to run after I found you holding a knife over a dead man and--"

"You took me for a cold-blooded killer." Cassandra's eyes simmered like hot cocoa. "I thought *you* were the killer."

He started to speak, but she stabbed a rigid finger at him, right beneath his nose, and he snapped his mouth shut.

"All I could think about was getting away before you killed me, too. That's why I ordered my dog to attack."

Nick held his tongue.

This wasn't going well. He didn't want to fight with her.

From across the room came a muffled snort.

They both turned. Cassandra dropped her hand and sputtered out a laugh. Her ferocious attack dog lay curled on the hearth, sound asleep.

Nick laughed, too. For the moment, they seemed to have reached a truce.

"I must say," Nick remarked as they walked to her CRV. "So far my vacation's been one hell of a trip. How about yours?"

"I'm not on vacation," she said.

Nick stopped beside her Honda. "Oh?"

She bit down on her lip and heaved a deep sigh. "The last six months have been... difficult." She slid on dark sunglasses, hiding her eyes.

"Then maybe it's time to put the last six months behind you." Rufus shot by them into the front seat when Nick opened the door. "I'd like to give you a call, Cassandra."

"My life's complicated right now. Being suspected of stabbing a man doesn't help. Besides, don't you think your being related to the officer investigating the case might be a problem?"

Nick closed her door, braced both hands on the vehicle's roof, and waited.

After some hesitation, the glass between them slid down. In one slick move, he plucked the sunglasses from her face and perched them atop her head.

"I don't see a problem at all, Cassandra."

"I'll think about it." She repositioned the glasses. "And... my friends call me Cassi."

She shifted gears and drove away.

*****

Cassi rolled down the window and let the wind tangle her hair. Upon entering the outskirts of Pine Bluffs, she adjusted her speed. Rufus stuck his head out the window and tested the breeze. She'd left Nick McGraw behind, standing all alone beside that charming log cabin with his hands thrust into his pockets.

Mentally, however, he'd come along for the ride.

The man fascinated her. His every move reflected calm inner strength, probably from being a cop. She'd never dated a cop before. They came to her club to keep fit, and remembering how he'd landed on her like a slab of pure muscle yesterday, she'd bet Nick worked out to keep in shape.

Cassi admitted she liked the way his jeans sat low and snug on his narrow hips, and how the fine lines framing his tawny eyes deepened when he smiled. The way his riveting gaze had pinned her after he'd snatched off her sunglasses had caused her heart to leap into her throat.

She stopped for a red light and reached over to tug gently on Rufus' silken ear. "Rufus, if I keep picturing him, I'll be hanging out the window, pantin' like you."

The light turned green, and they shot ahead. No, getting involved with Nick McGraw had complications written all over it. For example, what would his cousin, not to mention his uncle, think about him dating a possible suspect? And why the sudden interest? Yesterday he'd turned her in, and today he seemed eager to get close to her.

Maybe too eager?

She tucked away *that* disturbing thought. No, she wasn't about to get tangled up with Nick McGraw, even *if* she changed her mind and decided to see him.

Rufus plopped his butt on the seat and sent her a flat-eared, happy dog smile. Cassi gave him a quick head rub.

"It's just you and me, pal," she said, and then she laughed. The air whipping in the window had warmed, and a decision about seeing Nick McGraw could wait.

Back at the cottage, she explored her aunt's domain. Fragrant herbs and thick berry bushes covered much of the property. The land sloped toward the lake, and a brick pathway leading to the tall grasses along the shore beckoned her.

In great detail, Ada had explained how the borough of Pine Bluffs had been formed at the northernmost tip of Pine Shadow Lake. Everywhere Cassi turned, picturesque beauty unfolded before her like bold watercolors on canvas.

Tall evergreens, mixed with stands of maple, rimmed the hills at the southern end of the lake. She hadn't known Northwestern Pennsylvania had once been covered by a glacier.

Interesting stuff for a city girl.

According to her aunt, the natural collection of moisture from glacial lakes had created a fragile environment for plants and animals -- a bog -- and the rich peat harvested from it was valuable. Perfect for the lush gardens before her.

"Ready for lunch?" Ada's voice made her jump.

Rufus scrambled up the porch steps. "Ada, this is beautiful. It's wild and rambling. Yet there's an order, symmetry to what you've created."

Ada's gaze roamed her gardens, and warmth crept into her eyes.

"It's nice to see you appreciate what I've done with my little piece of heaven beside the lake. Come in," she said, sliding the door open. "I've made some fresh herbed pumpkin soup."

"Umm, wonderful." Cassandra followed Rufus inside.

They carried steaming bowls of soup, tall glasses brimming with iced tea, and a basket of fragrant rolls onto the porch overlooking the gardens and lake.

After dining in companionable silence, Cassi set her empty bowl aside. "Tell me about my mother."

Ada swallowed her last bite of muffin. "I came along eleven months after your mother," she began. "Allie -- what I called her instead of Alice -- was the center of our parents' world until I arrived. Every time she reached a goal, I was right behind her. I was fierce about keeping up with her; she was fierce to outdo me."

Rufus woofed softly. Cassi rose and opened the door. He bounded down the steps, darting about to investigate clumps of grass and wispy stands of dill.

"So much energy." Ada laughed, shaking her head.

Then her laughter died. Squinting into the afternoon sun, she relayed story after story, some obviously painful, about growing up with Cassi's mother.

Cassandra filed away the details, absorbing them like a dry sponge. This was her family history.

"Why was my mother so jealous of you?" she asked, puzzled by some of what Ada had said. "Did she get less attention?"

"I wouldn't call what Allie felt jealousy," Ada declared. "She was more driven than jealous. Mom and Dad loved us both, but we were very different."

Ada refilled her glass and took a long drink. "From an early age, I loved nature. My Grandmother Milnor, Dad's mom, grew gorgeous herb gardens. I learned the skill from her, and inherited her love for herbs."

A faraway look crept into Ada's eyes, and she turned toward her own lush gardens. Cassi followed her gaze. Parsley and dill ruffled in the breeze. But she sensed her aunt saw something more, if only within her heart.

"I dug in the dirt," Ada continued. "Alice partied. Her friends called me the 'nature freak.' I laughed along with them, but on the inside, I guess I cried."

Ada turned, eyes brimming. She raised a hand, halting Cassi's move to comfort her. "The tears aren't for me, honey. They're for the life my sister never got to live."

Cassi turned to face the lake. Ducks glided along the shore, trolling the water for food while Rufus, prancing at the water's edge, eyed them warily. She focused on them through tear-filled eyes, waiting until the lump in her throat loosened.

"Why didn't she want me?"

Ada knelt and closed her hands over Cassi's. "Oh, Cassandra, I'm sure that at the end, Alice regretted her decision. But by then it was too late. She turned to me, and God forgive me, I couldn't get past my own pain to help her or you."

She gave Cassi's hands a squeeze, rose, and walked to the end of the porch. Rufus clattered up the steps, trotted over to her, and thrust his wet nose against her leg.

She bent down to hug him." This is hard for me," she said, her voice cracking. "But I want you to understand."

Giving Rufus a parting pat, she straightened and leaned against the railing.

"Let me back up a little. Someone up there," she said, raising her eyes skyward, "smiled on me, and I met John Blaine."

She brushed away her tears with her shirt sleeve. "He was twenty-two; I was eighteen. We fell in love and got married."

"How did my mother feel about that?"

"I don't know. She didn't come to our wedding. Allie left after high school to 'see the world.' That was her dream. We didn't hear from her for years. And then everything changed."

"What happened?"

"Alice popped back into my life. Only she wasn't alone. You were with her, and she was ill. Childbirth had sapped her, and she didn't seek help. I checked you both into a hospital and called John. He was in Pittsburgh on business and said he'd bring Mom home to help."

Cassandra moved to the edge of her chair, alarmed by the catch in Ada's voice and by how pale she'd become.

"Everything happened so fast. An untreated infection was winning the battle, and Allie asked me to take you. I was stunned, but before I could reply she was gone. I left her room in a daze, praying John would get there soon."

Ada dropped her eyes and stared at the weathered porch floor. She gripped the railing with white-knuckled fingers. "A state trooper was waiting for me outside her room. He told me there'd been an accident. A tractor trailer had crossed the road, killing John and my mother instantly."

Several moments ticked by. "I still don't remember much about the first twenty-four hours. I had so many painful decisions to make."

She lifted her pain filled eyes to Cassi's. "The doctor who had treated Allie was a wonderful man. He helped me cope. Then he told me about the Burkes, who had been trying to adopt."

"Mom and Dad," Cassi whispered.

Ada relaxed. Color returned to her cheeks. "I knew you'd be loved and cared for, and that was all I could grasp at the time. I did insist on knowing where they lived, but I never contacted them. I kept track of you, though. I have an album of paper clippings highlighting your life from grade school, through high school, and beyond."

"When I heard about the Burkes' accident, there was no question. I had to get in touch with you. So I did."

Ada pushed off the railing and disappeared inside the house. She returned with more tea and refilled their glasses.

They sipped in silence, until Cassi finally spoke. "Now I see why your gardens thrive. You've given your life to them. It shows. I don't know if I'm that strong. I don't know if I'll survive losing those I've loved."

"I wish I had been a part of your life." Ada once more knelt before Cassi's chair. "But by the time I was able to get up in the morning and face the day ahead, you were happy and loved, and I knew that seeing you would open that wound again."

Cassi wrapped her arms around Ada and held on tight. Her uncertain future terrified her. Would she be able to fight her way back like her aunt had done?

Cassi breathed in the combined scents of soft cotton and tangy herbs. "I was so mixed up after the accident. When I got your letter, I didn't want to believe you. I'm sorry, but I was so lonely. Sure, I have friends. One of them, Lanie, talked me into getting Rufus to help me deal with the loss. She's the one who pushed me into coming here."

"God bless Lanie," Ada said softly.

"I'm glad I came," Cassi continued. "I hope you don't mind if I lean on you. Besides Rufus, you're the only family I have left."

"Lean on me all you want, child." Ada tightened her arms around her. "I'm here for you, whatever the future holds."

Chapter Five

"Holy shit. Sadie, come here!"

Sadie Mitchell's eyes popped open. *Crap.* She flopped onto her side, the ancient bedsprings protesting, and smashed a pillow against her ear.

"Now, Sadie. Damn it, you're on TV!"

What the hell's he talking about?

"All right. Quit your damned yellin'."

The pillow hit the floor, and she kicked a tangled knot of sheets and blankets aside. Maybe he could watch television all damn day, but she needed sleep.

After jerking on a tattered blue robe, Sadie staggered into the next room. She wrinkled her nose. The place smelled like day-old pizza and stale cigarette smoke.

Rick Andrews sat on the edge of their shabby sofa. The broken down piece had come with the flat, along with a sagging recliner, an oversized red ottoman -- looking as if the last tenant had owned several cats, or a small lion -- and two end tables that matched, much to her surprise.

Rick leaned forward, braced his elbows on his knees, and stared bug-eyed at the TV.

"Geez, Rick. What's so damn important on the fuckin' television? If you had a decent job, maybe you wouldn't be glued to that screen all day."

She was tired of repeating the same gripe, day after day. He tended bar. She waited tables. Between them they barely made enough to keep a roof over their heads. A roof that leaked like a friggin' sieve.

"Come here." Rick grabbed her wrist and yanked her down beside him.

"Get your hands off--" Sadie broke off and froze. She twisted her arm free and stared at the screen. "I'll be a son of a bitch."

Filling the screen was the face of a woman he identified as Miss Cassandra Burke. The still shot was striking. The announcer droned on in the background.

Mouth agape, Sadie listened.

"Miss Burke is the owner of a popular fitness center near Pittsburgh in Fox Chapel, Pennsylvania. She was apprehended yesterday in connection with a murder believed to have been committed in Pine Bluffs. While visiting a relative in the small borough located near Lake Erie in western Pennsylvania, Miss Burke was allegedly caught at the scene standing over the murder victim clutching a knife."

The announcer went on to say Miss Burke denied any involvement with the deceased or his murder, and that local law enforcement had no comment due to the ongoing investigation.

The camera panned to the clean-cut news anchor.

"Pine Bluffs is shaken by the discovery of the body," he reported. "Residents are anxious and waiting to learn more about the case. No charges have been filed, and Cassandra Burke has been released. We will report further details as they become available."

Dumbstruck, Sadie continued to stare at the TV.

The captivating face of Cassandra Burke filled the screen once more, and the announcer noted the picture was a recent promotional shot for Fox Chapel Fitness. Then they rolled grainy footage showing a woman of medium height leaving the police station. She kept her face averted, giving the camera only a quick glimpse of her profile.

Sadie collapsed onto the sofa beside Rick.

"Like lookin' in a friggin' mirror," she rasped, raising a shaky hand. Her skin, still caked with make-up from the night before, felt rough, and her fingers came away with smudges of mascara on them.

"Holy shit." Rick tore his gaze from the screen, raked it over Sadie, and curled his lip.

"Shut up. Just shut the fuck up!" She gave him a shove and stumbled to the bedroom, slamming the door behind her.

Rick -- the jackass -- had ogled the picture of Cassandra. Why didn't he look at *her* like that anymore? The cracked mirror above her ancient dresser answered her question with cruel reality.

The image of Cassandra Burke had been like a reflection from the past. Did Rick remember? Did he realize that when they'd first met, Sadie had looked almost identical to the accused woman?

She'd been curvy, with dark brown eyes and thick blonde hair. Now her eyes were puffy and dull. Her hair, nearly white from over bleaching, hung in strings, and her skin had turned pasty. Her body was more dumpy than curvy.

With trembling hands, Sadie lit her last cigarette. She crumpled the empty pack and tossed it aside.

"Got to quit," she mumbled, drawing deep and squinting at her face in the mirror. The jagged, dissecting crack distorted her features.

Too much booze, too many cigarettes, and too many hours working at a no-end job. No wonder she looked like shit.

She used to look like *her*. The woman on TV. Exactly like her.

Who in the hell was Cassandra Burke?

*****

Rick didn't follow Sadie. Let her be pissed off. He couldn't help it if she looked like crap most of the time. He grabbed a beer and cast a wary eye around the cluttered kitchen. A jumble of unwashed dishes filled the sink.

Her on and off attitude was beginning to wear thin. She could be sweet as a fuckin' pie, or evil as a wicked witch.

Drove him friggin' nuts!

Just last week a coworker had gotten fired. A waitress, like Sadie, blamed for stealing cash. Sadie had been all over her with phony sympathy, but behind the girl's back she'd laughed her ass off. The amount stolen didn't jive with what they'd found on the girl, only that didn't seem to matter. With the missing bank envelope sticking out of her purse, the boss didn't have a choice. He'd fired her on the spot.

Rick became suspicious when Sadie bought him a fancy bottle of booze and modeled her new leather jacket. Still, he'd looked the other way, letting the poor girl hang, and drowned his guilt in the earthy taste of Scotch.

He hated Sadie's dark side. Maybe it was time to get the hell out. Get away from her before that darkness within her took him somewhere he didn't want to go.

The bedroom door opened. "Rick, get your ass in here."

Shit. What did she want now? He shuffled to the doorway, sipping his beer.

"Call me in sick tonight."

"No fuckin' way. I'm the one who'll fry for lyin' to the boss. You call him yourself. I ain't doin' it."

"Rick, honey, I need you to do this," she whined, her voice grating on his already frayed nerves. "That story on TV tonight... I have to know more. You saw that woman's face." She clutched a fisted hand to her chest. "It was mine. I have to find out who she is."

He scowled at her.

She turned her back and swept across the room. Using a tissue, she rubbed furiously at the thick layer of cold cream covering her face. She squinted at the mirror and lifted a limp strand of her over-bleached hair. Her eyes narrowed.

Rick took a long pull on his beer. She had a cunning look on her face. Evil reflected back from the aged mirror and met his gaze across the room with heat that took his breath away.

Sadie didn't like anyone taking what was hers, and in Sadie's eyes, the woman on TV possessed something very personal. She had Sadie's face.

Turning away, Rick crushed the empty beer can. Nothing would stop her once she'd made up her mind. The woman was diabolical. Driven. He wanted no part of whatever scheme Sadie was about to hatch.

And as for Cassandra Burke... *heaven help her.*

Chapter Six

Nick found Infantino back on the front desk. He was on the phone again, his mouth set in a thin line. The calls were starting to come in already. He rolled his eyes.

Nick waited patiently and grinned.

Frank finally hung up. Raking stiff fingers through his hair, he leaned back and rubbed his neck. "Morning, Nick."

"Is TJ in yet?"

"He's with the chief. Go on back."

The station was a hive of activity -- phones ringing, keyboards clattering, accompanied by the underlying hum of voices. The kind of stuff Nick experienced every day in Philly; a chaotic pain in the ass for the guys in Pine Bluffs.

As he approached the chief's office, he recognized TJ's voice.

"Robert Morelli was stabbed to death, and he'd been dead between eight and twelve hours."

"Morelli," his uncle remarked. "Not a common name around here."

"He's from Strongsville, Ohio, just south of Cleveland," TJ said, then snorted out a short laugh. "The local PD was all broken up to learn of his demise. Apparently he's suspected of having connections with drug traffic stretching from Cleveland, Erie, and points east... maybe even into Canada."

"Interesting. I take it no next of kin have come forward to claim his body?"

"Not so far." TJ was helping himself to coffee when Nick reached the open door. "There were no clear prints on the knife, but the handle had a good set of teeth marks. They match the ones I got from Miss Burke's dog perfectly."

"How the hell did you get teeth marks from her dog?" The chief leaned back, causing the springs on his chair to protest.

"The dog turned up at the cabin where Nicks staying. I stopped and tossed Rufus, that's her dog, a stick. He latched on and... *voila*. Tooth prints."

"Voila? What the hell is 'voila'?" Tom paused, eyeing TJ over the brim of his cup.

"It means 'to call attention to something'." Both men turned at the sound of Nick's voice.

"I thought you were on vacation, Nick." Uncle Tom grinned, lifting his coffee for a quick sip. "Ever since you hit town, you can't seem to stay away from the police station."

The coffee's tempting smell lured Nick into the room. "Got any of that to spare? I'm trying to cut down on caffeine and skipped my morning dose. Now, after a five mile run, I've got a killer headache and my disposition is heading south along with my energy level."

Tom McGraw chuckled, and with a tilt of his head, Nick's uncle said, "Help yourself."

Nick closed his eyes after his first sip of the rich, dark coffee. *Heaven.*

"As I was saying," TJ went on, "Rufus caught the stick. His teeth marks match the ones on the knife, and that confirms Miss Burke's story."

Tom swiveled around to face TJ. "The story would have been hard to make up quickly."

"Good point." TJ took a moment, rubbing his clean shaven cheek. "For the time being, it looks as if she was doing exactly what she said. Taking her dog for a walk. Unless some connection turns up between her and Morelli, I guess she's off our suspect list." He scowled, scooping up the case folder. "Unfortunately, that makes our suspect list nonexistent."

Nick poured himself another cup of coffee. He liked the part about suspicion shifting away from Cassandra. So far his instincts were right on.

"Guess that's it for now," Tom said. "When we get a full report from the state crime lab, let me know. Till then, continue business as usual." He swung back to his desk and began sorting a stack of reports.

TJ moved toward the door. "Nick, come back to my office. We've hardly had time to talk since you got here. Plus, I want to hear how things went when Miss Burke came to get her dog."

Nick didn't comment. He followed TJ to his office, coffee in hand, and pulled a chair close to his cousin's desk.

"Well?" TJ tossed him a sly grin and shuffled papers on his desk. "Did she get Rufus?"

"She did. He was very happy to see her." Keeping his expression blank, Nick took a sip of coffee and changed the subject. "This is way too good for station brew. Ours usually tastes like used motor oil."

"That's Dad's personal stash. He makes a pot every morning. I suspect it's to lure us into his office. That way he doesn't have to chase anyone down to find out what happened on the second and third shifts. Seems to work."

TJ flipped through a pile of notes. Touching the computer mouse, he checked his e-mail.

"You look good, TJ, like a real cop."

TJ's head jerked up, and with a laugh, Nick raised his hand.

"Don't be so damn defensive. That was an honest to God compliment. I'm impressed. You handle yourself well. Pine Bluffs got lucky when they recruited you."

"Yeah, they got lucky, all right. We'll see how soon I solve this case. Then ask if anyone feels lucky." TJ dismissed the computer screen and turned back to Nick. "What made you decide to spend your vacation here?"

"Hell, I don't know. Maybe a great cabin with free rent. Or maybe just a chance to relax, visit the locals."

"Pretty quick with the glib answers, Nick. Could be you miss the locals. Maybe the big city isn't so great anymore?"

Nick tossed back the rest of his coffee. TJ's remark came close to the truth and stirred up a nagging itch he'd been trying to ignore. He needed to figure out where the hell he was headed. This vacation was the first step. "Speaking of locals, isn't the grape harvest in full swing over the ridge about now?"

"Ah, that's what drew you back. Our Fall Fest. Lots of folks who've moved away come back to town this week. Gonna look up some of your old acquaintances, Nick?"

Nick stared into his empty cup, not bothering to hide his smirk. "Maybe Rhonda Reeves will show up."

"Geez, Nick. You don't forget anything, do you?" TJ's face flushed when Nick burst out laughing.

"Hey, what kind of a role model would I have been if I hadn't provided condoms for my little cousin when it looked like he was going to get lucky for the first time with the one and only Rhonda Reeves?"

The phone's piercing ring interrupted them.

"McGraw," TJ answered. He scratched a few hasty notes on a pad. "Thanks for the heads up. I'll take care of it."

He stood and grabbed his hat. "Gotta go. The press will be here shortly. They want a formal statement. What are your plans for today?" he asked, straightening his uniform.

"Have you told Cassi Burke she's no longer a suspect?"

"No." TJ's head came up. "*Cassi* Burke?"

"Is there any reason I can't pass that along to her?"

"Thought you had me fooled, didn't you?" TJ settled his hat into place. "Shit, I've known you too long and too well, cousin."

Nick lifted a questioning brow.

"Yeah, go ahead and tell her. You might get points for being the messenger."

With a sly wink, Nick zipped up his vest and left by the back door. Getting involved with Cassi Burke could be damn complicated. So, he reasoned, he would *not* get involved. Hell no, he just wanted to make sure she didn't think he was some macho, insensitive jerk.

Nothing more.

*****

TJ made a hasty detour into the station locker room. The press was due at any moment, and he wanted to make sure he was squared away. How had Nick put it? That he 'looked like a real cop?'

Having Nick around was like old times. Speaking of which, he did remember that night with Rhonda, and yes, sir... it had been a lucky one, quite memorable for a sixteen-year-old-boy. TJ laughed. At the time, his *role model* had just completed boot camp.

Nick had it all. An exciting life in a big city, women probably lined up at his door. So why did TJ get the feeling something was going on in Nick's life?

Nick was quick with words, and he thought on his feet. Good traits for a cop. To search for words was out of character for TJ's macho handsome cousin, but that is exactly what Nick did whenever anyone asked about his vacation. He had a snappy come-back all right, but there'd been a telling pause.

TJ had been about eight when Nick had moved away, and it had been like losing a big brother. TJ had missed him. At first, he figured Nick would move back some day.

That day had never come.

Over the years, Nick's visits dwindled. He went to college, did a stint with the Marines that included a few days leave in Pine Bluffs -- thus, the condoms -- and then he joined the Philadelphia Police force. Years had passed since they'd spent any time together.

Opening his locker, TJ grabbed a pack of mints. This case was going to eat up his spare time, but somehow he'd find a way to see Nick. He had to. Something was bugging his cousin, and he sure as hell meant to find out what it was. He was a detective, after all. Wasn't he?

TJ checked his watch, time to meet the press.

*****

With his loose jointed, half jogging gait, Nick soon left the police station behind. The herd of reporters waiting for TJ had barely given him a second glance.

The sun chased away the morning chill as he moved along the lake, automatically following a familiar hard-packed footpath. When Ada Blaine's cottage came into view, memories slammed into him.

As kids, TJ and Nick had often come to Ada's. Aunt Mary brought them along whenever she bought juice-dripping berries and clumps of herbs. Nick would pull a wagon all the way from town with TJ aboard, bouncing with the bumps, grinning like a goose, clinging to the slatted sides. On the return trip, TJ's hair would stand out like a damn red ball among the greens.

Nick stopped, inhaling the clean, sharp scent of parsley. The roll of the land and the curving brick pathway to the lake hadn't changed. Like a still-life, the picture had remained in his mind.

He sauntered up the path. Once within earshot of the cottage, he detected muffled barking. The door opened, and Rufus wriggled past Ada and bounded down the steps.

"Morning, Nick. Sorry," she exclaimed, palms up. "I couldn't stop him. He usually barks and then cowers behind me." She tilted her head, her eyes on Rufus. "Although, he seems to have taken a liking to you."

"Aw, he's just a sucker for bologna and cheese," Nick said, scratching Rufus, who huffed happily and bumped against his legs. "Probably figures I'm a ready source."

Ada stepped back and motioned him inside. With Rufus trotting worshipfully behind him, Nick followed her into the kitchen. Sunlight spilled through windows running the entire length of the room. The wall of glass showcased Ada's gardens and the shimmering lake beyond.

Shoving his hands into his pockets, he just looked. "I'd forgotten how beautiful this place is. Time stands still in your gardens. Don't ever change it, Ada."

"You need to come home more often, Nicholas. I somehow can't imagine you among all the noise and pollution in Philly. You used to love roaming the bluffs and woods around here."

He shrugged. "Once Dad took the position in Philly, the move was inevitable. The teaching opportunities for Mom, all the artsy stuff. She loves the city."

"How are they?"

Nick fiddled with the sliding door, inching it open. "They're good. Dad's retired. Mom will, too, end of this year. They plan to move into a condo and travel."

"How about you, Nick? What are your plans?"

"Me? I'm okay, I guess. I've got my own place. My back yard isn't very big, but it came with a grill." He flashed a grin.

He couldn't remember the last time he'd used the rusting grill on the pitiful patch of grass behind his compact non-descript house. "But you're right. Being here reminds me how much I love this place."

Ada touched his arm, and he smiled down at her. He winked. "Don't spread it around, but, yes, sometimes I miss it."

He turned back to the window just as Cassandra came up the brick path from the lakeshore with long legged strides, her posture straight and tall. She'd removed her jacket and looped the sleeves at her waist, letting it trail over her hips. The knotted fabric pulled her blue tee shirt tight across her chest.

"I swear that girl doesn't know how to sit still."

Nick blinked at Ada's words, embarrassed that he'd been staring at her niece like a wide-eyed owl.

"She took Rufus for a walk, wore the poor guy out, and then spent a half hour lifting weights before she announced she was taking another walk. She's driven, and she's got a lot of self discipline. More than I ever had."

Nick pulled his eyes from the sculpted female body heading his way and leaned over Ada's shoulder, drawn to the muffins she was arranging on a plate. "I don't agree with you. You're pretty fit for a woman who must be--"

"Old enough to be your big sister." Ada broke in. She placed the muffins on the table and turned to her whistling teapot. They were laughing together when Cassi entered.

She drew back, taking a deep breath. "Hello, again."

"Hello, yourself, Cassi." He skimmed his gaze over her. *Eye candy* might well describe the type of woman Nick was usually drawn to, but Cassi Burke wasn't all frosting and fluff.

Oh no. She was taffy. Toned and sweet. No doubt providing melt in your mouth satisfaction when a little heat was applied.

"You must be exhausted, honey." Ada's voice cooled his thoughts. "Come join us and have some tea and raspberry muffins.

Cassi dragged her eyes from Nick's. "I need to freshen up. Give me a minute."

Rufus jumped up and trailed down the hallway behind her.

When the door to her room closed, Ada turned to Nick and asked, "I assume you know about the recent tragedy in her life?"

Nick nodded. "Aunt Mary filled me in before I got to town. Told me of your connection and how you'd kept it a secret all these years."

"I had my reasons," Ada said. "What has TJ told you about the investigation?"

He broke open a muffin and took a hefty bite, letting the warm center melt in his mouth. Nick chewed and swallowed, then took a sip of tea before responding. "Your niece is off the suspect list, for now. TJ said I could let you and Cassandra know. He would have done it himself, but the press was clamoring for a statement."

"What kind of statement are they releasing?" Ada pinned him with her no-nonsense stare.

He took another bite, stalling for time, deciding how to field her question. Ada would not be easily bamboozled with bullshit.

Accompanied by a flurry of movement, Rufus and Cassi reentered the room.

"Thanks," Cassi said, taking a steaming cup from Ada. While adding cream, she glanced from her aunt to Nick. "Did I interrupt something?"

"You're no longer a prime suspect. I stopped by to let you know," Nick volunteered.

"I guess that's good, considering." Cassi sipped her tea. "I talked to my manager today. The story is all over the news in Pittsburgh, and the whole mess could hurt my business. I hope they find whoever stabbed that poor man soon."

"I wouldn't call him a 'poor man' just yet," Nick said, studying Cassi's face carefully. "Indications are he was a bit of an unsavory character. Sometimes the company you keep isn't good for your health."

"Lie down with dogs, get up with fleas." Ada's sage comment made them smile.

They put a sizeable dent in the plate of muffins, enjoying the warmth of Ada's sunny kitchen. All while Rufus slept blissfully in a pool of sunlight streaming through the sliding glass door.

Nick was relieved. He hadn't learned much from TJ, but it was obvious, and rightfully so, that Ada wanted to know more. His position was precarious. Though TJ had indicated his interest in Cassi was diminishing, as an investigator Nick knew TJ would look closer. And this *was* TJ's investigation.

"I've got to get moving," Ada proclaimed, noting the time. "The Fall Festival is in full force, and I have fresh herbs to deliver for resale. Cassandra, I'll bet you've never been to the wine country this time of year."

"I've never been to wine country any time of year," Cassi said. "May I go with you?"

"Any other time I'd welcome your company, but I'll be gone all day. What would we do with Rufus?"

Cassi's shoulders slumped, and Rufus lifted his head at the sound of his name.

"The festival runs through the week-end." Ada bustled around the kitchen, loading the dishwasher. "I'll be busy delivering goods today, but then I'm free." Without breaking stride, she turned to Nick. "Why don't you take her to North East in the morning and show her the sights? Today will be very busy and I'll welcome a rest tomorrow. I can watch Rufus."

"Oh, I can't impose on Nick," Cassi burst out.

"No imposition at all," Nick assured her. "It would be my pleasure to introduce you to wine tasting, and all that autumn along the lakeshore has to offer."

Cassi glanced at Ada, indecision evident on her face. Nick waited patiently, and Ada busily dried a clean muffin pan.

"Well, all right, Nick, if you're sure you have the time."

Her chocolate eyes met his questioning gaze, and God help him, all he could think about was warm taffy.

Chapter Seven

Rich McConnell's Ace Hardware was a staple in Pine Bluffs. When growing up, Nick had often accompanied his uncle to the timeless old business.

He liked Rich. The man was forty-something, maybe early fifties, and was also a former Marine. He had that clean cut, fit look. Aunt Mary called him a *handsome devil.*

Nick always made it a point to see Rich whenever he came to town. He couldn't remember the last time they'd talked, so he figured a visit was long overdue.

After setting up his date -- and he did consider spending the day with Cassandra just a date, and nothing more -- he'd returned to town and meandered into the hardware store. He immediately spied Rich struggling with an awkward display. Nick jumped right in and helped to assemble an unwieldy carousel of keys,

Approaching footsteps thudded on the store's wooden floor, and his Aunt Mary rounded the corner, her feet eating up the distance between them.

Rich glanced up and then returned to the stubborn bolt he'd been working on. "Mornin', Mary."

"Good Morning, Rich. Nicholas. Have either of you seen the chief? I called the station and TJ said he had to run out for something. I know darned well he headed right up the street to this store."

A slow smile crossed Rich's face. He nodded. "Check over there. He's lookin' for a new crescent wrench, claims one of his best ones up and disappeared." A final twist finished the job, and Rich turned to Mary. "You look a little upset there, woman. What's the problem?"

She let out a disgruntled huff. "I swear we should sell all our cabins and invest the money. The aggravation is just not worth the hassle sometimes."

His aunt was usually unflappable, but Mary McGraw's distressed tone made something inside Nick tighten. Nothing specific, just that little red flag cops sometimes heeded, and he asked, "What happened, Aunt Mary?"

"I rented out one of the cabins near the edge of town early this week. The man insisted he only needed it a few days. So, I let him pay a deposit with the agreement he would settle up when he left." Her pretty brow furrowed. "He seemed nice enough, though he wasn't the usual type to rent a remote cabin."

"What'd he do, skip out on you?" Nick asked.

"I'm not sure." Mary narrowed her eyes. "Here it is almost a week later, and I haven't seen or heard from him. So I went to check. His car was still there, but something just didn't look right. The place seemed deserted, and when I knocked the storm door came loose and almost hit me."

"Aunt Mary," Nick cautioned, "you shouldn't have gone there by yourself. If he--"

Tom rounded the corner.

"My dear, I can hear you from clear across the store." He clutched a rather large wrench and moved with his usual lanky ease. Mary's frown disappeared when he pulled her against him and placed a quick kiss on her nose.

Nick loved being around his aunt and uncle. He never tired of hearing their story. How they had met, fallen in love, and remained married close to forty years. Even in casual clothes, Aunt Mary was still an attractive woman. Uncle Tom's hair showed a touch of gray around the edges, but was thick enough that if he didn't keep it short, it tended to get unruly.

Keeping one arm around the petite, smiling blonde at his side, Tom looked down, his warm hazel eyes intense.

Nick hated to ruin the moment, but something about that broken door bugged him. "Did you see anything else unusual at the cabin?"

"What cabin?" Tom asked.

She placed her palm on Tom's chest. "Hon, something's not right at our cabin on Border Road. The door's broken, and the man who rented it has disappeared."

"Did you go out there by yourself?" Arching one brow, Tom gave her a squeeze. The gesture gently admonished her.

Mary rolled her eyes. "Nick asked me the same thing. I've been checking on our tenants for years 'all by myself'." She made little air quotes. "Let me finish. Like I was saying, his car was there, but he didn't answer when I knocked. That's when I noticed the door."

"We'll check it out," Tom said, "but until we have more data on this murder case, I'd feel better if you don't go off by yourself that way."

"Humph," Mary snorted. "That poor man you found was probably a drug dealer someone killed and dumped off. Whoever did it is probably back in Cleveland or Buffalo by now."

Nick was inclined to agree with her. Considering what TJ had discovered in Strongsville where Morelli had last resided, Mary's quick conclusion could very well be correct.

Tom glanced at his watch.

"Rich, put this on my tab," he said, lifting the wrench while guiding his wife toward the door. "I'll settle with you later."

"No problem," Rich said. "Let me know if there's anything you need to fix that busted door."

Nick fell into step beside Mary. He was still mulling over the missing tenant. Tom, too, seemed lost in thought as they left the store and turned toward the station.

"Do you have the man's registration on file?" Tom asked Mary absently. "I can find him quicker with that than just his name, which is?"

"Morelli. His name is Robert Morelli."

Tom stopped.

Mary took several steps before she noticed he wasn't with her, then glanced back at him. The chief grabbed her. Before she could react he folded her in his arms and crushed her against him.

A cold knot coiled deep inside Nick's belly. His eyes flew to Uncle Tom's. Mirrored in their depths was the sickening realization of what might have been.

Nick was hot and ready to tag along, but something told him TJ wouldn't appreciate his presence at a second crime scene in as many days. When Aunt Mary had revealed the name of the missing tenant, his heartbeat had faltered. From the look on his uncle's face as he made Mary promise to go straight home and let him handle things, Nick would've bet Tom McGraw's pulse had altered considerably, too.

His long overdue visit with Rich had been cut short when Mary had arrived, and he needed to talk to his old friend. So when the chief rushed off to the station, Nick headed back to the hardware store.

Still dealing with the stubborn display, Rich looked up when Nick approached. "Hey, Nick. Forget something?"

"Yea, I forgot how much I like to shoot the shit with a crusty old Marine."

Rich grinned. He motioned for Nick to follow, leading the way to his office at the rear of the store. "Have a seat."

He crossed the room, lifted a near-empty coffee pot and shook his head. "I've had my caffeine allotment for the day, but what the hell. I'll make us a fresh pot. You cops still put away at least a gallon a day, right?"

"Probably closer to two or three," Nick said with a wry smile. "And that's before lunch."

Rich left the room laughing, and Nick surveyed his surroundings. The room was a prime example of organized clutter. Odd pieces of furniture crowded every available space, yet the shelves and cubicles were neat and organized. Nick lifted a sturdy rubber mallet from the scarred surface of an oak desk. He grinned, examined the hefty tool, then put it down exactly where it had been.

Soon a rich aroma rose from the hissing, groaning coffee maker.

"You're in good shape for an old guy." Nick took his first sip and eyed

Rich over the rim of his cup.

"I can still beat your skinny ass, *Detective*," Rich scoffed, carefully placing his steaming cup on his desk. Propping his feet on an overturned box, he leaned back. "It's been a while since you've been in town. What brought you back to Pine Bluffs?"

Nick strolled to the window and peered out, taking time to watch a truck loaded with drywall lumber toward the street. For the second time in as many days he carefully chose his words. "I had vacation time built up, seemed like a good place to come. So, here I am."

The explanation was vague, and he suspected Rich would see through his glibness. Though the part about vacation time was accurate, a veritable tangle of reasons had brought Nick back to his hometown. He propped his hip on the windowsill and met Rich's unwavering gaze.

"Have you met Ada Blaine's niece?"

"No." Rich shook his head. "Not yet, but I hear she's pretty easy on the eyes."

"I'm taking her to the wine festival tomorrow."

"Sounds like a nice way to relax on vacation." Rich arched a brow and reached for his coffee.

Nick stared into his cup. "Yea, that's what I thought at first. Now I'm not so sure."

"Nick, what's chappin' your ass? There's sure as hell something on your mind. Could you spit it out before the friggin' sun sets?" Rich's volley of words cracked like automatic rounds, making Nick jump. But when he looked up, his friend grinned at him.

His shoulders relaxed. Rich's cut-the-crap approach uncoiled a boatload of tension. He drained his cup and went for a refill, then dragged a chair close to Rich's desk.

"She's not just easy on the eyes," he said, "she's gorgeous. Smart, too. But I'm not sure I can be impartial dealing with the woman."

Rich drew his brows together. "*Dealing* with the woman? It's a date, for Pete's sake. Why the hell are you beatin' yourself up over taking her out?"

"I'm attracted to her, Rich. Getting involved with a murder suspect isn't smart for any cop."

"That's bullshit." Rich dropped his feet, propping crossed arms on the desk. "Tom told me they'd cleared that up. What's really eating you, Nick?"

Nick averted his eyes and took a deep breath. "Something happened on the job that almost shut me down." His nerves jumped just saying the words out loud.

"An old Marine buddy once told me that keeping things locked inside is like swallowing acid. Sooner or later it'll burn a hole in your gut. What happened, Nick?"

"Stats pointed to a rise in the incidence of police shootings." Focusing on a shaft of light dancing on the floor, he finally unloaded what had been bothering him. "Gun violence was up and suspects had gotten increasingly brazen and were much quicker to use a weapon. In turn, homicides committed by police officers on duty increased substantially. Done in the line of duty they were justified, but the press was yammering and citizens were griping. That combination twisted the city fathers' tails, who in turn prodded the mayor, who then jumped on the department."

"Shit flows downhill," Rich concluded.

Nick nodded agreement. "Our instructions: get the bastards, but don't shoot them. To my mind, that's ass backward thinking."

"I agree," Rich said. "But those are the demands you face as a cop. How do they affect your relationship with women?"

"During that time I met a woman." Nick rose, paced the room, and rubbed the back of his neck. "Things moved fast, and before I knew it, we were pretty hot and heavy. The guys teased me, said I was snagged."

"Were you?"

"She was a little off center. You know, different. Not the kind of woman I usually date, but no, I wasn't *snagged*. She took the edge off some rough times. What man doesn't like his ego stroked?"

"We're all prone to have top heavy egos, Nick. And we don't always think with what's perched on our shoulders."

Nick laughed. "Not that kind of stroking."

"Quit pacing and sit."

"Okay." Nick poured more coffee and sat. "I was putting in sixteen hour days and seeing Kat. Her name was Katrina; she went by Kat. I'd just walked in the door after a mind blowing shift and she showed up."

"She followed you home?"

"In retrospect, that's exactly what she did. At the time I just thought she wanted to be with me."

"What changed?"

"We'd been working a case in the Old City neighborhood. Timing and secrecy were crucial. Everything was in place and all we had to do was close the trap." Nick paused. Dredging up the details made his gut burn. "That night, when I got the call, I shooed Kat out the door and headed out. Everyone was wired. We were finally going to put away some real slime balls we'd been after for months."

"Weapons?" Rich asked.

"Oh, yeah. Big time. But we'd barely gotten the place surrounded when all hell broke loose. Two of our guys went down." Breaking out in a sweat, Nick shook his head. "I can still hear rounds thunking into the ground, pinging off parked cars. Officer Parks screamed and dropped, almost at my feet. He and another good cop, Amenta, were only wounded, thank God, but the incident was still unacceptable."

Discovering his coffee had cooled, Nick set the cup aside. In his mind's eye he could still see the two downed officers and the dark pools of blood forming beneath them. Tamping down the image, he continued. "Like rats scurrying down holes, half of those dirtbags got away. We were downtown, booking the ones we'd nabbed, when it hit me. I'd been keeping company with the head rat's sister."

"How'd you find out?"

"One of the perps was barely alive. He made it to the ER, but most likely knew he was a goner and begged someone to call his sister. I made the call."

"Did she get there in time?"

"No. She didn't." Nick returned to the window. The sun peeked through colorful maple leaves to cast odd-shaped patterns on the ground, and in the distance, Pine Shadow Lake shimmered. "The number was Kat's."

"Shit," Rich declared. "She must have tipped them off."

"She sure as hell did." Nick braced his hands high on the rough hewn window frame. His fingers contracted until splinters bit into his skin.

Once Nick had shared the worst of it, more words spilled out. Rich listened to details of the long buried incident. He was a good listener, and his comments made sense. Especially when he pointed out how Nick's fast thinking had helped identify Kat as the leak, leading to her apprehension and providing the authorities with valuable information.

Talking with Rich helped put some of the self-doubt Nick had been carrying around into perspective. But ferreted away deep inside, his reluctance to share more than casual feelings with anyone remained.

*****

Bright yellow crime scene tape stretched across Border Road. The tape surrounded the McGraw's rental cabin centered in a rough-cut clearing, angling from tree to tree. The cabin's windows were stark, vacant looking. And the gaping screen door, hanging by a single hinge, made the small structure look deserted.

Wide plank steps led onto the porch fronting the cabin. With one foot resting on the bottom step, TJ balanced a clipboard on his knee while jotting notes. Along with Montroy and Long, he had a new crime scene to process.

Step by step, Jake and Chuck combed the area. Using a spiral search pattern, the two men worked from inside the cabin in a tight outward circle. Tedious work.

TJ skimmed over his notes. Robert Morelli had been at the cabin prior to his death, and the bog where his body had been found was less than two miles away. More than they'd uncovered up 'til now, but not by much.

The mid-afternoon sun beat down on the clearing. TJ slipped off his sunglasses. After tucking them into his pocket, he shook his head.

"I can't believe I overlooked something so obvious."

"TJ, we're all guilty of sometimes overlooking what's right in front of us." Checking off a list of his own, Jake stopped in front of TJ. "You were looking for a suspect to fit the crime. Maybe someone lurking, acting covert or suspicious in our peaceful little town. People come on a regular basis to rent these cabins, and that put it way down on your priority list."

"Maybe." Jake's sound reasoning didn't ease TJ's guilt. What if his mother had checked on the tenant sooner? What if she'd walked in on a murder in progress? Despite the hot sun, the chill in his body went bone deep.

Found inside the cabin and tagged as evidence was a wind-breaker, a ring of keys lying on the table, and an empty duffle bag. Morelli had traveled light. They'd also located a long sleeved denim shirt. He'd been shirtless when discovered, and speculation was he'd been getting dressed when the killer arrived. There was no visible blood on the shirt, but if it was deemed important, he was sure they could find other DNA on it that would verify it was Morelli's. For now, though, they'd hold it as evidence.

TJ's mother had given him a list of items provided for guests. The list included several guest towels, a number of which were missing from the Border Road rental.

Jake followed TJ inside the cabin. Together they studied a highly visible dark stain just inside the door on the plank floor.

"Looks like blood," TJ remarked to Jake.

"I'd bet my ass that's where Morelli spent the last moments of his life." Jake bent down to take a closer look. "Ya know what I think?"

"Probably the same thing I do." TJ said. "If those missing towels turn up, they'll be soaked in the same blood. Ninhydrin will confirm if that stain is blood."

"That's a chemical developer, right?"

"A good one." TJ gestured to the wood planks beneath their feet. "It's perfect for porous surfaces like wood."

Jake looked at TJ and grinned. "Ah, technology. Even in Pine Bluffs."

Crunching gravel alerted them to an approaching car, and they stepped outside. A police cruiser appeared. Its driver carefully navigated the narrow road lined with Pine Bluffs patrol cars and parked at the foot of the steps.

Chief McGraw alighted from the vehicle. He placed one foot on the bottom step and looked up at the TJ and Jake.

"Afternoon, gentleman. How's it going?"

"About as I suspected. How's Mom? She seemed frazzled when I stopped by for an inventory list."

"She's fine. More mad than upset. The thought of a murder being committed in one of our cabins pisses her off. Now we not only have to replace a door, we also probably have to rip up half the floor. The upside is that dealing with those problems is distracting her. Seems to take the edge off reality for the time being."

The chief looked grim. TJ figured the *what if* factor would haunt both of their imaginations for quite some time. His father stood in the afternoon sunshine. His demeanor usually garnered respect and confidence, but for the first time TJ noticed weary lines around his dad's eyes.

TJ joined his dad at the bottom of the steps. "Tell Mom she did the right thing when she backed away. We went in there knowing nothing had been contaminated."

Jake joined them. "Mrs. McGraw's quite a woman, sir."

Tom's smile transformed his strained expression. "That she is. I can't begin to tell you what ran through my mind when she told me Morelli was the man who had rented the cabin. How in the hell did I overlook checking the connection?"

"You and TJ should go have a beer and quit feeling so damn guilty about something that any number of people missed," Jake said. "Present company included. Shit happens, Chief. And everything considered, finding out any sooner would not have changed much."

"Maybe not," TJ pondered. "But knowing would have given us a head start. A more recent lead on who came here, and when."

"You may be right," Jake agreed. "We can ask around again, now that we have a better timeline and location, but chances are nobody saw anything. My guess is that whoever did this came and went without causing a ripple in Pine Bluff's daily routine."

"Why don't you plan on having dinner with us tonight, TJ?" his dad suggested as Jake moved away. "Having you there will keep your mother from dwelling on all of this."

"I'll try, Dad. You're right, though. Mom will worry the details to death. Maybe together we can steer her in another direction." TJ checked his watch. "I still have a lot to process. Six o'clock okay with you?"

"Sounds good. Okay if I come by tomorrow and get measurements so I can order repair material from Rich?"

"I'll let you know." TJ glanced at the cabin. "When we rip out those boards, I'll make sure we put something in place to keep critters from getting in until you can replace them."

The chief departed, and TJ spotted two officers he'd sent to comb the woods.

"Anything?" he asked when they approached.

"Nothin' unusual," Long replied. "Someone could have easily reached the bog from here without being seen. The grounds soft and spongy, not good for lifting footprints. Moisture is a constant in that area and tends to erase or obliterate evidence as time passes.

TJ agreed. Right now, time was the enemy.

He recalled Jake to his side. "One of you needs to help Jake take out those stained planks. I don't want a hint of what happened left behind. Jake, I want you to accompany the evidence to the crime lab."

They removed the planks and secured plywood over the hole. The stained planks, the empty duffle bag, the jacket, the shirt, and Morelli's keys were sent off to the lab. Inside the duffle bag they detected a powdery substance resembling drug residue. TJ was confident the lab would confirm their suspicions.

The murder looked more and more like a drug deal gone bad, making the chances of ever knowing who stabbed Morelli and dumped him in the bog slim to none.

*****

When Nick left Rich's hardware store, he decided to let the proverbial dust settle and spend the afternoon exploring. As Rich had pointed out, his date with Cassi tomorrow was only one date.

"Don't get your shorts in a twist over nothing," his friend had advised.

Nick planned to take that advice.

Some of the new stores on Main Street drew him to their windows filled with wreaths of grape vines, stacks of wooden crates with *Welch's Grape Juice* stamped on the side. All designed to pull in tourists for the Fall Festival, and it seemed to be working.

He strolled by the school he'd attended with Marcy, and came upon the Pines Dinor. Pausing a moment he chuckled, studying the sign above the door. He'd forgotten the unusual way they spelled *diner*, with an 'or' instead of an 'er' in this western wedge of Pennsylvania.

Time rewound when he stepped inside where gleaming chrome accents and red vinyl booths triggered his long forgotten memories.

He strolled to the counter and straddled a stool anchored to the floor.

A cheerful, gum chewing waitress appeared. She reached up and plucked a pencil from behind one ear. "Hi, there. Isn't this a great day?"

Nick folded his arms on the counter and grinned up at her. "The best I've seen in a long time."

They exchanged small talk about the weather and the upcoming festival. She talked fast and fussed with a single strand of hair that kept escaping from behind one ear.

Nick didn't know her, but her tee shirt with *Pines Dinor* stamped on the front pocket looked like the ones he remembered from way back when.

He ordered coffee and indulged in a generous slice of berry pie. And gauging from the fresh berries and melt-in-your-mouth crust, he'd bet his last dollar the berries had come from Ada Blaine's garden.

By the time he returned to the street, heavy purplish-gray clouds hid the sinking sun. He turned up the collar of his jacket and set off at a brisk walk toward his cabin. Near the end of town, a police cruiser approached him.

The car rolled to a stop, and the window glided down.

"Hey, cousin, where're you heading?" TJ slipped the car into park.

"Back to the cabin. I've been tripping down memory lane, but the chill in the air makes me want to start a fire and kick back with a cold beer, or maybe hot coffee laced with something to kick it up."

"Come on over to Mom and Dad's. Dinner's at six, and there's always more than enough to go around."

"How'd things go today?"

"I'll fill you in over dinner. I've got to run, or I'll never make it there by six." TJ shifted the car back into gear.

"Hard to pass up Mary's cooking," Nick admitted, stepping away from the cruiser. "Can I bring anything?"

"Do you know anything about wine?"

"What's she fixing?"

"Don't have a clue. Give her a call. She'll be thrilled that you're coming, and you can find out what's for dinner." TJ said, and then he sped away.

Nick continued on to the cabin, showered, and changed. He opted not to call Mary; better to surprise them. On his way out the door, he selected both a merlot and a nice, well-chilled pinot grigio.

He climbed into his Honda, whistling cheerfully, and headed for the McGraw's. The evening ahead promised something that was hard to beat: reconnecting with family. Time spent talking with Rich had pushed the past way down on his stress-o-meter, and tomorrow he had a date with a very interesting woman.

Things were looking up.

Cassi would be a nice diversion while on vacation. She was attractive and fun, not to mention smart. Then by next week he'd have decided about his job in Philly and put the *nice diversion* behind as he moved on with his life.

Chapter Eight

The brim of Sadie Mitchell's cap and the turned-up collar of her denim jacket hid her features well. Exactly what she wanted. Cassandra Burke was a visitor in Pine Bluffs, so Sadie's resemblance to her might not draw attention.

Sadie couldn't take the chance that it might.

The jostling, relaxed crowd in town for the wine festival had provided perfect cover as Sadie roamed the streets after her early morning drive from Brecksville, Ohio to Pine Bluffs. The drive had taken over two hours. Sadie grimaced, thinking of the long trip home facing her.

The afternoon faded and fancy street lights winked on. Sadie drove to the outskirts of town, frustration gnawing at her like a ravenous rodent.

She'd yet to lay eyes on her look-alike, and her need to see the woman in the flesh was insatiable.

She wanted answers, damn it.

Who is this woman? This person who looked like her? As if she'd stolen Sadie's face.

The young girl at the library sure knew how to find stuff out. All Sadie had done was tell the bubbly little twit what she wanted to know, and the girl had almost tripped over herself showing Sadie how to dig up crap from the past.

Once she knew how to find most of what she wanted, Sadie had drummed up a few tears to fit with the long lost friend crap and sent the silly broad off to file something. Then she'd sifted through what she'd uncovered.

She and Cassandra Burke had been born only days apart in western Pennsylvania. Big deal. So had a million others.

She tightened her grip on the wheel. Sure, they'd both been orphans, yet *Miss Cassandra* -- fancy fricking name -- got adopted and led a charmed life. If Sadie believed all the crap newspapers had printed, the bitch was a damned saint.

Sadie sped up, aiming for a hapless cat crossing the road ahead.

"Shit," she snapped when the skittering feline disappeared into the roadside brush. "I hope you starve to death. I almost did, abandoned like a damn cat," she muttered, remembering the greedy foster homes with pawing hands at night.

Hell, at least four legged strays went to descent shelters. She'd bounced from one filthy, greedy foster home to another, putting up with sly pats and pawing hands. Christ, no wonder she'd run away every chance she got.

"But I got smart, and I got mean. Nobody messes with mean. So damn it, I survived."

Downtown Pine Bluffs soon disappeared behind her and the distance between houses along the road became greater. She had the address of Ada Blaine's Herbs. Digging into the recent murder investigation had produced that gem. She cruised along, scanning mailbox numbers along the way.

The road curved, skirting the lake, following the shoreline. Damn, this place was pretty.

She slowed the car to a crawl. Had to be getting close.

Then Sadie saw her. She eased her car beneath the branches of a roadside willow tree. Cassandra knelt on the ground trimming sprigs from a row of bushy plants and putting them in a basket. Other plants and bushes surrounded her, creating gardens that seemed to cover every inch of ground clear down to the lakeshore.

She was fuckin' beautiful. The setting sun behind her outlined every curve. Every stupid curve. Sadie sucked in her gut and sat up straighter. Long willow branches brushed the car, scraping the windshield and setting her nerves on edge. The same breeze that stirred the branches lifted the heavy sweep of hair framing Cassandra Burke's face.

Sadie glanced in the rearview mirror. The road behind her stretched empty and dark. She started to look away but her reflection, stark in the fading light, caught her eye.

Her face was an eerie duplicate of Cassandra's. The face she'd seen on TV, with gracefully curving cheeks, an almost-square chin, and one brow arching slightly higher than the other. But the camera hadn't captured Cassandra's inner glow and natural beauty, and the true difference between them made Sadie's blood boil.

Her gaze shifted back as Cassandra rose and walked away, carrying the basket. Once she disappeared into the cottage, Sadie whipped the car around and raced back into town. Her insides burned as if they'd been shredded by a dull razor blade, and the pain cut a direct path to her heart.

She stopped at a spot overlooking the lake and reached for her cell phone. Twice it slipped from her grasp. Finally, with a vivid curse, she dialed the familiar number and slapped the phone to her ear.

Her fingers tapped a wild rhythm on the steering wheel. The sun had dropped below the trees, making the surface of Pine Shadow Lake look flat and black.

"'lo," Rick answered, his voice drugged with sleep.

"Hey, wake up. I saw her."

"Who?" he croaked out after a long pause.

"That Burke woman, that's who. The one who looks like me. Shit,

Rick, where do you think I've been all fuckin' day?"

She was exhausted. Her head throbbed, and her nerves, fed by nicotine and about a gallon of caffeine, drove her.

Rick coughed. "Will you be back in time for work tonight?"

"Tell the boss I'm sick," she demanded.

"Ah, hell. Sadie, he knows you're not sick. Quit your damn screwin' around and get back here. You're goin' to end up losin' your job." He sounded wide awake now, and pissed.

"All right, already. I'm on my way." She cut the connection and tossed the phone aside. A dark compact truck sped by, and for a brief moment, oncoming lights lit up the truck's interior. The man driving had been in the diner earlier. He was a looker, all right. She'd been in the last booth, keeping out of sight while he'd sat at the counter sipping coffee and flirting with some simple-minded young waitress.

There'd been something about the way he watched things, the way he moved, that marked him as *authority*. He stood out from the locals and tourists in his snug jeans and dark pullover.

If her instincts were correct, Sadie mused as the evening shadows swallowed up the truck's taillights, the man was law enforcement through and through. She did *not* want to pop up on his radar anytime soon.

Much as she wanted to linger, she feared Rick wouldn't cover for her. So she headed back to Ohio.

She'd be back. Like a damn moth to a fuckin' flame.

Chapter Nine

Tom and Mary McGraw's cedar-sided home rested on the uppermost slope of a rolling field. Hills dropped away from the house on three sides, offering a priceless view of the surrounding woods and Pine Shadow Lake. The lake's surface, lit by the sun's final dazzling display, shimmered.

The hills he and TJ had once used for sledding seemed more rolling and gradual now. Catapulting down the icy slopes at breakneck speed had been a great way to spend cold winter afternoons. Aunt Mary always kept a close eye on them. On occasion, she'd come outside and stand at the top of the hill, her hands on her hips, and chew out their young asses for performing wild and crazy antics.

Cinnamon, wood smoke, and a hearty aroma that no doubt came from the main course, surrounded Nick as he stepped through the door.

"Nicky, what a nice surprise."

Lifting a dishtowel tucked into her waistband, Mary wiped her hands. She brushed a flyaway wisp of hair behind one ear and hurried toward him, looking much like she had years ago riding herd on him and TJ.

He set the wine he'd brought aside, wrapped his arms around her, and lifted her off the floor. She laughed. Nick inhaled warm vanilla and spice. Ah, Aunt Mary.

He set her down and scooped up the wine. "Hope this makes up for my being an uninvited guest."

"What do you mean *uninvited?* You have a standing invitation, and you know it, Nicholas McGraw." She pulled the towel from her waist and hastily swiped it across her cheek.

"I thought I heard your voice, Nick." Uncle Tom strolled from his study, part of the evening paper clutched in one hand. "Here, let me take your jacket. You're staying for dinner, aren't you?"

"Of course he is," Mary said. "And TJ called. He'll be here any minute, late as usual. Do any of you cops ever actually leave work when the clock says it's time to go?" She turned her back, not waiting for a reply, and returned to the steaming pots on the range.

Nick and Tom exchanged a look. Mary had been a policeman's wife for years, and although her remark seemed critical, her tone belied the ingrained acceptance Nick knew would be there until Tom retired.

A blast of cool air announced TJ's arrival. He closed the door with a snap.

"Hey, Nick, ya' made it. Maybe we can relax and catch up." He placed a smacking kiss on his mother's cheek. "We've got the best food in town, great wine, and family. Perfect."

Tom set out wine glasses, and Mary retrieved a corkscrew.

"Nick," she said. "Would you do the honors?"

"Yes, ma'am." He grasped the opener and uncorked the chilled pinot.

The evening passed way too fast. With their long legs stretched before them, Nick, Uncle Tom, and TJ sprawled beside the fireplace, polishing off the last of the smooth merlot.

"Aunt Mary, I won't fit into my clothes when I go back to Philly. First Ada Blaine tempts me with homemade muffins, and now you stuff me with melt-in-your-mouth pork loin and enough mashed potatoes to choke a horse."

Mary came to stand behind his chair and rested her hand on his shoulder. "Any chance we can talk you into staying here?"

Nick drained his glass and pondered her question in silence. At that precise moment, her suggestion didn't seem so remote.

"One of these days, I just might surprise you." He gave her hand a gentle squeeze, then rose from his chair and stretched.

"Uncle Tom, TJ, I'm heading back to the cabin." He plucked his jacket from a hook by the door. "Thanks for bringing me up to speed, TJ. What's next?"

"I hope to hear from Strongsville PD by tomorrow," TJ said, also preparing to leave. "They're supplying background on Morelli. Maybe something will point to a local connection. Though, in all honesty, I doubt there is one."

Nick fished his keys from his pocket. "So you feel that Cassi really is in the clear?"

"I've double checked her statement." TJ picked up his jacket. "She's accounted for most of her time prior to the murder, and as near as I can tell her story holds up."

"Most of her time?" Nick repeated. He bit back another comment, reminding himself again that the investigation was *not* his to question. He'd already given his account, laid it out succinctly in the report he'd left at the station for TJ.

"One of her employees thought she'd left Fox Chapel earlier the day, *before* she stumbled over the body," TJ explained. "Her trip up here took longer than what I calculated, but I'll know more after I talk to her manager. She was unavailable when I called."

"So you haven't spoken with Cassi again?"

"Yes, I did." TJ shrugged into his coat. "I stopped at Ada's late this afternoon. Cassandra seemed uneasy, and I asked if being there alone made her nervous. She pointed out that she had Rufus to protect her."

Nick couldn't suppress a smile.

TJ laughed and added, "That dog slobbered all over me when I came to the door, so I guess I looked a little skeptical. She actually broke into a laugh. Not a bad looking woman when she loosens up."

"Can't argue with that," Nick agreed.

"I advised her to lock her door behind me." TJ looked straight at his mother. "Right now, I'd advise everyone in Pine Bluffs to do the same."

Tom wrapped his arm around Aunt Mary's waist.

"Don't worry about me," Mary said, smiling at her son and nephew. "I sleep with a policeman who carries a very big gun."

TJ's face turned sober, and he leaned in and placed a gentle kiss on his mother's cheek. "Goodnight, Mom. And please, stick close to that policeman."

Nick caught the look that passed between TJ and his uncle, and he wondered just how close Aunt Mary had come to meeting the murderer face to face.

Once outside, he and TJ paused beside Nick's truck.

"Goin' to be a chilly night," TJ said, buttoning his jacket. He turned to Nick. "Will I see you tomorrow?"

"Nope." Nick flipped up his collar against the chill. "I'm going to introduce an attractive young lady to the joys of wine country in autumn."

"So-oo, you figured a way to lure Cassandra away from her protective aunt, huh?" TJ said. He rested one hand on his car. "Enjoy yourself, but keep your guard up, okay?"

Nick opened the door to his truck. "What, you think she might seduce me, maybe stick a knife in my chest?"

"Don't be a smartass. We have bigger concerns here. I've considered unknown connections. An accomplice might not take kindly to Cassandra spending time with a cop. Someone did stick a knife in Mr. Morelli, Nick. Just be careful, pay attention, and use the organ that thinks."

Nick's conversation with Rich sprang to mind. His cousin's words of warning hit a nerve, but right now he wasn't about to bring up his past mistakes. He bumped TJ's elbow to defuse the building tension. "Hey, you don't happen to have a couple of condoms I could borrow, do you?"

"Very funny, you jackass." He shook his head. "Catch you later."

TJ got into his car and drove away.

Nick took a deep breath. Damn, he hated being at odds with his cousin. Cassi was off the short list of suspects, but TJ had made no attempt to hide the fact that he was still keeping tabs on her, and that didn't sit well with Nick.

Deep inside he understood, however, and that annoyed him as well. Guess he'd have to keep tabs on Cassi, too.

Chapter Ten

Sadie raced across the interstate back to Ohio, her thoughts keeping pace with the climbing speedometer. Her past had never seemed important. She'd always buried her head in the sand or did a line of coke, in an effort to forget those lost years. They'd never seemed important. Now her past loomed like a dark puzzle with a lifetime of missing pieces.

Her life hadn't been memorable or happy. In her estimation, foster care had been the pits. And pleasing anyone but herself hadn't been high on her list. Perspective parents always tossed her after a few weeks, sometimes after only a couple of days. Then tight-lipped case workers would grit their teeth and shuffle her back into the system.

Stifled anger and hurt bubbled up from deep inside her, tormenting her.

Damn, she needed a drink. Or a man. Men helped to dull the pain, too. For when a man held her and stroked her, she forgot about her empty life for a while. Her encounters were brief and purely physical. Yet that was the only time Sadie ever felt close to other human beings.

Even Rick, who had outlasted all of the others, would someday leave her. He used to tell her she was funny and pretty.

Not anymore.

Before too long, all the shit he'd put up with would hit the fan, and he'd walk. And as always, she'd be left alone to wallow in her own misery.

Violent shivers raced through her. She closed the car window and snuffed out her last smoke. *Who the hell cares?*

Grabbing a quick shower and changing clothes would eat up precious time, but what the fuck? She was already late.

A short time later, Sadie slipped through the side door of Al's Bar, looked around, and breathed a sigh of relief. Rick was tending bar, and her boss was nowhere in sight.

Al's had once been a popular neighborhood hangout. The cozy wooden booths lining the walls had been full every night. But the surrounding neighborhood, located on the seedier side of ever-growing Brecksville, had gone downhill. Brightly lit sports bars with customers waiting in line now dotted strip malls and shopping centers. Al's had taken on a used, outdated appearance. The booths were scarred and dull, and the ancient barstools now sported wide strips of tape to keep their seats intact.

Tonight, lazy country music echoed off the walls, and a motley mixture of patrons were scattered throughout. Sadie pegged most of them as college students. Al's staff never paid much attention to hastily flashed IDs.

She donned a well-worn apron while Rick worked his way down the bar, clearing dirty glasses as he approached.

"Hey, Rick." She darted a quick look around the room. "Is Al around?"

His eyes bored into hers. "He had to go get supplies and left about the time you were due to show up. Before he left, he asked me where you were. He looked pissed, too."

"What'd you say?" She tucked a pad and pen into her pocket.

"Nothin'. I'm done making excuses. My ass is grass if he finds out I'm covering for you, so from now on you are on your own." He ambled away to wait on a customer.

Cold air hit Sadie's back, and a whiff of sweetness accompanied Tina Hayes as she dashed in the door. Tina was as thin as tissue paper, except for her very impressive and questionably authentic breasts, and she habitually chewed one sweet stick of gum after another.

She spotted Sadie and made a beeline for her. Turquoise blue eye shadow framed Tina's gleaming eyes, and a rapid stream of words tumbled from her candy red lips. "They bumped him off! Just stuck a knife in him and dumped him in some swamp."

"What the hell are you talking about?" Sadie frowned. With her jaw going a mile a minute, Tina stopped dead in front of Sadie. Liberally applied blush, combined with her excitement, gave the skinny waitress an electric look.

"Bob."

"Bob who? I don't know what you're--"

"Morelli."

Sadie froze. Tina's jaw stilled, and she gawked with unabashed interest.

Oh. Oh, no! Robert Morelli.

The connection hit Sadie like a sledge hammer. "Holy shit." She'd been so fixated by the girl from Pittsburgh she'd paid no attention to the murdered guy, including his name.

Fuck!

"You knew him," Tina accused, her eyes narrowing. "You had a thing going with him once, didn't you?"

"Shh," Sadie cautioned, lowering her voice. "I didn't know him that well. We had a few laughs, shared a little weed last summer. That was before I moved in with Rick."

"Oh." Tina blinked rapidly.

Sadie forced a smug smile. "Rick made it real clear he didn't want another man hanging around. I already suspected Bob was gettin' in deeper than doin' a few hits with friends. So I told him to get lost."

"Have you seen him since then?"

"No." she said, emphasized with a firm head shake. "Not me. Last I heard, he'd moved to Strongsville and was living high on the hog."

They jumped apart as Rick slapped a couple of beers down on the bar. "I hate to interrupt you ladies, but could one of you deliver these to table four sometime tonight?"

Tina scooped up the drinks and mouthed, "Later."

Then she sped off.

Ignoring Rick's sarcasm, Sadie went to work. She couldn't wait for her shift to end. Al soon returned, and he tracked her as the crowd swelled and business hummed. To her relief, he wasn't in sight when the final customers drifted toward the door.

Sadie approached the bar.

"Rick, I'm heading home. It's been one hell of a day, and I'm beat." She dumped an untidy pile of bills and change on the bar. "Cash this in for me, will ya? Keep some. Treat yourself to some scotch."

She grabbed her jacket and scooted out the side door. Her tips made the difference between paying bills and creative juggling at the end of each month. Maybe another bottle of scotch would even the score between her and Rick.

The minute she burst into their apartment she dashed into the bedroom, tossing aside her coat and purse on the way. Clutter greeted her when she opened the closet. She grimaced at the mess, and then yanked a tattered shoe box from beneath a pile of magazines. After taking off the lid, she dumped the contents on the unmade bed and rifled through them.

She pounced on a photo in the scattered debris and held it up to the light.

The frozen image showed a couple at The Waterfront in Cleveland, laughing as wind tangled their clothes and whipped their hair into wild disarray.

The man in the photo was the late Robert Morelli. And leaning into his embrace, smiling up at him, stood Sadie.

Chapter Eleven

Fresh from her morning shower, wrapped from head to toe in an oversized towel, Cassi eyed the clothes she'd chosen. She wanted to be comfortable, but she wanted to look good, too.

Nothing wrong with that, she mused, donning a pale green, long sleeved pullover. No, there was nothing wrong with wanting to look good for a handsome man.

And Nick McGraw is one handsome man.

He'd readily agreed to Ada's suggestion about their trip to wine country.

"My pleasure," he'd said, and Cassi had to admit the idea of sharing any *pleasure* with Nick enticed her. She looked forward to letting him introduce her to wine tasting... and anything else she might want to taste.

She pulled on a pair of comfortable tan slacks and twisted to view her rear in the mirror. A reflected photo of her parents caught her attention. She turned and lifted the tiny oval frame off the bedside stand. Her mood shifted.

"I miss you both, so much," she whispered.

Fresh pain washed over her. Yet she sensed they would understand her need for this day, this time for herself. They'd want her to get past the grief and turmoil shadowing her life. Blinking back tears, she placed a fingertip kiss on the curved glass and returned the photo to her nightstand.

With brisk strokes, she put the finishing touches on her hair, then again checked the mirror. Her well toned, tidy reflection gave her confidence, and that was well worth the effort and time she put into maintenance.

"Okay, Nick, let's make this one unforgettable day." She stepped into the hallway and almost collided with Ada.

"It's nice to see a smile on your face," Ada said. "I don't blame you for anticipating a day with Nick."

Amidst laughter, they said together, "Hunky."

They entered the kitchen laughing, and discovered that Nick had already arrived.

"Good morning, ladies." He gave them a quizzical look and strolled in the door, clean shaven and accompanied by the clean, crisp scent of his aftershave.

Cassi caught her breath.

"It's an exceptional morning, Nicholas," Ada replied. "Today is going to be one of our classic fall beauties. So don't waste a minute of it."

Nick's gaze moved to Cassi. "Ready?"

"I am," she replied.

He claimed her hand. "Then let's get the day started."

He tightened his grip and led her out the door.

"Thanks for watching Rufus," Cassi tossed over her shoulder.

Ada stood in the doorway, and the dog appeared by her side. He whined softly, gently waving his tail.

Nick helped Cassi into the passenger seat and rounded the truck, moving with tiger-like grace. Surreptitiously, her eyes traveled the full length of his body. He slid into the driver's seat and shot her an easy smile. Cassi returned the smile. She wanted to say something clever. Anything, for Pete's sake. So far, her end of their morning conversation consisted of *I am* and thanking her aunt for watching Rufus.

Brilliant.

They pulled away, and she turned her attention to Ada and Rufus. "I hope Rufus behaves for her. If he gets bored, he can get into all kinds of trouble."

"I doubt he'll get bored. Quit looking so worried." He reached over and squeezed her hand as he turned onto the highway. "I'm sure Ada will do fine. She used to have dogs of her own, you know."

"Really? When was that?" Every time Cassi felt as if she were getting to know her aunt, something new turned up.

"When she first moved to Pine Bluffs, she was alone and kept to herself. I was just a kid and didn't pay much attention, but I heard my mom and Aunt Mary talking." Negotiating the curves with ease, Nick shot a brief glimpse at Cassi. "I used to roam the bluffs, and on one of my outings I crossed the edge of Ada's property down by the shore. Two dogs charged at me, barking like hell. I nearly jumped into the lake."

"I can't imagine you being afraid of anything."

"I was afraid of those dogs. They were huge."

Cassi laughed at the way his eyes rounded, and her earlier tension uncoiled. "Did they attack you?"

"No. Ada called them and they stopped and just stood there, kind of eyeing me up. I was shaking all over. Couldn't move. She walked over and stood between them, just stroking their heads. 'Come here, young man,' she ordered. I looked at her, then looked at the dogs. Looked back at her, and just shook my head."

Cassi giggled. "What did she do?"

"Ada came toward me. I considered running, but figured my two legs wouldn't get me out of there quicker than the eight big legs on those dogs. She walked right up to me and brought them with her, told them to sit -- and son of a gun, they both smacked their butts right down."

"I wish I could've seen you."

"When my voice came back, I said I was sorry, figuring that was the best way to save my skin. She seemed okay with that, and to cut this story down to size, I ended up in her kitchen eating the best muffins I'd ever tasted."

Nick went silent for several moments. Driving along, he cast quick glances out the window. Were there more youthful memories woven in the changing tapestry of the landscape?

Finally she asked, "Did you visit her often after you got to know her?"

He broke into a wide grin. "Oh, yeah. I stopped by pretty regularly, and then I started bringing my friends. Marcy... you remember her? She and I would take TJ, dump him in a wagon, and haul him around. We often ended up on Ada's porch drinking cold drinks and eating cookies, muffins, or whatever."

The mental image made Cassi smile. How enlightening to picture this man as a young boy. To imagine what had helped shape him, mold him.

"I think at first your aunt's herb gardens were something to occupy her time. But then people started wanting her plants. Local restaurants inquired about buying the herbs, and so on and so on." Nick's hand did a rolling motion.

"So her business just kind of *grew*," Cassi concluded, causing them both to laugh.

The road Nick took from Pine Bluffs threaded north through thick stands of sugar maples, dotted with evergreens. They passed rolling fields of corn, some already harvested with stubby stocks dotting the earth-turned rows.

Classic oldies rolled from the Ridgeline's hidden speakers, and Cassi began to relax. They bounced from one topic to another. Nick proved easy to talk to, as well as being a good listener. Once she got past the zip and sizzle, she liked him, really liked him, and wanted to know more about him. Not that the sizzle went away, oh no, but discovering he was more than just a drop dead handsome man warmed her heart.

Toned, fit guys came to her club on a regular basis. She'd dated a few, some more than once. Then she'd lose interest and concentrate on her business. Nick definitely fell into the toned and fit category, but Cassi suspected there was much more to him than the physical. Layers more. Though their casual conversation told her a lot about the man, Cassi felt she'd only scratched the surface.

When they topped a ridge she stopped mid-sentence, spellbound by what lay before them. Lake Erie stretched as far as she could see, blending into the horizon and running east to west like a shimmering blue ribbon.

Every picture, calendar, or ad she'd ever seen for the Great Lakes fell flat in comparison to what lay before her eyes. The beauty, the shades of blue. Colors changing where water met the sky. Blending together, yet separated by an almost invisible line.

"Hey," Nick reached over, gave her hair a tug. "You still in there?"

Cassi blinked. "Oh, sorry. It's just so, so..."

"Stunning, incomparable... like nothing else in this world."

Cassi looked at the man beside her. He'd grown silent, his attention focused on what lay before them. A barely visible smile curved his lips.

On a surge of emotion, Cassi reached for him. When her fingers touched the warm skin of his arm, he glanced down. His eyes met hers, and then returned to the road. He cleared his throat, and when his eyes lifted, the smile holding secrets turned into a broad grin.

"Welcome to Great Lakes Wine Country," he said, and sped down the ridge.

A major thruway hummed with traffic and followed the line of the lake. They passed beneath it, sweeping around a winding curve. Then the land flattened, and acres of rolling grape vineyards surrounded them.

One after another, perfect symmetrical rows as far as the eye could see were covered with lush vines and leaves flipping from green to gold in the breeze.

*****

Nick checked his rearview mirror, then slowed and edged the truck off the road. "Roll down your window."

Cassi looked doubtful, but did as he asked. He touched the button on his door to lower the glass on his side, too.

"Now take a deep breath." He inhaled deeply. "God, I forgot how potent this is."

He turned to Cassi. She'd stuck her head out the window. Eyes closed, she inhaled like a kid in a candy store.

"Oh, Nick. I can smell the grapes, almost taste them." She plopped back into the seat, relaxed against the headrest, and looked over at him. "I could fall in love with this place. Can we just sit here and sniff?"

"We could." He checked traffic and pulled from the roadside. "But we have a lot more than grapes to see, so let's get started. We've got all day."

Hours later, Nick glanced at the time. Holy shit, where had the day gone?

For him, strolling through farmer's markets and tasting local wines wasn't new. But he had to admit, as the day shot by, doing them with Cassi had put a new spin on things he'd done a million times before.

Her tenacious curiosity charmed him. She'd hung on the tour guide's every word when tasting local wines. Her eyes lit with delight, and sometimes, her nose wrinkled with indecision.

At one point, she bit into an Ida Red apple, laughing and fumbling for a Kleenex in her bag. He'd stilled her hand and wiped the sweet juice from her chin with his thumb. Then he'd leaned in and planted a quick kiss on the spot.

He stepped back, noting the quick flush of color that stained her cheeks, laughing when she grinned and quipped, "Works for me."

We've one more winery to hit." He helped Cassi load bags of apples into the truck. "Unless you're getting bored."

"Never." She scrambled happily into the truck. "Lead the way. There's so much stuffed into my brain about tasting wine, I'd feel cheated if I didn't visit every vineyard."

The look of delight on her face when they entered their final wine stop alerted Nick that they'd be there a while. They found the place crammed floor to ceiling with wine paraphernalia.

Nick discovered he could learn a lot about a woman by spending the day with her. Cassi admired a few items, chose a quirky wine opener, and moved on to the tasting bar. No lingering, no sorting through every shelf. She was a focused, decisive woman. He liked that.

She had paid attention throughout the day, he observed. Deliberately, she sipped the wine, and a little frown appeared as she tested it, tilted the glass, and swallowed. Her moist lips glistened.

Nick bet if he touched his tongue to those tempting lips, he'd taste an earthy quality not found in any bottle of wine.

Cassi's concentrating frown disappeared, and she handed her empty glass to the clerk. She checked another box on the order form. "Nick, this is amazing."

"I know." He leaned in to view her selections, placed his hand on her shoulder, and brought her against him. "You've made good selections. I go for the drier wines, too, but usually first timers lean toward sweeter wines. Catawba's, Niagara's... those are the popular choices made from local grapes grown right here along the lake. I think you should--"

Cassi hung on every word, but her chocolate brown eyes simmered with humor when he stopped mid-sentence.

Her closeness frayed his train of thought. He'd asked for it, using that sneaky move that had tucked her right against him. He wasn't prepared for the shot of heat. And her scent, somewhere between earthy and sweet, nailed his senses and fogged his brain. He intended to move away, but instead, he pressed closer to her.

She raised a delicate eyebrow and slid to one side. He suspected the maneuver was a deliberate attempt to maintain some invisible boundary. Nick respected the silent message, though he kept his hand cupped on the curve of her shoulder.

"I enjoy a good glass of wine." She dropped her eyes and studied her wine selections. "But I prefer semi-dry whites and reds like a merlot or good Chianti, served with the right food, of course. Not bad for a first timer, huh?"

She tilted her head. Amusement danced in her eyes, and she added, "The right company is a prerequisite, too."

"Okay, smartass," he said after a moment. "Let's look at what you've picked."

Cassi tapped her finger on her list. "Some of these are interesting, and I admit many are unfamiliar."

"Such as?" Nick queried.

"Chambourson is new to me. The taste is earthy, maybe a little sharp. For some reason pairing it with chocolate comes to mind, kind of a decadent desert."

She had Chambourson checked on her order. He smiled at her. "You have quite a shopping list going there. This is our last stop. Let's get your selections and stop at the chocolate shop in town. Then we'll go back to my cabin for the decadent part of the evening."

Cassi laughed and handed her list to the clerk. They loaded the wine, and within minutes, entered the quaint, sinfully sweet-smelling Cocoa Treats Chocolate Shop in North East.

The setting sun had turned Lake Erie's surface a dazzling shade of gold. As they left the little borough behind, Nick sneaked peaks at the impressive display in his rearview mirror.

"Oh look, Nick. What is that? They look like tractors on stilts." Cassi almost dumped the chocolates on the floor when she whipped around to look.

Nick snatched the ribbon wrapped brown box just in time, keeping one hand on the wheel. "They are."

She gaped at the cumbersome blue grape harvesters. One swung wide and started down another row. "Can we stop and watch them a minute?"

Nick signaled and pulled over. He turned and rested his arm along the seat behind her.

"See how they move through the rows, straddling the vines? They're harvesting grapes. Conveyors move the grapes into bins following along behind. You should see them after dark." He winked when she looked at him. "With lights on, they look like monsters rolling through the vineyards."

Cassi laughed. "Yes, I believe they would. I'd love to see that sometime."

When the slow moving machine disappeared from sight, they continued up the road. As they topped the ridge, she looked at him.

"Thank you, Nick. Today was wonderful. Who knew there was such a place in western Pennsylvania? What I saw and experienced today was something I'd expect in California... or Italy." She frowned. "You grew up here, yet you moved away. Don't you miss it?"

Nick considered his reply before answering. He made a habit not to let women he dated, or anyone he spent time with, for that matter, delve into his private thoughts or personal feelings.

Sure, he missed the town where he had grown up and the aroma of ripening grapes. Yet, to admit any of that was personal. Close to his heart.

When he touched a woman and held her soft, lush body close that was... well, just physical. A touch, a caress, and the final deep plunge that ended with the earth falling away, like plunging over a mile high water fall, was all just physical. He shared his body and enjoyed those with whom he shared it, but to peel the layers from his heart and mind, to share a want or a need, was foreign to him.

Until now. Until Cassi.

He drove along in silence, keenly aware of her dark eyes on him. He'd shown her vines heavy with grapes and trees dense with apples.

Sharing these things with her stirred up past memories imprinted on his mind and in his soul. Her attention and interest touched him.

"I do," he admitted at last. His eyes met hers. "I miss everything you saw today."

He lifted one hand, indicating the fields and hills ripe with color in the fading twilight. "And I miss Pine Bluffs, too. They'll always own a piece of me."

Her eyes softened, or was the fading light playing tricks on him? They drove on, and the shadows deepened, hiding autumn's splendor like a curtain closing on a spectacular show.

When they entered the outskirts of Pine Bluffs, Nick snapped his fingers close to her cheek, making her jump. "Hey, you went from laughing at monster grape pickers to somewhere that took all the fun from those come hither eyes. Don't look so serious. We're about to get to the decadent part of the day."

He turned the truck sharply and followed the curving drive in the gathering twilight. His cabin beckoned through the trees.

They rolled to a stop, and he turned to her.

She smiled and picked up the chocolates, and Nick's plan for a fun, casual date went straight to hell.

Chapter Twelve

His cabin smelled woodsy. Like cedar and the scent left behind when roaring fireplace logs turned cold. Nick brushed past Cassi and disappeared into the shadowed room.

"Wait here," he said. "I'll get the light."

A dull thud, followed by a muffled curse, made her smile. Nick returned, rubbing his left thigh. She crossed her arms and gave them a brisk rub. He placed strong, warm hands over hers, stilling the movement. "Cold?"

She couldn't move. She didn't want to. He rubbed one thumb across the back of her cold hand. Heat shot up her arm. If nothing else, she was getting warmer.

Nick raised her hand and placed a gentle kiss on her fingers. "I'll start a fire to chase away the chill."

Cool air whispered over the spot where his lips had touched her skin. Cassi's knees almost buckled. She didn't dare move, but fixed her gaze on Nick as he crossed the room. The solid wood floor muffled his footsteps, and the lamp he'd lit cast a circle of light that chased the shadows into far reaching corners.

He knelt on the raised stone hearth and clicked a long-handled igniter. Dry kindling erupted with a whoosh. The instantaneous flames created a vivid pattern, highlighting knotty pine throughout the room and doing a primitive dance on the cabin walls. Crackling flames raced over the bank of logs, and warmth crept across the floor. The heat surrounded Cassi like a subtle, steamy caress.

Nick rose. With one hand braced on the stone carved mantel, he gazed into the growing fire. Cassi lingered outside the expanding circle of firelight, scrutinizing six plus feet of man.

She admired his broad shoulders. As well as his long, lean, tapered torso and the firm curve of his drool-worthy backside hugged by snug denim. She found the outside package stimulating. But the inside was very complex... like a good wine waiting to be sampled.

And wouldn't it be interesting to sample Nick McGraw?

She dragged her reluctant gaze from temptation to scrutinize the room. Two night-darkened skylights were set high above them between honey-colored beams. The room was spacious, open from the kitchen to the stone-faced fireplace. An oversized sofa, covered with well-worn fabric and a myriad of colorful pillows, faced the hearth.

For a man on vacation, he seemed quite at home in his surroundings.

Several empty beer bottles were lined up on the counter. A cup, neatly inverted on a paper towel, sat next to a coffeemaker. And nearby, a tee shirt hung haphazardly over the back of a chair.

A neat pile of manila folders rested on a time-worn wooden table next to his laptop. And stacked beside a large, lumpy-looking chair rose a mini-tower of paperbacks.

Organized clutter. He was trying to relax, but judging from the laptop and what she'd bet were files from work, he hadn't quite succeeded in leaving his job behind.

As Nick braced the bottle of Chambourson and twisted the corkscrew firmly in place, Cassi emerged from the shadows, pulled to the hearth by the dancing flames.

"You handle that wine opener very well," she teased.

The cork released with a subtle pop, and with a slow, lazy smile, he said softly, "I handle a lot of things very well."

Not missing a beat, he scooped up two wine glasses from Presque Isle Winery's gift pack.

Cassi edged closer to the fireplace while Nick filled the glasses with a robust, deep red wine. He sauntered across the room, balancing both glasses in one hand and clutching a small box of chocolates in the other. Cassi drew in a deep breath and released it slowly in an effort to calm her racing heart. Her cheeks flamed, heat from the fire engulfing her. That warmth was tepid, though, compared to the heat building inside her as Nick closed the distance between them.

He placed the filled glasses and chocolate on the hearth, then tossed several bright sofa cushions to the floor at her feet. His hand closed over hers and gave it a quick tug.

She laughed and tumbled onto the makeshift bed.

Nick placed a brimming wine glass in her hand and tilted his glass, touching hers. The red wine sparkled in the firelight, and he sealed the silent toast with a tender kiss.

He pulled back and looked into her eyes. Using one arm, he tugged her closer, and together they sank into the cushions. They sipped wine in the flickering firelight. And between long, sweet draughts of one another, they shared bites of melt-in-your-mouth, cream filled chocolates.

He closed his mouth over hers. He was demanding, yet gentle. She hadn't known his kiss would be like this, and when his hand brushed with feather lightness against the side of her breast, she quivered, wanting more.

Twice he topped off their glasses. The tangy wine mellowed when they sampled the rich, dark chocolate. His firm lips tasted anything but mellow. She kissed him, savoring the moment.

Hot. Sweet. Male.

He grazed a burning path with his teeth, nipping the tender flesh of her neck, nudging, nuzzling, and driving her to wild distraction.

Cassi closed her eyes on a long, deep sigh. Was it the wine, or the scent of his heated skin making her head spin?

"More wine?" Nick murmured, his voice deep and rich, like the potent combination of wine and chocolate they were sharing.

She tipped back and gazed into his mesmerizing gold-flecked hazel eyes.

Unknown territory. *Dangerous* territory.

"I think I'll pass." She placed a restraining hand on Nick's chest. "It's hard to know if the warmth I'm feeling is from the fire, the wine, or... the company."

"Do you have to know?" He touched his mouth to hers. "As long as you're enjoying the warmth."

Cassi shifted and put distance between them. She fought the helpless sensation of standing on the fast crumbling bank of a raging river. If unchecked, she'd be swept into unknown swirling currents and be dragged under.

Nick's intentions were clear. He wanted her. And to be perfectly honest, she wanted him, too. But could she handle a brief fling?

Nick was on vacation. All too soon he'd return to his job, his life. A life she knew nothing about. How could a man like Nick *not* be seeing someone?

What would happen if she let go? If she gave herself, and her body, to Nick McGraw, and he walked away. Could she pick up the pieces? Could she go on unscathed?

"Cassi?" He lifted one of his eyebrows a fraction and offered her more chocolates. For a crazy moment, she stared at the sweet confections. Why didn't they melt? When Nick's hands were on *her*, she nearly pooled at his feet.

She studied the assortment, and then chose an orange truffle.

"I really shouldn't," she said, biting into the creamy delight. "I'll have to double my workout tomorrow."

"I can't see that you have much to worry about." Nick's bold gaze roamed over her. He readjusted, settled her against his side, and then one-handedly topped off her glass. "Tell me how you got to be the owner of a fitness center."

Licking remnants of the truffle from her fingers, Cassi focused on the simmering coals. Talking about something familiar brought her back to center. Allowed her to step away from the abyss of emotion and physical need.

She pursed her lips, tasting remnants of wine, chocolate, and Nick. "I grew up a part of the fitness craving generation, exposed to everything the

YMCA offered. Aerobics, nautilus training, yoga, Pilates. Fit TV created a demand for all of them. I loved the challenges and did it all."

"You got bit by the fitness bug at the YMCA?" Nick's hand rubbed lazily up and down her side.

"No," she covered his hand, stilling the movement. "My dad was the Y's executive director. I went there every day after school. When mom finished work -- she was a teacher -- she'd meet us, and we'd all go home together. It worked for us as a family, and over the years I got hooked."

Nick took a sip of wine. "And then what?"

"After college I worked at a fitness club in Fox Chapel. When the owner decided to sell, I was ready to make the move. That pretty much covers my rather ordinary life."

"You're an achiever, Cassi," Nick said, brushing her hair aside and touching his lips to her neck. "Not only did you challenge yourself physically, you went further. You got educated, you worked, probably very hard, and *that* is not ordinary."

She shivered.

"That," he whispered, "is admirable." His warm breath tickled her neck, and he inched his hand slowly up her body.

They were right back where they'd been before the little detour into her formative years. Nick pinned her to the cushions. He kissed her hard this time, rocketing her pulse and blasting reason all to hell. Cassi wrapped her arms tightly around Nick's neck and returned the kiss.

Her conscience screamed, *be sensible, stop now!*

She was so damned tired of being sensible.

The taste of wine and orange truffles and Nick stoked a need he'd so adeptly primed, and her split second of indecision vanished. She surged upward and pressed her body to his.

His bold hands stroked her body's curves and valleys. Being possessed, explored, and needed made her mind reel. Lost in the moment, Cassi clung to Nick. Stunned by her hunger to be held, to be set on fire, scorched by passion and aroused to a fever pitch like no man had ever done before.

He skimmed the sensitive skin beneath her chin with hot, lingering kisses. She pulled him closer. The rigid muscles running the length of his back hardened like coiled steel beneath her hands.

Watching her steadily, Nick rolled the hem of her shirt upward. She lifted her arms. He tugged the shirt over her head and tossed it aside. His eyes darkened. Hidden promises and unleashed desire flickered in their tawny depths.

"You're beautiful, Cassandra. So beautiful," he rasped, burying his face in her tender flesh. Pleasure spread and sizzled through her like melting butter. He kissed the soft swell of her breast, setting her afire with coaxing, gentle nips, hot enough to sear the skin from her bones.

Her transparent bra hid nothing. Being exposed so brazenly drove her wild, excited her, like being caught getting dressed... or undressed. Erotic thoughts exploded in her head. Thoughts so shocking, so blatant that shyness rushed over her.

Cassi made an effort to cover herself.

Nick claimed her hands and halted her attempt to hide herself from him. His eyes wove a sensuous spell, and she crumbled.

His fingers fumbled with her bra. He muttered a soft curse, and seconds later, the lacy garment lay on the floor.

A moan escaped her trembling lips when he closed his mouth firmly over one thrusting breast. Cassi arched up, enveloped in the hot, wet sensation of his tongue on her bare flesh.

Without warning, Nick jerked away.

"Shit," he muttered, and Cassi's eyes flew open. "Honey, we've got company."

For a brief moment, his blazing eyes lingered on her. He cursed and rolled to his feet.

Confused, Cassi jumped up. "Where...?"

He scooped up her discarded clothes and pressed them into her hands. He pointed down the hall. "First door on the right."

Sharp knocking resounded as she dashed away.

"Hey, thought you might have already hit the sack."

She recognized that voice and stopped to look behind her.

Nick stepped back and motioned his cousin TJ into the cabin.

Chapter Thirteen

The pungent scent of late season parsley flourishing amongst twiggy oregano filled the air. Rufus scrambled down the porch steps, casting about, reading unseen messages only a dog's nose could decipher.

Cassi deposited a pair of free weights onto Ada's porch. Keeping fit was hard work, but worth the effort. This morning she craved a workout. Taking the time, making the effort, guaranteed she'd feel good. Plus, the familiar routine would take her mind off last night's fiasco. She needed to put things in perspective, evaluate something else that made her feel good.

The touch of Nick McGraw's hands.

She likened TJ's arrival to a dash of cold water on an out-of-control blaze, and she found it thoroughly embarrassing. She'd scurried into Nick's bathroom like a frightened rabbit. Then while struggling into her crumpled top, she'd overheard Nick and TJ's heated exchange through the closed door.

As soon as Nick's cousin left, she'd insisted he drive her home. The interruption had caused a definite mood shift, and the evening had come to an end.

"Good morning." Ada's voice, husky with sleep, came from behind her. "You're up early."

Cassi's face grew warm. Avoiding Ada's eyes, she returned the greeting. Last night after Nick had dropped her off, she'd given Ada an abrupt, "Good night." Then she'd hurried to her room. Inexcusable behavior, and this morning Cassi struggled with guilt.

Rufus bounded onto the porch, creating a distraction. He bumped her and woofed softly, splitting his generous affection between them. Ada produced a bone-shaped treat from her pocket, and Rufus smacked his furry rump down onto the porch. He focused adoring eyes on her and waited.

Ada laughed and tossed the bone. Rufus snapped it up, losing nary a crumb.

"Good boy," she crooned, and then said, "Okay."

He sprang from the porch, racing in happy circles before stopping with a flourish to lap noisily from his water bowl.

"How'd you do that?" Cassi declared in amazement. "One day with you, and his behavior surpasses the past couple of weeks with me."

"It's not so hard," Ada replied, settling into a chair. "I used to have dogs, big beautiful guys, and they were as docile as lambs. Their looks could scare the pants off strangers, but they were soft-hearted lugs."

Affection and maybe a little wistfulness came through in her voice.

"Nick told me about them." Cassi sat on the top step and leaned against the porch railing. "He admitted being scared to death the first time he met them."

Ada chuckled. "He was at first. Then I think he came around to see them as much as to visit me."

"I'd be willing to bet the goodies you provided for him and his friends had something to do with his visits," Cassi scoffed.

Her aunt smiled down at her. "He told you about that?"

"Yes, on the way to North East. I asked him how long he'd known you."

"Ah, so you learned a little about both of us."

Cassi couldn't take it. She owed her aunt an apology, and the words tumbled out. "I'm sorry I went to bed so quickly last night. We stopped at Nick's for wine, and I was tired when he brought me home. Tired... and a little cranky."

"Honey, look at me," Ada coaxed. "Cassandra, I'm not about to pry into what went on between you and Nick. And I fully understand why you would want to learn more about me. So let's quit dancing around and wasting time. Your visit will go by in the blink of an eye. We don't have time to beat around the bush. Trust me. If I were upset, you'd know it."

Feeling a bit ashamed of her assumptions, Cassi gave her a weak smile. This relationship was all new territory.

"You were starting to land on your feet when you arrived," Ada continued. "Then you got smacked down again through no fault of your own. I'm not here to judge what you did last week or last night."

"Even if I'd stayed out all night?"

Ada shook with quiet laughter. "My dear girl, if a man like Nicholas McGraw plied me with wine and his charming manner, I wouldn't think twice about spending the night with him." She reached down and took Cassi's hand. "Why, you must be asking yourself, would a stuffy old woman like me be so... so liberal?"

She laid her fingers against Cassi's cheek. "Because I haven't forgotten what it's like to lose yourself in the moment. To be kissed blind, deaf, and dumb while the combination of good wine and a handsome man makes it all so tempting."

Cassi cupped her hand over Ada's. Her breathing hitched. Ada's trust was reflected in the depths of her eyes.

"I want you to know me, Cassandra. If talking to others about me helps you get answers, then do it. And *I* want to learn about you."

"Your trust overwhelms me." Cassi laced her fingers with Ada's and she studied her aunt's strong hand, with its neat clipped nails. "Almost since the day I arrived, my life's been all tangled up, and I've dragged you into the middle of the whole mess."

"Cassandra, I know in my heart you did not stick a knife in that man. Maybe it's because you're my flesh and blood, but I guarantee all the investigating and sniffing into your background is just going to tell them what I already know."

Her words humbled Cassi. After all these years, for whatever reason, she and her aunt had been brought together, and she desperately wanted to return Ada's unconditional love and trust.

Cassi clutched her aunt's hand tighter and thought back to a time not long ago when loving and trusting family had been as natural as breathing. With only a few words -- *you're my flesh and blood* -- Ada had assured Cassi she wasn't alone now, either.

*****

Caffeine hummed through Nick's veins as he tipped back cup number three. Agitation, fueled by the coffee he kept downing, simmered within him.

Damn that TJ.

Nick had been totally immersed in Cassi last night when his cousin's unexpected visit had sent her dashing into his bathroom. Granted, he'd almost broken the vow he'd made not to get involved. Hell, maybe he should thank TJ for stopping him.

But after TJ had found out Nick had company and discovered who it was, he'd given him a bunch of shit about her still being a possible suspect. Due to Nick's state of mind at the time, his cousin's attitude had just plain pissed him off.

Either she was a suspect, or she wasn't. Nick wasn't on the case. He didn't even live here anymore and... oh, crap.

TJ had a point. A good one. And after his sudden ill-timed appearance, the evening had come to an abrupt halt. Nick admitted that *that* was what had really pissed him off.

Cassi had been quiet on the way back to Ada's. He hadn't been ready for the night to end, but he'd backed off when she'd made it crystal clear she wished to leave.

He'd respect her wishes. For now.

At the door to Ada's cottage, she'd thanked him -- politely, formally -- for a great day. He'd forced himself to keep the goodnight kiss brief, because if he'd tasted her too much he might not have let her go.

Instincts are second nature to cops. What bugged Nick was that his instincts were... well, blurry. If he only had more facts, more information with which to work, maybe something would click. TJ had readily admitted there was a lot of speculation.

Currently, Nick's biggest concern was a time lapse. Apparently, Cassi's account of her drive from Fox Chapel to Pine Bluffs lacked detail, and that didn't suit TJ -- Mr. By-the-Book McGraw. She hadn't been able to tell him exactly what time she'd left her apartment, and had forgotten how many times she'd stopped, or for how long. This left gaps in her story, unexplained time TJ seemed hell-bent to pin down.

Nick tossed out his remaining coffee, grabbed his keys, and headed to his cousin's duplex. He was on a damn vacation and should just back away, not get involved.

Yeah, right. The friggin' stack of case files from Philly he passed on his way out the door was proof that detectives were *never* on vacation.

As he drove across town, he rehashed last night's encounter, chewing over every steamy detail. Remembering the glow of flickering firelight on Cassi's creamy skin made his mouth water. TJ had known he'd planned to see Cassi, had even joked with him about the date. Yet when his cousin had arrived and found them together, he'd gotten all bent out of shape.

Why the turn around?

He had accused Nick of complicating *his* friggin' case by zeroing in on Cassi. Then he'd had the gall to suggest Nick use his head and pursue some other female. What the hell had TJ uncovered that was making him act like such a damn jerk?

Locating TJ's place was easy.

Nick delivered several hard knocks to the well-polished hardwood door and waited, hands thrust into his jeans.

"Took you long enough." He brushed past TJ, striding into the apartment when the door opened.

"Oh, please, come right in," TJ spoke to the empty doorway, then he shut the door with enough force to tilt a picture on the wall. He paused to straighten the picture and proceeded to briskly rub a towel over his wet hair. Looking weary, he turned and draped the towel over his shoulders. "How about some coffee?"

"I've already had my daily allotment and half of tomorrows," Nick said with a tight smile. He scrubbed both hands over the stubble on his face. "Aw, shit. Sorry to bite your head off. Can we talk?"

TJ nodded. Using his fingers to comb his tangled hair into place, he ambled into the kitchen. A narrow counter separated it from the rest of the room, and sunlight spilled through the window.

Nick claimed one of two high-backed stools while TJ poured himself some coffee.

"Nice place," he remarked, scanning the room. "How long have you lived here?"

"I bought the whole unit about three years ago," TJ said, sliding onto the stool beside Nick. "Figured that by living in one side and renting the other, I could pay off my mortgage sooner. Then maybe I'll move into a single and rent both apartments."

Nick grinned. "Taking tips from your folks?"

"Yeah," TJ acknowledged. "Owning all those cabins they've accumulated over the years will provide a nice income when Dad retires." He frowned and took a tentative sip from his steaming cup. "Although, after what happened on Border Road, they might consider selling some now."

"Anything new turn up at the site?"

TJ shook his head. He stood, opened the freezer, and extracted some frozen bagels. "Mind if I eat while we talk? I have to be at work in half an hour."

"No problem. Throw one of those in for me too. My breakfast consisted of three cups of coffee."

"Hell, no wonder you're so wired and grumpy." He microwaved several bagels and popped one into the toaster.

While moving about the kitchen grabbing butter, jelly, and two bananas from a bowl on the counter, he filled Nick in on new developments with the case. "We're almost certain Morelli was killed at the Border Road cabin. I'm betting the blood stains found on the floor will match his. The items inside, along with the car parked out front, are his. So far, though, no one we've talked with remembers seeing or hearing anything unusual prior to the body being found."

"Has time of death been established? Last night you said the time of Cassi's arrival in town could be suspect. What's that all about?"

"Sorry about my timing last night." TJ used wooden tongs to lift a steaming bagel from the toaster. "I'd forgotten the plans you mentioned after dinner at Mom and Dad's."

He placed the hot food on a plate and slid it toward Nick. "I went over Cassi's statement again, carefully. The vagueness of her travel time bothers me. Like I told you, there is a window -- granted, it's small, but it's there -- of unaccounted for time." TJ pinned him with a hard, direct look. "I *have* to look at everything, Nick, and separate personal feelings. I'm trying to be objective here."

Nick spread sweet-smelling jam on a warm bagel and mulled over the circumstances. The fact that the jam was some of Ada Blaine's finest hit home. He took a bite and relished the sweet taste. Whether they wanted to admit it or not, the tapestry of entanglement did make TJ's investigation personal, on so many levels.

"Got any juice?" he mumbled around a mouthful of bagel.

"In the fridge," TJ said, swallowing his last bite. Then he added, "I'm going to talk to Cassandra again, and I want to talk to a woman by the name of Elaine Delacor, her manager at Fox Chapel Fitness. I'll contact

Miss Delacor this morning."

"Are you serious about your cockeyed accomplice theory?" Nick raised one eyebrow. "That would involve a lot of coincidences. She came to Pine Bluffs to meet her aunt, not help plan a murder. Come on, TJ."

He poured a glass of orange juice and took a gulp. "That's really stretching it."

"In theory, I agree." TJ picked up his plate and cup. "But until we can make sure she had absolutely no connection to Morelli, I have to play it out. You know he was a dirtbag druggie, and I'll be the first to point out he sure doesn't seem like Cassandra's type. But I've got to run the data, and I've got to ask questions. That way, she's either cleared or we take a closer look."

Nick stared at TJ's departing back, then walked over to the door and waited until his cousin returned, buttoning his uniform shirt.

"Trust me, okay?" TJ said.

They both walked outside. He pulled the door shut behind them and pointed toward a dark green kayak leaning against his garage.

"Take my kayak and do what you came here to do. Relax, for God's sake, and enjoy your vacation."

They stood in TJ's driveway, staring at the kayak.

"Okay." Nick heaved a sigh. Why not? Part of him agreed with his cousin. The cop part. He knew how to run a tight case, and that's exactly what TJ was doing. He clapped TJ on the shoulder. "Let me back up my truck and load her."

The personal dilemma he'd waded into sent up red flags. His own personal Fourth of July celebration.

Maybe TJ was right. He'd spend a day on the lake and take a step back from the tangle of feelings being with Cassi had woven into his head.

Chapter Fourteen

Ada pulled Cassi to her feet. "Come on. Enough serious talk. If we're going to keep these hot bodies fit, we can't be sitting on the porch all day."

With Rufus in tow, they set out to walk around the lake. Ada couldn't help but wonder if Cassi realized that a few moments ago she'd called the cottage *home*.

Once they'd left the cottage behind and the path became more remote, Ada unsnapped the leash and let Rufus run ahead of them.

"You asked me about your mother, Cassandra. Now you tell me about the Burkes. I never knew much about them, only that they could provide a good home for you."

"I never wanted for anything. Not important things, anyway. Unless you count my need for designer jeans or my own TV, neither of which I got without working my teenage butt off."

"So you were a working teenager."

"Oh, yeah. I worked at Arby's, pushing roast beef sandwiches all through high school. In college, I did the work study deal. Those were the days." Cassi rolled her eyes.

Ada chuckled. "So they weren't pushovers as parents. You seem to have survived their rules of discipline."

"Discipline tempered with lots and lots of love." Cassi picked up a stick and tossed it. Rufus scrambled ahead, tail whipping with glee. "They loved me. I never had to wonder about that. But what got me, what really, really set the bar high, was their love for one another."

They'd slowed to a stroll, and Ada draped her arm over Cassi's shoulder. "Could be that high bar is what's kept a bright, attractive woman like you unattached, still single."

"Oh, God. If I had a dollar for every time someone's pointed out my single status, I'd pay off the whopping mortgage I have on Fox Chapel Fitness." Cassi stooped and snatched up the slobbery stick the dog dropped in her path for one more toss.

As was typical for fall, the sun had chased away the morning mist and then retreated behind drifting clouds. The air had turned cool, and a brisk breeze rattled the leaves drying on the trees. Ada and Cassi settled on the porch with steaming mugs of tea after their walk. Rufus curled against the door and promptly fell asleep.

"What made Nick's parents move from Pine Bluffs?" she inquired, curious about Nick, TJ, and their friends. "He seems to belong here, and I have to wonder why he never came back when it's obvious he loves the place."

"Alan and Elisa McGraw are a lovely couple. I wasn't around when Alan was in law school. That's where he met Elisa, the daughter of one of his professors, and fell head over heels for her. She's quite beautiful. Reed thin, with chestnut brown hair and big blue eyes."

"Alan is probably like all the McGraws I've met so far." Cassi grinned. "Drop dead gorgeous."

"You've noticed." Ada laughed.

"They must have lived here while Nick was young. He seems to have a real tie to the area."

"True. I've always felt Nick fit better in Pine Bluffs, but after he was born I believe Elisa got restless."

Cassi's eyes widened. "Was there trouble in the marriage?" She chewed her lip thoughtfully. "Maybe that's why a man like Nick is still unattached." Then she frowned. "If he *is*, in fact, unattached."

Ada shook her head. "If there's a woman back in Philly pining away for Nick, I'm sure it's one-sided. Far as I know, he's been a tough one to pin down. And no, his parents' marriage wasn't troubled. Elisa just wasn't cut out for small town life. Mary, TJ's mother, is very different from Elisa. Nevertheless, they became friends. Mary's told me she all but raised Nick those first few years, and Lisa -- that's what Alan calls Nick's mom -- started doing freelance decorating work. She left Nick in Mary's care."

"Why did Mary wait so long to have TJ? He's got to be eight or more years younger than Nick." Cassi scratched Rufus' ear absently. He was awake now and sat leaning against her chair.

Ada considered her comment for a moment. "Mary wanted a big family, but I guess it wasn't in the cards. She loved Nick like a son, and when TJ came along, she was in heaven. Lisa, on the other hand, felt unfulfilled career-wise and made the choice to not have more children."

"Understandable," Cassi mused, "and that explains the bond between TJ and Nick. What caused Nick's parents to leave Pine Bluffs?"

"Elisa had a degree in interior decorating, and when the opportunity to pursue her career in Philadelphia came about, Alan stood behind her. Her dad pulled some strings and helped him land a job with a prominent law firm in Philly. Nick was a teenager when they moved."

"Hmm... I'll bet he wasn't too happy about moving away."

"Ah, yes," Ada rolled her eyes. "Nicholas was quite a handful. He ran away once and hitched all the way across the state. Everyone was frantic until he showed up on Tom and Mary's doorstep."

"Did he finally accept the inevitable?" Cassi asked.

"Of course." Ada smiled. "Being the handsome young man he is, he soon made friends. He went on to college, did a stint in the Marine Corps, and then went back and joined Philadelphia's finest. He shot through the ranks in record time, and from what Mary's told me, he's one fine investigator."

Ada's tea was cold. Leaning over the railing she dumped the last of it. She couldn't help but smile, remembering all the years she'd know the McGraws.

"Times change." She gave Cassi a rueful look. "For years, they visited regularly. I remember one summer in particular. Nick came by a few times, but didn't stay long. Something was different. From what I heard, the girls summering with their parents in Mary's cabins had their hands full."

A mischievous twinkle lit Cassi's eyes. "Wouldn't it have been fun to park by a moonlit Pine Shadow Lake with a young, handsome, and I'm sure very quick-handed, Nick McGraw?"

Chuckling, Ada nodded in agreement. "I'm glad you had a good time yesterday," she said, moving toward the door. "This time of year is the best. This evening you'll get to meet some of my friends. The committee for the Fall Festival is meeting here."

"Will Mary McGraw come?" Cassi said, following Ada.

"Yes, she will." Standing aside, Ada let Cassi and Rufus in through the open doorway, and added, "I'm sure she has plenty of interesting stories about Nick."

"Oh." Cassi shrugged as she washed her hands. "I'm not really interested in hearing more about Nick McGraw."

Ada's brows rose. *And the leaves won't fall from the trees this fall.*

*****

Nick enjoyed the quiet solitude of Pine Shadow Lake. This time of year, he had it all to himself. He steered the kayak to the far end of the lake, using powerful strokes, and then drifted along the shoreline. Frequent workouts kept him in prime condition, but he hadn't kayaked in years. He suspected he'd pay the price.

His aching muscles would recover. Today he needed to clear his muddled head, to put his job and personal entanglements aside. Physical exertion provided a release valve, and until recently, a good session at the gym usually did the trick.

He glided along the lake's glass-like surface. The day slipped away, and with it the tension that had been coiled inside him like a spring since last night.

He stopped to explore, pulling the kayak ashore under sheltering branches. The familiar haunt stirred sharp, poignant memories of endless, lazy summer days long ago.

Winters had been Currier and Ives perfect, and then, of course, there was autumn. The lake around him reflected reds, golds, and crazy splashes of yellow. Off to his left, bringing with it the smell of burning leaves, a hazy cloud hung low over the treetops. He drifted and a light breeze sprang up. God, he loved this place.

Evening approached quickly. He steered the kayak through reflected images on the lake. Whether by design or simple coincidence, Nick found himself rounding an outcrop of tall water grasses and moving toward Ada Blaine's cottage.

He pulled the paddle from the water and laid it across his lap, then tilted his cap back for an unobstructed view. The trim craft drifted into the wide, copper-colored ribbon cast by the setting sun. He and the kayak became one, their dark outline casting a solitary silhouette.

Voices interspaced with static bursts of laughter -- female laughter -- carried across the water. He narrowed his eyes and probed the encroaching shadows. Outlined in the fading twilight, several individuals lounged on Ada's sprawling porch.

After quietly making his way to shore, he stepped from the kayak and pulled it onto the bank. He took a sweatshirt from his duffle, tossed his cap aside, and pulled on the shirt. Running a hand through his wind-tousled hair, he trudged up the path through Ada's gardens.

"Evening, ladies," he drawled, approaching the porch.

Six pair of eyes swung to him as he emerged from the shadows. Several candles, scattered about on tables and stands, highlighted their features in flickering light.

"Well, good-evening, Nicholas." Ada glanced toward his upturned kayak. "Out on the lake a little late, aren't you?"

He placed one foot on the bottom step, shoved his hands deep into his pockets, and smiled up at the assembled group.

"Let me introduce my friends," Ada said before he could reply. She pulled the chain on a tiny tabletop lamp, and soft light spilled across the porch. Whimsical dragonflies etched into the shade danced across the wall and the low porch ceiling.

"You know your Aunt Mary and Cassi, of course, but I'm not sure you remember Molly Hirtzel, Millie Banks, or Lois Farrell. Millie and Lois are sisters. Their parents used to run the dairy bar in town. Ladies, meet Nicholas McGraw, Tom and Mary's nephew.

"I met you at the police station a few days ago," Molly offered. "I was filing a complaint."

"I remember. Did they get whoever was responsible for damaging your gardens?"

Molly looked pleased when he recalled her plight. "As a matter of fact, Officer Allen called me the next day. We have a top notch police department in Pine Bluffs."

"I agree." Nick crossed his arms and leaned against the porch railing. He looked at Millie and Lois. "I remember great milkshakes at The Brown Cow. Does your family still own it?"

"Lois and I inherited the Cow when our parents passed away several years ago," Millie responded. "My husband Dave and I run it now, and Lois helps. Stop by, Nick, and I'll make you a shake. What's your favorite?"

"Root beer, hands down."

"Root beer's one of our best sellers. Come by while you're in town, and I'll treat you to a super-duper sized shake."

"That's an offer I can't refuse." He sent her a wide grin and then glanced at his watch. "Guess I'll have to hoof it back to the cabin," he said, straightening from the railing. "Ada, is it okay if I leave TJ's kayak here? I'll come by for it tomorrow."

"Of course. But that's quite a hike, Nick. I'm sure Cassandra will be happy to run you home. We've been boring her to death with our committee meeting."

Cassi opened her mouth, and then closed it. She blinked several times. "Ah, yes... I can do that." She shoved herself to her feet. "I'll get a sweater and meet you out front."

Nick's gaze followed her swift retreat across the porch and through the door. She'd been caught off guard; her expression gave that away. She did not want to be alone with him. And maybe, like him, she wondered how far things would have gone the other night if TJ hadn't shown up.

Suddenly aware of five curious faces observing him, Nick expressed pleasure to have met the other women, gave Aunt Mary a quick kiss on the cheek, and said goodnight. Then he dashed to the kayak for his duffle and hurried to meet Cassi.

*****

Cassi donned a hoodie and zipped it before she stepped out the door. Rounding the corner, Nick fell in step with her, and side by side they approached her CRV. He opened the driver's side door for her and she slid in, starting the engine as he circled around to the passenger side.

He settled in beside her and swept his gaze over her as he snapped his seatbelt in place. The sexy-smelling, broad-shouldered man filled a good portion of the CRV.

Heat built inside her.

At a loss for words, she stared straight ahead trying to banish the memory of Nick's mouth closing over her naked breast. She sneaked a glance at his profile, outlined in the glow of her dash lights. That didn't help. Now breathing took so much effort she feared she'd start gasping.

He draped his arm along the back of the seat and brushed her shoulder with his lean fingers. He caught her eye and curved his lips. She reversed down the lane and swung onto the highway, thankful for the diversion. Because if he kept smiling at her like that, she'd melt like hot wax.

"Ada has some nice friends." He refocused his attention on the road ahead.

"Yes, she does." Cassi pounced on the topic, anything to take her mind off the heat building in her like a stoked furnace. "They're energetic, and all of them have a terrific mindset. Once they learned about my background, they hit me with a million questions. Before I knew it, I'd volunteered to give them a few impromptu workout sessions."

She was babbling. But at least she had cooled down.

That is, until Nick's tone changed.

"No kiddin'?" He sounded surprised... and *amused*?

Maybe she had only imagined the amused part. Slowing to pass through the center of town, she chanced a fast look at him. The dark interior of the CRV revealed nothing, so she continued, "Ada and her friends aren't ladies who meet just to chat and knit. Far from it. They're all for fitness and healthy living. I suspect that's a result of Fit TV; they all admitted to watching it, but I told them I'd be more than happy to create a fitness regime for them anyway and..."

No question about it; Nick's shoulders shook with laughter. She frowned and tightened her grip on the wheel. They'd arrived at the cabin turnoff, and she hung a sharp right.

"Something funny about that?" she asked, clenching her teeth while she slowed to negotiate the lane to his cabin.

"You bet." He chuckled, absently rubbing his eye. "I had a quick flash of Aunt Mary doin' a little dance routine like 'Sweatin' to the Oldies'." He gestured, feigning arm curls.

They'd reached the cabin, and Cassi stomped the brake.

Nick slapped both hands on the dash as they rocked to a stop and yelped, "What the hell are you doing?"

She shoved the gearshift into park and cut the engine. Gripping the keys like a weapon, she whipped around to face him. Nick's hazel eyes were dark and narrowed to mere slits.

The man is pissed. Well, too bad.

"First off, a serious fitness session is *not*," Cassi snapped before switching to a cutesy little chant, "'a little dance routine.'"

He widened his eyes a bit and smirked.

Now *she* was pissed. Releasing her seat belt, she leaned toward him.

"I believe in warming up, stretching, and using proper form." She bit off each word. "Good nutrition's a *must* for strength, endurance, and weight control."

They were eye to eye now, their noses mere inches apart.

He curved his lips into a full-fledged grin. Then his features blurred as the space between them closed. Nick shot out his hand and clamped onto her neck. He yanked her close, and his lips crashed down on hers. The firm, heated feel of them shot straight to her toes.

Her hand went limp, and she dropped the keys. They hit the floor with a loud clatter, jolting her back to reality. She placed shaking hands against his rock hard chest and pushed him away. Beneath her palms his heart hammered, a perfect match to her own erratic beats, and his clear hazel eyes burned into hers. Every nerve in her body jolted to life as if it had been hit with an electrical surge.

Neither of them spoke.

He loosened his hold and caressed the base of her neck, a tantalizing gesture combining gentleness and restraint. His warm, sweet breath fanned over her heated cheeks.

She ran her tongue over her lips, savoring the taste of him. Then she cupped his beard-roughened cheeks and pulled him back for another kiss.

Nick didn't hesitate. He invaded her mouth with his tongue, sampling what she offered. She twined her arms around him. His warm, hard chest brushed her soft breasts, making her moan. She squirmed closer, and the shelf between the seats jabbed her hip. Pain shot down her leg. Though reluctant to tear herself from Nick's sweet torture, she had to stop or risk bruising her tender flesh. Still, she let her hungry lips linger on his until she ran out of breath, forcing her to let go and move back.

Resting his arm on the seat behind her, Nick threaded gentle fingers through her hair.

She leaned her head against its steely warmth and murmured, "Why did you do that?"

"I seem to have a hard time keeping my hands off you, Cassi." His lazy, heat-infused smile held her spellbound. He toyed with the ends of her hair. "Those stubborn lips were only inches from mine. What'd you expect?"

"Not the kiss, Nick." Tears threatened, and she looked away. "I know why you did *that*. Why did you make fun of what I do?"

*****

Nick stilled his hand.

Shit. He'd rather have her spitting mad than on the verge of tears. What the hell was this about?

"Hey, I was only teasing." He lifted her chin and touched his lips to hers.

She straightened, loosening his hold on her.

"My career is important to me, Nick." She brushed moisture from her cheeks. "Maybe all the attention inflated my ego. But I'm flattered. I respect Ada and her friends. They're vibrant, successful, and happy. The way they've managed to come so far, to overcome roadblocks and take control of their lives, is impressive."

This side of Cassi surprised him. What had suddenly shaken her rock solid self confidence? He wanted to pull her into his arms. To comfort her and bring back the feisty, sexy woman who faced her own roadblocks head on. Yet all of a sudden, Cassi seemed remote. She'd withdrawn and gone somewhere inside herself he didn't understand, so he held back.

"Aren't you happy, Cass? I can understand why you're a little off balance right now. You've been through one hell of a rough spell, but you've done a lot with your life."

"I know." Her moist doe-like eyes met his.

An almost violent need to have her crashed over him. He wanted her. In the worst way, he wanted her. Yet this strong urge to comfort her, to protect her and kiss away her tears, threw him -- all new territory for Nick.

Her voice wavered, and she knuckled away an escaping tear. "I've worked hard, and my business, my club, is a tremendous success. You must think I'm an idiot."

He waited for... something. Maybe more about her work or more insight into her life, or hell, maybe just an explanation for the sudden personality shift.

But Cassi offered nothing. Her eyes looked sultry, despite the tears, and his loins tightened, despite his resolve.

He tugged a silky strand of hair. "I have to retrieve TJ's kayak tomorrow. Maybe I can locate another, and we'll do some exploring. Have you ever kayaked?"

Cassi drew in a shuddering breath. "No, I haven't. Any other time I'd love to, but I have to go to Erie tomorrow." Seeming to recover her composure she offered, "Could I take a rain check?"

He tucked an errant strand behind her ear. Starting fresh and taking things a bit slower, at the moment, made sense. "How about the day after tomorrow?"

She wiped lingering moisture from her cheeks. "I'll call you, if that's okay. I promised Ada I'd meet with her friends Tuesday, but I don't know exactly when."

"You can let me know." He took her hand and pressed his lips to her soft fingers. She didn't stop him, but she didn't respond, either. Nick reached for the door. "There's no phone in the cabin, but I'll give you my cell number. Come inside. I need something to write on."

Cassi stopped outside the cabin door. "I'll wait here."

Nick didn't press the issue. He unlocked the door, flipped on a light, and went to dig out one of his cards.

After writing his number on the back, he returned and pressed the card into her hand. "Call when you get back from Erie."

He followed her back to her CRV. After she got inside, he snapped the door shut and tapped on the roof. The window glided down.

"Call me," he repeated.

She nodded a silent good-night and drove away. Nick shoved his hands into his pockets and watched until her taillights disappeared into the darkness.

High above him, scattered stars winked through smoky gray clouds. And from somewhere far up a towering maple, the lonely, two-toned call of an owl broke the silence.

When he'd given her his card, she'd studied it and solemnly read it aloud, "Nicholas T. McGraw, PPD Homicide Division."

Then she'd taken a step backwards.

Had she been stepping away from Nick the man, or Nick the cop? And why was she stepping away at all? What ran below her passion, Nick wondered?

Sadness, regret, or guilt?

Chapter Fifteen

"Finally." Sadie exhaled, sank low in her seat, and fixed her gaze on Cassi's approaching CRV. "Stupid bitch. Probably out screwing that Philly cop."

Before returning to Pine Bluffs, Sadie had done more digging. Her assumption had been right. Nick McGraw *was* a cop. A detective from Philadelphia vacationing in Pine Bluffs. She knew exactly who McGraw was, but she had no facts, no proof, nothing that would help her answer the persistent question gnawing away inside her.

Could Cassandra Burke be her twin sister?

The possibility made her want to vomit. She'd found no written proof, but to Sadie, the proof was in the mirror.

Someday, she vowed, if there was such a connection between them, she'd find out why she had been the one left behind. Before those foggy, early years in foster homes, only a black, empty hole marked the beginning of Sadie's life.

Cassi's headlights swung perilously close, briefly illuminating the interior of her car. Sadie held her breath.

She'd parked amidst underbrush on a neglected side road. Keeping out of sight was important, especially since her recent whirlwind trip to Cleveland.

Her altered appearance pleased her, but the transformation had been costly. After a salon visit and shopping spree, her bank account was empty; her charge card, maxed out.

She'd taken a photo of Cassi, one she'd clipped from the newspaper, and gone to a young, eager stylist to have her look copied. Right down to her honey-colored hair.

Sadie had almost choked when the clueless girl had remarked how much she looked like the woman in the picture. She'd agreed. The perky stylist literally bubbled when Sadie had included a big tip.

The salon visit and shopping had been fun, but this day in Pine Bluffs had been one bitchin' long one. She'd found the nearly abandoned side road while walking, and had followed a secluded path back into town. In late afternoon, she'd returned and backed her car into the heavy undergrowth.

How did cops do it? In movies they seemed so cool, sitting for hours, eating pizza, watching their prey.

Fuck. She was cold and hungry. The sub she'd bought was long gone. And squatting to pee while bushes poked her in the ass was no picnic.

At dusk, she'd left the car and crept through the woods. Finding a well hidden spot, she'd eavesdropped as Cassi, her aunt, and a friggin' bunch of old ladies who'd all gathered on the porch, cackled like a flock a' hens.

Then that stupid dog had started barking his fool head off. The son of a bitch had been headed right at her. She'd crouched down, frozen in place. But the aunt had called him back and put him inside. So Sadie had stayed put and overheard Cassi's plans.

The distraction created when the cop showed up gave her time to slip back to her car unnoticed, where she'd waited until he left with Cassi.

Now Cassi was back, and she was alone. Not as alone as Sadie wanted. But she'd bide her time, like a damn alley cat, until her prey was unaware -- and unprotected.

Inching her car onto the highway, she left the cottage behind. She smiled into the mirror, low light glinting in her eyes, and smoothed her newly styled hair back into place. She needed sleep, and she needed food. But her long wait had paid off.

Sadie would be making a trip to Erie tomorrow, too.

*****

As the sun's first rays stole across Pine Shadow Lake, Cassi began her morning run. Running was something she forced herself to do, and she preferred to do it at dawn, letting the cold, crisp air drive sleep from her mind and body.

Rufus huffed along by her side, his ears flat, his tongue lolling. At the three-mile turn around, they paused. Cassi stretched while Rufus gulped noisily from the lake. Feeling limber and refreshed, at last she was prepared to face the day.

To occupy her mind, she'd compiled a list of things the ladies needed for her class. They hadn't batted an eye at the projected cost of hand weights, floor mats, or shoes.

She'd stressed the shoe issue, and they'd paid close attention. After pointing out the need for good ones, she suspected that by tomorrow they'd all be sporting brand new cross-trainers.

Drawing near the cabin, she slowed to a long-striding walk and climbed the slope from the lake. Rufus stopped to investigate the kayak Nick had left beside the lake the day before. His tail wagged as he nudged the trim craft with his nose.

Cassi stopped, letting him sniff.

"You like him, don't you?" she said. Rufus looked up, his tongue dangling, and gave her a sloppy doggy grin. She sighed, pushed the image of Nick's rugged, athletic frame away, and nudged the dog along. "Come on, boy. I've got to shower before I leave for Erie. Maybe you'll get to visit with Nick when he comes for the kayak."

Actually, she was glad she'd be out of reach today. Last night had been crazy. She'd gone from blazing anger, to practically climbing all over the man, to sobbing like a baby in the space of a minute. Had to be all those hormones he'd slapped awake by trumping her angry tirade with a steamy kiss.

What had suddenly made her so damn sensitive about her job? She'd always been confident. She was smart, educated, and personally didn't give a good rat's ass what any man thought. Until now. But then again, Nick McGraw wasn't just *any* man.

They entered the cottage, a flurry of clicking nails and movement. Uttering several soft woofs, Rufus made a beeline across the kitchen straight to Nick McGraw.

Cassi stopped cold and pushed her tangled hair aside. His unexpected presence floored her. Judging from his attire, he'd been running, too. And damn it, why did a sweaty man in scruffy clothes look both rugged and handsome when she looked like shit in her old shorts, grubby shirt, and no makeup?

After losing it last night, the least she could have done was look halfway decent the next time them met.

"Good morning." He smiled, scratching Rufus as the silly dog rubbed and bumped against him.

"Hi." Squaring her shoulders, Cassi strolled into the kitchen, poured tea from a flowered porcelain pot, and carefully selected a muffin. "You're up early."

"Needed a run. You, too?"

"Yes. I try to do six miles a couple of times a week." She took a healthy bite of muffin. Her good humor returned, and she locked her gaze with his as she chewed and swallowed. "That way, I'm in shape to teach my little *dance routine.*"

Nick laughed, making Rufus wriggle with renewed vigor.

Cassi relaxed. For the time being, they were back on solid ground. "Did you come for your kayak?"

"No. Not yet. My run took me in this direction, and the smell of apple muffins sucked me in." He seemed relaxed, his eyes warm and crinkled with humor. "I'm going to see TJ today. I'll ask if he has another kayak. Are we still on for tomorrow?"

"Maybe," Cassi hedged. "I don't know exactly when the ladies want to get together. Aunt Ada is trying to find a place to have class. I'll have to call you tomorrow."

Ada entered the room. She headed straight for the steeping tea and filled a mug to the brim. "Good morning, Cassandra. Did I hear you say you came for your kayak, Nick?"

"Will it be in the way if I leave it? I'm trying to scare up another one for Cassi."

"Won't be in my way, and you don't have to look very far. I've got a nice one-man craft in my storage shed." She turned to Cassi. "You're welcome to use it."

"Guess that solves the problem," Nick said.

Glancing at the clock, Cassi gulped down her tea. "I've got to get moving. Nick, I don't know how long I'll be in Erie today. It could be late," she stated, rinsing her cup. "I'll call you tomorrow when I'm free."

Nick nodded, devoured another muffin, and leisurely finished his coffee. He'd begged until Ada brewed a small pot for him. He liked tea, but had insisted apple muffins called for a more robust drink.

"Did you find a place for us?" Cassi asked Ada.

"I'll check with Rich McConnell. There's a large empty room over his hardware store he might let us use."

Cassi turned to Nick, edging away as she spoke. "I'll be in touch tomorrow."

His eyes slid over her, once more making her conscious of her scruffy attire, and he winked. "I'll be waiting."

Her face burning, Cassi hurried away to shower and dress. Nick was gone when she returned, and she stepped out onto the back porch.

Angled over her lush plants, Ada was busy trimming and weeding. Rufus lay nearby, stretched out frog-style on a patch of cool grass beneath the overhanging shrubs.

"I'm leaving," Cassi called out.

Ada removed her gloves, lifted the brim of her hat, and walked to the edge of the porch. She gazed up at Cassi. "Have a good day, honey. Take your time, but be careful. Peach Street in Erie can be crazy at times."

"I will. Thanks for watching Rufus today." Cassi dug in her shoulder bag for her keys. She chuckled as the dog rolled over and stretched. "He loves it here. I almost dread having to take him back to my tiny yard."

After a quick wave, she headed for her CRV. Rufus came up to Ada and sat. Leaning against her legs, he gave a giant yawn. While stroking his head, she remarked, "She's right, fella. But I wonder if she realizes how confining that small space will be for her, too?"

She stooped and wrapped her arms around his soft body. "When Cassandra moves on with her life and you both leave Pine Bluffs, my space will seem empty."

*****

Cassi's drive to Erie brought to mind several clichés. Colorful, sweeping and picturesque all applied, and she loved every passing mile.

Last night, Lanie had called to check on her. She'd left her feisty assistant in charge of Fox Chapel Fitness, and Lanie had reassured her that all was well.

"Thank God for Elaine Daphanie Delacor," she whispered to herself.

She and Lanie had met in college. At first, Cassi had feared she'd drawn the roommate from hell. At barely five-foot-two, Lanie was compact, firm, and lush, with striking green eyes. She envied her friend's lushness. Cassi had often been called sleek and curvy, but never *lush*.

One never knew how Lanie would appear. She'd come to work one time with her dark hair spiked and tipped with shamrock green.

"To match my eyes," she'd declared that day.

From neon colors to subtle taupe and black, her wardrobe surprised Cassi every day. But Cassi loved her and depended on her; in fact, she didn't know what she would have done without Lanie the past few months.

After her parents' untimely deaths, Lanie had stepped in and helped hold things together. From running the club, to dealing with the sudden entrance of Ada Blaine into Cassi's life, Lanie had been a rock. She'd made arrangements, adjusting her own life and agreeing to run the club so Cassi could visit Ada.

If not for Lanie, Cassi wouldn't have adopted Rufus. She smiled wryly, though the jury was still out on whether or not the dog was providing the peace of mind Lanie had assured her came with a pet.

Thoughts of a jury steered her in another direction. She'd had no contact with the Pine Bluffs Police Department for several days, except for her brief meeting with TJ at Nick's cabin. And she'd been a bundle of nerves before meeting Nick's Aunt Mary, who just happened to be the police chief's wife.

But last night, Mary McGraw had never mentioned the case.

Since Cassi's close encounter with a dead man and the long day at Pine Bluffs PD, the only cop she'd had contact with was Detective Nick McGraw. With *contact* being the key word. His interest in her couldn't be denied, at least physically. Maybe his goal was to do a little undercover work. The possible irony left her feeling hot on one hand, and grim on the other.

In the past, she'd been able to resist good looking men. But her attraction to Nick went beyond the physical. Granted, his touch caused her inhibitions to fly, but beneath his eye-catching exterior lurked a considerate, funny, competent man, and she found the combination irresistible.

The exit for Peach Street came into sight, and Cassi took the busy ramp. Ada had been right. As Cassi waited at the light, a steady flow of traffic passed before her, heading north. When the light changed, she joined the pack and merged onto the busy road. Like a picture postcard, Lake Erie appeared on the distant horizon, pristine and never-ending.

Ada's directions were good, and within only minutes Cassie reached the plaza where the Erie Sport Store was located.

*****

Sadie slammed her hand against the steering wheel. She'd parked her beat-up sedan well away from Cassi after struggling to keep up with the fast moving CRV all the way from Pine Bluffs to Erie.

"No wonder I'm in such a piss-poor mood," she muttered. "Getting up at the crack of dawn would make anyone cranky."

This morning, after grabbing some lukewarm coffee and a day old sweet roll, she'd returned to the secluded spot near Ada Blaine's cabin and remained undetected. After a short wait, she'd fallen in behind Cassi and followed her to Erie.

She tracked Cassi across the parking lot with her tired gaze. The sun highlighted the woman's golden hair as she moved confidently with long legged strides.

When she disappeared into the sprawling sporting goods store, Sadie grimaced. Why in the hell would anyone shop in a sporting goods store? She opened her window, shut off the motor, and slouched down in her seat to wait. Maybe Cassi was buying something to help her suck up to the cop. He sure seemed to be panting after her.

Blinding sunlight streamed into Sadie's car. She flipped down the visor and fumbled in her purse, searching for her sunglasses. Jealousy simmered within her, and more than one scenario came to mind that would even the playing field. Or better yet, remove a player *from* the field.

How fuckin' unfair. Sadie made a fist and rapped the steering wheel again. Her life had been one stupid fight after another just to survive. She scraped out a pissy living, and all her life she'd put up with shitheads like Rick. Scowling, she rubbed her bruised hand and slipped on her sunglasses.

Aw, hell. Rick tried. He really did. But other than tending bar so he could kick in his part of the rent, he was a slug.

Time passed, and Sadie waited. Her eyes drooped, her stomach growled, and her fingers tapped a steady rhythm on her thigh.

"To hell with this," she ground out at last, and cranked her car to life. "I'll see you another day, *Ms Burke*."

Why sit and stew about shit she couldn't control? Right now she had better things to do. She left the parking space and shot up Peach Street to I-90.

Her old haunts in Cleveland crept into her mind as she drove. Places for cold beer, great food, and if she were lucky, some old buddies to help her pass the time.

Maybe she'd even score some weed.

Yeah, that's what she needed. A hit of magic grass. Then she'd be able to think and work out her next move. Cassandra Burke wasn't going anywhere. Even if she left Pine Bluffs, Sadie knew where she lived.

And Sadie *would* find Cassandra, when *she* was damn good and ready.

Chapter Sixteen

Jack LeFavor lifted his glass and sipped, savoring the smooth, amber-colored drink. Scotch on the rocks. Good scotch, too. Top shelf. Nowadays he fuckin' liked requesting *top shelf* liquor when ordering drinks.

Because nowadays Jack was feeling lucky. And smart. The boys back in Detroit thought he was smart, too. They valued him because he had connections in Ohio *and* Pennsylvania. That is, ever since he'd wised them up about Ecstasy. Yeah, ever since he'd enlightened them, letting them know how every single pill in Erie brought in an easy twenty bucks instead of the measly five to eight they'd been getting in Detroit.

His income, and theirs, had skyrocketed, along with the constant demand for crack cocaine. And neither the feds, nor the locals had squat on him. Odds were, they never would.

Jack took care of problems by eliminating weak links, and Bob Morelli had been one *big* problem. A bumbling creep like Morelli had to be dealt with before he could rat you out to save his own skin, or before he made some dumbass mistake that would lead the cops right to your frigging door.

Jack had been laying low in Detroit until yesterday, when he'd learned the investigation into Morelli's death was going nowhere. He'd been smart, just plain brilliant, to have picked a backwoods town like Pine Bluffs as the place to do the deed. The cops there were still running around with their thumbs up their asses.

Almost lunchtime. Jack eyed his surroundings. He needed to stem the buzz scotch had created in his near empty stomach. He was about to signal the waitress and head for a table when the door opened, and in walked Sadie Mitchell.

"Well, shit," he muttered, plunking down his empty glass. She stopped to survey the room. Jack couldn't remember the last time he'd seen Sadie, but damn, she looked good. Actually, she looked much better than he remembered. Sadie was one partying-kind-of-woman. She wasn't a true druggie, but she had no problem getting high on occasion. If he remembered correctly, Sadie had a much softer edge after she'd sniffed a line or two.

As she crossed the room, she passed through dim lighting that cast orange patterns throughout the downtown Cleveland bar, and she looked even better.

Jack ran a quick hand through his coarse, gray-peppered hair. He thumbed a mint into his mouth, leaned casually against the bar, and waited. "Well, hell-o there."

Sadie stopped and squinted, edging closer.

"Remember me, Sadie?" He skimmed his gaze over her.

Jack was close to six feet, and Sadie had to look up. Her eyes widened, and if he wasn't mistaken, she seemed real pleased to see him.

"Jack! You old son of a bitch. How ya been?"

He'd been right. She all but crawled up the front of him with her fuckin' hello hug.

"Let's grab a table and catch up, sugar," he drawled, patting her ass with one hand while motioning for a waitress with the other.

Shit, he'd felt lucky just enjoying a good scotch. Imagine how good it was going to feel gettin' cozy with Sadie's curvy little body.

She followed him to a table where he ordered drinks and two specials for lunch. They laughed together, devouring shrimp cocktails like candy and sipping expensive drinks. Him, more scotch; her, frosty, dark ale.

They lingered in the secluded corner. He'd just charm the hell out of her, cater to her every whim, and spare no expense.

Then he'd see what the afternoon offered.

*****

Raife Samuels tapped his fingers in rough tempo to the pulsing background music. He occasionally glanced from side to side, outwardly showing no interest to anyone in particular. But Raife's keen eyes had been scrutinizing Jack LeFavor and his female companion for quite some time.

The bartender stopped before him.

He exchanged a few words with the man, then shook his head, and the bartender moved on. Raife had been tipping his drinks into a nearby potted plant, hoping like hell the damn thing didn't wilt on the spot and draw attention to his covert activity.

He slipped his cell phone from his pocket and hit redial. Rocking in time to the music, he waited.

"Yeah. Connors," a clipped voice answered.

"They're getting ready to leave. Try and get some shots when they come out. I don't recognize the babe, but they seem awful chummy. She could be a connection, or just some slut he wants to pass the afternoon with. Either way, I want all his contacts documented for posterity."

Conners chuckled. "I hear ya. When we finally nail this bastard, the whole damn connection will fold and go down with him."

Raife glanced sideways and tucked away the phone. He agreed with Conners. He'd been partnered with Fred in the Ohio Investigative Unit for over two years. They worked well together. Surveillance on LeFavor was ongoing, and they'd been involved from the start.

The deadly side effects of the Detroit-to-Erie drug traffic had increased. A trail of overdose victims and dead-end drug busts had spilled over into Cleveland and the surrounding towns. They knew Jack was involved up to his ass. But he was slippery, and he was smart.

The Pennsylvania authorities had ratcheted up their pressure on the operation, too. They were pissed about the influx of easy-to-get drugs in Erie, a city once referred to as a farm community with lights. Erie was growing, its growing pains made evident by the increase in drug use in the city by the lake.

As Jack and the woman stepped into the late afternoon sun, Connors turned, cell phone in hand, and snapped pictures of them until they climbed into a dark gray Mercedes.

Raife stepped outside the bar and waited until the distinctive taillights disappeared. Then he walked down the block, glanced around, and slid into a parked, beat up Chevy.

"What'd you get?" he asked, settling into the worn upholstery.

"Take a look." Fred passed him the cell.

Thumbing through the shots, Raife frowned as he studied each frame. "That girl looks familiar. The light was dim as hell in there, but damn. She reminds me of someone. I know I've seen her before."

Fred shrugged. "Maybe she'll turn up when we compare these with our other surveillance shots."

"Okay. Let's get these blown up and added to the file. I want to nail this guy. Among other things, it chaps my ass that he's driving around in a friggin' Mercedes.

Fred snapped on his seatbelt, glanced over his shoulder, and shot into rush hour traffic.

Chapter Seventeen

TJ dreaded making the call. Poking that hornet's nest wasn't a great way to start the day. He'd sifted through the new facts they'd gathered, and revisited old ones. So far, neither had told him anything he didn't already know.

Crap. All that time spent studying how to solve crimes, and he was coming up with zilch on his first homicide.

He was jolted from his commiserating by a solid knock at the door.

"Enter," he barked.

"Hey, TJ. You missed your coffee stop this morning," his dad remarked, sticking his head in the door.

"Sorry, Dad. I'm so damn wrapped up in this case. Come on in. I'll have a cup with you later, but first I have to make a call, and I'm draggin' my feet about doin' it."

"Anything I can help with?"

"I'm afraid I'm on my own with this one," TJ said as his dad took a seat. He appreciated the respect implied by his father's offer to help, not to dictate. "I'm going to call Fox Chapel Fitness and hopefully interview the acting manager."

"Why the dread?" Tom's eyebrows rose.

TJ pushed away from his desk, stood, and walked to the window. He stared at the street below and ran his fingers through his hair. Dropping his hands, he turned and spread them out, palms up.

"Am I the only one who still doubts Cassandra Burke? Nick's all but drooling after her, Mom's going to take an exercise class from her, and you've been as tight lipped as an old maid school teacher. Am I being too hard-nosed? Am I missing something you all see in her?" He dropped into his chair, leaned in, and placed crossed arms on his desk.

Tom blew out a long breath. "Son, you have a job to do. And nobody, and I do mean nobody, has the right to keep you from doing it. You're going by the book, and that's good. Follow your leads and your instincts. If something doesn't seem right to you, don't ignore the itch. Scratch it until you find the source."

TJ leaned back and weighed his dad's words. "I feel like something is missing, Dad. Something important. I look at that woman, and I can't imagine her involved in drugs, let alone murder. I see the same things you all do. That's what's keeping me up nights."

"I know the process often feels like you're going in circles. But it's a process every cop I've ever known goes through. Instincts often feel like they're pointing in one direction, but end up showing us something entirely different."

"You're right about the circles." TJ picked up a pen and fiddled with it. "I keep circling back to prod at her background. Calling this manager is not going to be fun. From what I've learned, she's totally devoted to her boss."

Tossing the pen, he grabbed a file and flipped it open. A dark-haired beauty stared up at him with sultry eyes. That smile probably had men dropping at her feet. Trying to get a sense of who Elaine Daphanie Delacor might be, he stared long and hard at her picture.

"She's a looker," Tom said, tilting in closer. "What have you got on her?"

"She met Cassandra in college. They were roommates and both worked on the school's newsletter. She carried a four-point-oh grade point average and graduated in the top ten percent of her class."

"Sounds like Miss Burke made a good choice for manager." Tom stood and adjusted the gun resting on his hip. "Make your call, son. Maybe she'll surprise you."

He left TJ alone, closing the door behind him.

TJ rolled his shoulders, took a deep breath, and reached for the phone. He tried to focus and not overthink what he had to do. Just track down the facts and see where they led.

A crisp, efficient-sounding voice answered on the second ring, "Fox Chapel Fitness. May I help you?"

"Elaine Delacor, please."

"Whom may I say is calling?"

"Officer McGraw, ma'am." He sensed the woman's hesitation and offered, "I'm with the Pine Bluffs, Pennsylvania Police Department."

"One moment, sir, I'll see if Miss Delacor is available."

"Thank you." TJ tilted his chair back to wait and tapped a pen rhythmically on his notepad. The receptionist was no doubt conferring with *'Miss Delacor.'*

What if she didn't accept his call? He huffed out a sigh, studied the ceiling above him, and continued to wait.

"Elaine Delacor speaking." Her voice caught him by surprise, and he let his chair drop forward with a thump. His tapping pen slipped from his hand, rolled off the desk, and hit the floor.

"How may I help you, Officer McGraw?" She spoke with an easy maturity and a soft, purring undertone that was... well, a surprise.

TJ had expected someone more bouncy, like the fitness channel girls. Elaine Delacor's voice was more 'Come hither' than 'Come feel the burn'.

"Miss Delacor, thank you for speaking with me." He opened his desk drawer and snatched out another pen. "I'll try not to take much of your time. I have some questions regarding the owner of Fox Chapel Fitness."

"Cassi? You want to ask me about her? Has something else happened? I just spoke with her and--"

"No, no, of course not." He pulled at the neck of his shirt. "Sorry if I gave you that impression. I just need to ask you a few questions. That's all."

An uncomfortable moment of silence passed between them.

"I see. Why more questions?" She finally said, not missing a beat, although the 'come hitherness' had disappeared from her voice. "I thought that crap about Cassi stabbing someone was all straightened out. Do you know what her life has been like the past few months? Or have any idea how hard it was just to get her to meet the only living relative she has left in the world?"

Taken aback, TJ shifted, changing ears. "Miss Delacor?"

"I'm here." Forget come hither; her tone had shifted to *mind your own business*. She had dug in her heels, and as he looked down at the emerald green eyes smiling up at him from the photo in her folder, he gritted his teeth. The woman was a pain in the ass.

"I'm just trying to verify some dates and times prior to the incident," he said.

"Incident? Finding a carved up body in your town is an *incident*? I'd call it murder, plain and simple. If you had any idea about what kind of person Cassandra Burke is, you'd be out there looking for the real killer."

TJ bit back his response. Damn, her voice had changed again. And something, some throaty undertone, made the muscles low on his belly tighten.

He plunged right back in, ignoring her prickly question. "Can you tell me what day and the approximate time Cassandra left Fox Chapel last week? Also, how far in advance did she ask you to take over management duties during her absence?"

Another lengthy silence followed. Was she weighing her answers? He was about to prompt her when she spoke.

"She contacted me a few days prior to leaving. I don't know exactly when she left for Pine Bluffs."

No cooperation. He closed his eyes and shook his head.

"Actually, I manage the club quite often when Cassi is away," Miss Delacor added, sounding a tad smug.

After a moment's contemplation, TJ tried another approach, striving for an easy-going style, putting as much admiration into his voice as he could muster. "I understand. She seems to have a lot of faith in your abilities."

"I've worked with Cassi since before she bought the club." She'd toned down her smugness a notch. "We have the same approach to the business, but--"

"Your temperaments tend to be rather different," TJ jumped in. He awaited her reaction. Could she tell he'd simply made an educated guess?

"How could you know what my temperament is, Officer McGraw?" Her voice had gone low and throaty again,

At a loss for words, TJ opened his mouth, then snapped it shut. His mind had gone into overdrive, and his body had shifted to semi-alert. At least, part of his body had. What the hell was the matter with him?

Shit. He was getting turned on by the voice of a smart mouthed woman he'd just met.

"It's my job to know about people I come in contact with," he finally managed, struggling to get both himself and the phone interview under control.

"Officer McGraw," she purred. "I really don't see us coming in contact with each other any time soon. However, for the record, I'm Cassi's polar opposite. I'm not sweet, level-headed, or cooperative." Her voice had developed a distinct edge. "So unless you have more questions, I have a business to run."

"I'm sure you do, Miss Delacor." Talk about hot and cold. TJ scooped his outspread fingers through his hair for about the third time. "Thank you for your time. I'll be in touch."

He hung up before she could use that low, throaty voice on him again, and headed for the men's room.

"How'd the phone call go?" his father asked moments later, when he came in the door.

Reaching for a paper towel, TJ glared into the mirror above the sink. "Like shit."

He tossed the wadded up towel and tried to comb his unruly hair into place with his impatient fingers.

"That bad, huh?"

"That woman is a real piece of work. First hot, then cold, like a faucet gone amuck. Basically, she gave me nothing. Nada." Satisfied his hair was finally under control, he reflected on something she had said. "Although, she 'often runs the club when Cassi's away', as she put it. We may have more unaccounted for time to consider."

TJ's dad smoothed his own thatch of red hair in silence, and clapped TJ on the back as he left.

Returning to his office, TJ decided to wait and contact the Strongsville, Ohio Police Department the next day. They might have more information on Morelli by then. Today had been a bust. He had nothing. So... screw it. He'd go home, grab a beer, and see if he could con Nick into going out with him tonight.

The first shift had ended, and guys were reporting for second. Chuck Long was off duty, and he stopped to report that Ms. Burke had not yet returned to Pine Bluffs. TJ thanked him for the info and noted that and the time in his notebook. He started to call Nick, then as an afterthought called out to Chuck instead

The officer peered around the edge of the doorway. "Yeah, TJ?"

"I'd appreciate it if you kept my request for you to watch Cassi Burke's movements to yourself for now."

"No problem," Chuck said. Then he continued down the hallway.

TJ cleared his desk and closed the door behind him. If Nick knew he was keeping tabs on Cassi, he'd sure as hell chew his butt for doing it. Regardless of what his cousin thought, TJ's instincts pushed him to watch her.

Where the hell had she been all day if she was so damned set on getting reacquainted with her long lost aunt?

*****

Nick relaxed in a high-backed rocker on Mary's front porch, stretched out his legs, and crossed them at the ankle. His aunt occupied an identical chair, and between them, the squat wooden table held a bottle of wine, a plate of sliced apples, and an ample chunk of sharp cheddar cheese.

A cool breeze kicked up, and Mary suggested they move indoors just as Uncle Tom's car turned up the winding drive. Tom emerged from it loosening his tie as he strolled toward them.

Leaning down, he gave his wife a warm kiss. She cupped the back of his neck, a gentle gesture, and he smiled into her eyes. An invisible signal seemed to pass between them, a connection forged over the years.

Tom straightened. "Evening, Nick. Stayin' for dinner?"

"No, not tonight. I'm waiting for TJ. We're going to head over the ridge, have a few beers, and catch some food."

"Sounds like a good idea. You're sure to get an earful about his day." Tom chuckled. "He spoke with Cassandra Burke's manager, and I can't ever remember TJ letting a difficult woman get him so rattled. He was pulling his hair out, literally, after he talked to her."

Tom eased one hip onto the porch railing, shrugged his jacket off, and reached for Mary's wine.

Puzzled, Nick asked, "Was she in town?"

Tom sampled the wine and passed the glass back to his wife. "No, he called her. He's like a pit bull with this case. Granted, murder is not the norm for us, but he seems to have taken this one personally."

"Uncle Tom, do you feel Cassi is somehow involved with that man's murder?" Nick sipped his wine and gauged his uncle's response over the rim of his glass.

"Honestly?" Tom rolled up his shirtsleeves. "I don't see a scrap of evidence to support that theory. However, I put TJ in charge, and he's unconvinced about something. Though I'm not sure he knows what that something is."

As Mary gathered up the wine and cheese, Tom hastened to open the door for her. She smiled her thanks and entered the house.

Nick tipped his glass and drained the last of the crisp Chenin Blanc. "I remember when you would be on top of every case that rolled through the door, Uncle Tom. What I've seen the past few days is a definite shift of authority."

Tom paused and readjusted the holster on his hip. He stretched his arm toward the door, indicating for Nick to go inside. As Nick obliged, his uncle placed a hand on his shoulder.

"I'm in a bit of a quandary," he said as they moved through the foyer into the heart of the McGraw household. Mary proceeded into the brightly lit kitchen at the far end of the room. A wall of windows showcased the lake beyond, and mouth-watering aromas permeated the air.

Tom followed her with his gaze. "I'm ready to retire, been thinking about it for months. The idea became a reality when TJ joined the force. It's always been my desire to see him succeed in our profession, and I have no doubt that he will."

"Why do I get the feeling you're not happy about that?"

"TJ's the one I don't think is happy."

Stunned by his uncle's words, Nick studied him closely. He hadn't talked with TJ about his work. The days since his arrival had been anything but conducive to meaningful conversation, but he took what his uncle said very seriously.

He was about to pursue the subject when TJ burst through the door.

"Hey, big cousin, ready to tear up the town?"

A short time later, TJ eased his silver Camry onto the highway and punched the gas, pressing Nick back in his cushy gray leather seat. He admired the high-end Toyota's nicely appointed interior. Strange. He drove a truck -- granted, it was a sporty compact, a Honda Ridgeline, but it was still a truck. The guys in Philly had razzed him about being a country boy at heart. Here was TJ, the real country boy, driving a sleek, streamlined gray bullet like a true urbanite.

"Nice car," Nick said, running a hand over the butter-soft leather. "Where'd you get it?"

"Erie," TJ said. "Always wanted a car like this, and when I knew I'd have steady work, I drove in the old hatchback, handed over her keys, and never looked back. Ya like it, huh?"

Eyes alive and alert, TJ accelerated, negotiating curves and handling the wheel with ease. He wore a smug, self-satisfied smile. The smooth engine hummed undetected and edgy rock guitar rolled from well-placed speakers.

Nick threw back his head and laughed. "You look like a man who's just had great sex."

TJ grinned. "And how would you know how I look at that very personal moment?"

"Good point," Nick conceded. He stretched, relaxing into the forgiving leather, and then dove right in. "Are you happy with your life, TJ?"

His cousin shot him a look, as if checking to see if he was wading deep or just shooting the shit. Nick played it cool, focusing on the scenery as they topped the ridge. Lake Erie spread out before them like a wide, shimmering path. The sun teetered on the horizon, and for one breathless moment, he couldn't tear his eyes from the ever-changing portrait.

"Guess I could ask the same of you," TJ said, turning his attention back to the road. "I remember you used to come here often to see these sunsets. Where do you watch sunsets in Philadelphia, Nick?"

Touché. Nick leaned back and watched the vibrant orange ball slip from sight as they rolled off the ridge and into the outskirts of North East.

A bold sign displayed in The Corner Bar claimed the wings served within hadn't changed in years. Nick agreed. An impressive pile of bones grew on the plate between them after they settled into their booth, and he washed down the tangy sauce with beer from a cold, frosty mug.

The place looked the same as it always had. Low lights, heavy wooden tables, and chairs that scraped loudly against the rough plank floors. The pitchers of beer were generous, foam-topped, and well chilled. And the wings... oh, yeah. The wings. Smothered in sauce that stung your tongue, coated your fingers, and had you reaching for that frosty mug between bites.

"You asked if I'm happy," TJ said, picking up where they'd left off earlier. He made use of a paper napkin from the stack between them and emptied his mug with a sharp tilt of his head. Then he poured another, meeting Nick's eyes across the table. "I take it you think that because I drive a spiffy car, I don't fit into Pine Bluffs's 'home boy' culture?"

Nick grinned. "Spiffy? Voila? Hell, it's a wonder you haven't been run out of town for not speaking the language."

TJ laughed and sipped the overflowing foam from his mug. Nick hoped the beer and the great evening had TJ relaxed enough that his cousin wouldn't resent what he was about to say.

"A car has nothing to do with happiness," Nick said. "We both know that. You weren't raised that way." He made a point to use *you* and not *we* when referring to how they had been raised. "You're one hell of an investigator. Pine Bluffs PD is lucky to have you."

"But?" TJ prompted.

"But it's a damn shame if it's not where you want to be. Doing a job well is one thing; enjoying where you are while doing it is another."

TJ lowered his mug and locked his intense gaze on Nick's face.

He's not a dumb kid anymore, Nick assessed before he continued, "Your dad suspects you're not happy. He started telling me just as you arrived this evening. The conversation didn't go any further. And this one won't either, if that's what you want."

TJ's eyes never left Nick's face. "Let me ask *you* something."

"Shoot."

TJ's grin broke through. "Bad choice of words for a cop."

"Cut the crap."

"Okay." TJ turned serious. "When your parents moved from Pine Bluffs, you threw a fit."

"I did. According to my parents, I was a royal pain."

"Now, when you look back, do you wish they hadn't made the move? Do you ever think about coming back, living here again?"

Nick stared at his cold mug. He turned the glass slowly, making trails in the moisture with his fingers. TJ was skirting close to something he'd thought about, but had never said aloud.

"I have a great job," he explained. "Busted my butt to get where I am. Personally, I have a neat little house, a small back yard, even a grill. Professionally, the work is never-ending."

Nick shifted in the hard chair. "One hot Sunday in mid-summer, five people were shot dead in a neighborhood bar. Their deaths brought the total killings in the city to two hundred thirty-two so far this year, probably even more by now. The city's murder rate is escalating, on pace to be the highest in a decade."

TJ's eyes widened with interest as Nick refilled his glass. He blotted up moisture left by the weeping pitcher, drank some beer, and then continued, "Flip side of the coin would be that less than two thirds of the way through this year, the men in our department have shot and killed sixteen people. That's the highest annual total of fatal police shootings in the city of Philadelphia in the past quarter century."

In answer to his cousin's unasked question, Nick shook his head. "They aren't bad cops. Gun violence is up, and all those brazen suspects are quick to use their weapons. It's not repeat shooters among the ranks, or people not following policy. They're defending themselves."

TJ angled his head and listened in silence.

"I don't want to defend myself, TJ." He lowered his voice and narrowed his eyes. "I want to defend the public. Our code of honor states that as our goal. Yet every day, doing it gets harder. Would I like to work for a small department like you do? On days like that Sunday when five innocents died, you bet."

TJ looked down. When he lifted his eyes, a grim smile tugged at his lips. "Sounds like we ended up opposite from where we want to be."

"Will you listen to a suggestion?" Nick asked, lifting a napkin from the generous stack on the table and blotting his fingers.

"Might not act on it, but you've got my attention."

"If you feel you want more than what a small department has to offer, look into joining one of the best." Nick placed both elbows on the hard wood. "Pennsylvania's State Police force is one of the most respected in the country. Check it out."

TJ plucked up the last french fry and dragged it through a river of ketchup. He popped it into his mouth, chewed thoughtfully, and then swallowed. "Believe it or not, I've already done some preliminary investigating into how to go about applying. But thanks."

Lifting his mug and digesting their exchange, Nick glanced around as the door opened and two attractive women entered. They'd covered enough serious ground for one night, so he gave a meaningful nod at the pair. "Anyone you know?"

TJ eyeballed the two as they headed for the bar. The snug fit of their jeans -- one pair slim and tight, the other nicely rounded -- was clearly in his sights.

"Not yet." He brought his eyes back to Nick and nodded toward the bar. "Shall we?"

By the time they'd mulled it over and examined the possibilities, it was too late. A couple of locals had already moved in and flanked the two young women, charming them into giggles.

Just as well. Nick relaxed as he sat back in the Camry a few minutes later. His heart wasn't into pursuing anonymous females tonight.

As they wound their way back to Pine Bluffs, another female popped into his mind. For the past six months, he'd been seeing a woman named Michelle. *Michelle Norris of the Brin Mawr Norris',* as his mother described her. She'd introduced him to Michelle, a suspicious move on her part, but he'd graciously followed through anyway. Michelle was attractive, and her tousled black hair and clear blue eyes had caught many an eye.

His mom had been pleased, smug with her success at matchmaking. She had also acted as the engine that kept the relationship rolling along. The set up worked, mainly because Nick's trust issues hadn't come into play.

Michelle had been more or less dropped into his lap. He hadn't sought her out, and for the time being, that suited him just fine. Ever since the disaster with Kat, he'd been reluctant to date any woman more than a few times.

He felt safe with Michelle. They'd drifted into dinners out and attended all the *must see* plays and concerts around town. He was comfortable with her. No strings, no commitment. The sex was, in a word, *satisfying*.

But in the past couple of days, Cassi Burke had pushed Michelle Norris right out of his mind.

Chapter Eighteen

Cassi sprinted from the shower and slathered on lotion, followed by a generous layer of sunscreen. Nick and Ada's voices drifted in through the open bedroom window. After tugging on a pair of thigh length shorts, she shrugged into a tee shirt, then tore open the box holding the new water sandals she'd purchased on her trip to Erie.

Earlier that morning, her first workout with the Pine Bluffs ladies had run longer than expected. The group had arrived on time and spilled into Rich McConnell's upstairs room bursting with enthusiasm. The session had been intense. Ada's friends were great students. Cassi had been pleased with them, but she wasn't pleased now that she was running late.

Anticipation bubbled up inside her. After she'd put Nick off, she'd thought maybe he would give up and forget about her. After all, he was on vacation. No man who looked like Nick McGraw would sit around by himself for long. But when she'd called him early this morning, he'd been relaxed, friendly, and upbeat.

And as he'd laid out plans for the day, his voice had held a promise that made her shiver.

*****

Nick slid the door open, stepping aside to allow Ada and an enthusiastic Rufus to enter the cottage. "Ada, that's a fine craft. When was the last time you took her out?"

The trim one-man kayak they'd retrieved from storage had been covered with a fine layer of dust, but was in pristine shape.

"Early summer, I guess. Before I got wrapped up in my gardens." Ada glanced up from washing her hands. "Not using chemicals is time consuming. When my plants start to produce, there's a lot of maintenance. It keeps me busy."

She dried her hands and pumped lotion from a bottle on the sink. Crossing to the refrigerator, she opened the door and pulled out several containers.

When it dawned on him what she was up to, Nick smiled. He stepped closer and inspected several of the containers as she packed them into an ice chest. He and Cassi would not starve on their outing today.

Cassi helped cart the kayaks to the shore, and he let her take the lead out onto the lake. She set a good pace, her measured strokes strong and fluid.

They glided along, cutting through the calm lake surface beneath cloudless skies and a sun guaranteed to bake unprotected skin. Today was one of those unexpected September days that would have air conditioners humming back to life.

He admired Cassi's legs. Hard to ignore all that exposed skin gleaming with a skim of moisture. They were quite a distance from shore when she pulled her paddle from the water, laid it across her knees, and twisted to face him. The full curve of her breasts thrust out, and he grinned, enjoying the view.

"Do you know someplace we can land to eat? I can't stop thinking about the stuff my aunt sent with us. I'm starved."

Nick stopped paddling and drifted. Reaching out, he grasped the rim of her kayak and pulled on the craft until it bumped his. "I know a couple of places. The county park should be deserted now that school's back in session. The view is terrific, and there are... facilities."

Cassi titled her head and scrunched up her face.

Nick had to chuckle. "Or do you like hiding behind trees to ah..."

She laughed, a rolling, full out whoop that made him want to reach out, pull her in, and touch her. No rigid, formal stiffness today. Today she looked relaxed and soft.

Tempting.

"I'm sold," she declared. "Even primitive plumbing is a plus for me."

Nick widened his grin. "Follow me, then."

He was right; the park was deserted. The lunch containers Ada had sent overflowed. What a feast. Thin sliced roast beef on homemade rolls and sprigs of sweet, green grapes, for starters. The assortment of cookies made his mouth water, but when he foolishly went for them first, he got his hand smacked.

They discovered a thermos filled with tart, chilled apple cider tucked into a duffle bag. Nick spread a blanket on the ground in the shade of a nearby tree, and they dug in until he couldn't eat another bite.

He lay back on the blanket and closed his eyes. Could this day get any better?

Cassi slipped away and strolled closer to the lake. She sipped cold cider and gazed into the distance. Leaves reflected on the water's surface created a never-ending pattern, a myriad of colors shifting and rippling in the breeze. Her serious, melancholy expression drew Nick to her.

"A penny for your thoughts?" He moved in behind her and placed his hands on her shoulders, waiting out a long pause until she heaved a shuddering sigh and spoke.

"My dad used to ask me that."

Her voice hitched, and he turned her in his arms. Still clutching the cider, she settled against him. He stroked her back, rubbed to soothe and comfort. Her shoulders relaxed, and his pulse hammered.

"I'm okay," she said, resting her forehead against his chest. Placing his cheek on her silky hair, he inhaled her scent. Then sweeping her hair aside, he pressed his mouth to the soft spot below her ear.

Cassi shivered. Locked in his embrace she seemed so fragile, yet judging from the way her kayak cut through the water, her muscles were toned and strong beneath her soft, pliant skin.

Disengaging herself from him, she stepped away. "Memories of my parents are strong, things they said or did. Don't feel you have to coddle me every time I leak a little when I remember them."

"Point taken." Using his thumb, Nick smoothed a single tear from her cheek. Then he removed the cup from her hand, set it down, and pulled her back into his arms. "This time I'm being selfish. This time it's strictly for my pleasure." He lowered his mouth to hers.

She tasted of apples and spice and -- heaven help him -- sweet, hot afternoon sex. He deepened the kiss, molding her body tighter to his, losing himself in the moment.

He broke the kiss, and not taking time to catch his breath, took her hand and pulled her to their blanket spread beneath the towering maple. He dropped to his knees and she slid down to join him like melting wax. His hungry lips reclaimed her sweet, willing mouth, and they sank onto the blanket.

Above them, a colorful canopy of leaves fluttered in the breeze, soothing his heated skin and ruffling her thick, honey colored hair. Nick became lost in her, drowning in her alluring taste and the exciting way she fit in his arms.

He'd wanted women before, had desired them. And he'd had many beautiful women. He was a man, and a healthy physical specimen to boot, but his growing affection for Cassi was more than physical. That scared the shit out of him.

When she'd spoken of her father, a very profound love had surfaced from deep inside her and was reflected in her eyes.

Nick admired her strength, admired the brave way she'd faced life after losing her parents. A woman like Cassi had many layers. Did he want to discover them, one by one, like sampling a good wine?

That first sip never failed to get Nick's attention; it slapped his taste buds awake. Tasting Cassi surely had gotten his attention. Holding her awakened his body. But would more than a sample of Cassi Burke involve more then he wanted to discover?

He skimmed his hand over her breast, testing her response. She arched up, and he closed his hand over that supple curve. Perfect. The thrust of her nipple against his palm sent a welcome signal. Encouraged by her deep, throaty purr, he worked his fingers beneath her top. Touching, sliding his hand over her heated skin, inching beneath the lacey barrier under her shirt.

The crunch of gravel and the distinct hum of an engine froze his exploring fingers. He opened his eyes. Reluctant to stop, however, his lips held the kiss. Then he jerked away.

"Not again," he muttered. "What the hell is TJ up to now?"

Cassi's eyes flew open. Frowning, she followed the direction of his gaze. They scrambled to their feet as a marked patrol car rolled to a stop nearby. Nick put his hand on Cassi's arm, stilling her movements as the door opened.

TJ stepped out and walked to the front of the cruiser. He leaned against the fender, crossed his legs, and carefully pried the lid from a takeout cup. Steam rose as he lowered his head to sip the hot liquid. He stopped when he caught sight of Nick arrowing toward him and straightened away from the car.

Getting right in TJ's face, Nick demanded. "What do you have, fuckin' built in radar?"

"Hey, I came up here for some privacy. A coffee break without interruption." TJ's brows shot up, and he raised one hand, palm out. His eyes moved past Nick. "Hello, Cassi."

"Sorry about that." Nick knew he'd lost it, and that Cassi had no doubt heard his crude comment to TJ. He stepped back. "I forgot myself."

"Not a problem." Cassi brushed dry leaves from her shorts. "I've heard worse."

To Nick, it was a big problem. His emotions were usually more disciplined, and the way he'd reacted, without thought, embarrassed him.

Lifting his coffee, TJ drank deeply. His eyes drifted from Cassie to Nick as he asked, "Did you kayak all the way here from Blaine's?"

"Yeah, we did." Hands on his hips, Nick stared at the ground.

TJ replaced the lid on his cup. "Guess my coffee break is over."

He opened the cruiser's door and folded his arms on top of it. Nick lifted his gaze, and TJ smiled ruefully. Nick relaxed his stance and let out a short, rough laugh.

"I owe you a case of cold ones." TJ grinned and got into the car. As he drove away, Nick tilted his head back as if reason would somehow appear in the drifting clouds above. Sensing that Cassi had moved away, he joined her as she gathered up the blanket and cooler.

"You're smiling," he said in accusation. He took the cooler from her hands. "Does that mean you see some kind of twisted humor in the way our trip to paradise is always interrupted?"

Cassi choked out a laugh. "Paradise? Aren't you afraid your ego might sink your kayak?" She didn't wait for his answer. "I was smiling because for once, I didn't get the feeling your cousin had me under a microscope. He actually smiled at me."

"He did, didn't he?" Nick thought about that as they eased the kayaks out onto the lake. Had new evidence shed light on the case? Did he dare hope that whatever was happening between him and Cassi might be spared the complication of her being a suspect?

Cassi remained quiet on the way back to her aunt's. Despite another interruption due once again to TJ's bad timing, the feeling of something inevitable about to happen plagued Nick.

Rufus appeared as they hefted the cumbersome watercraft onto Ada's weathered dock and rushed madly about while they returned Ada's kayak to her shed.

"Do you have any plans for dinner?" Cassi's question caught him by surprise.

"Is that an invitation?" he countered, snapping the tailgate of his truck into place. He'd planned to drop the borrowed kayak off at TJ's. Leaning against the truck and crossing his arms, he waited for her to answer his question.

"It might be." She crossed her arms and imitated his stance. Those tempting lips curved, and she flicked her gaze over him. "I'll call you, if that's all right. Maybe we can work something out."

"Got my phone right here." Nick tapped his pocket. "I'll be waiting."

*****

While Cassi was getting dressed, her aunt returned. Rufus woofed several times, nails clicking as he trotted to the door. A crescendo of howling enthusiasm met Ada's murmured greeting. Cassi entered the kitchen amidst the rattle of paper bags as Ada restocked the cupboards. She glanced over her shoulder.

"Cassandra, how was the kayaking?"

"Wonderful. I loved it."

"You're hooked," Ada declared. "I remember the first time I went. How I glided along quiet and easy. I would paddle out to the middle of the lake and sit there, all alone." She closed the door and paused. "Oh, are you going somewhere?"

"Yes. As a matter of fact I am. I'm going to dinner at Nick's. That is, if you can help me out. I'm providing the dinner. Any suggestions?"

A flicker of surprise crossed Ada's face. She purposefully closed the pantry door. When she turned around, a smile teased the corners of her lips. "I have several solutions. I'll raid the freezer; you get a bottle of wine from that hoard you've accumulated."

She started away and then swung back. "Make that two," she added, disappearing into her pantry.

About the time shadows crept across the lake, Cassi called Nick. He seemed both surprised and delighted by her proposal. So, after carting a sumptuous-smelling crock of beef barbecue to her vehicle, she returned and tucked crusty rolls and a container of salad greens into a large basket.

"All you have to do is warm up the barbecue, toss the salad, and open the wine." Ada wiped her hands on a dish cloth tucked into the waist of her slacks. "Oh. What about dessert?"

Cassi held up a neatly wrapped box of Cocoa Treat Chocolates.

"Wine isn't all I've been hoarding." She grinned and slid the box into the basket alongside two bottles of wine. When she looked up, Ada stood with her hands on her hips and her head canted.

Cassi flushed and bit her lip. "I... um... I'm not sure what time I'll be home."

Ada wrapped her in a hug, making her breath catch.

She laid a hand on Cassi's cheek and gave it a gentle pat. "Honey, enjoy yourself. He's a handsome, exciting young man. I trust you are both responsible adults and will have an evening to remember."

"Aunt Ada..." She covered her aunt's hand and whispered, "Thank you."

Then she headed for Nick's. Her plan was to totally surprise that handsome, exciting young man.

Cassi's decision to wear soft green cords and a cream-colored long sleeved top had been easy. Selecting scanty items which caressed her skin beneath the simple outfit had taken time. She wanted to knock Nick's socks off.

She wasn't a stranger to relationships, physical or otherwise. They were never casual, but one thing or another never fit. Mostly she kept to herself, much to the frustration of her outspoken manager, and even more so since the deaths of her parents. Lanie was forever pointing out great-looking men, and they encountered them on a daily basis. Yet the inside never quite measured up to the visible exterior. Not one had held her interest for more than a few dates.

In contrast, her attraction to Nick had exploded the moment he'd pinned her to the soggy ground in the bog. Of course, the fear factor had played a part, followed by indignation.

Now she couldn't keep her mind off him. Maybe her bold decision was a mistake. She'd always set goals and worked toward them. The goal this time? To simply enjoy the man. She had no idea where her involvement with Nick might lead.

Lights glowed from the windows as she approached the cabin. She parked and cut the engine. Silence engulfed her.

She squirmed, enjoying the silkiness of her hip-hugging briefs and the subtle caress of her lace-fringed bra, and she had to grin. For in her mind's eye, she pictured Lanie saying, "Yes!" with a wicked, wicked grin.

Chapter Nineteen

Jack LeFavor wanted to punch somebody's face in. He'd been sure the cops in Erie weren't sharp enough to notice the crack cocaine business he'd set up in the run-down duplex right under their noses.

He'd been wrong.

Now he could end up behind bars. The bust went down mid-morning just as he left the eastside Erie duplex.

Fuckin' cops. Who the hell pulled a drug bust in broad daylight? Jack hadn't been holding, and unless they could connect him to the operation he'd walk, and soon.

One of the cocky young men they'd nailed along with him shot him a sneer as he was escorted out of sight. Smug son of a bitch. The cop accompanying Jack tightened the grip on his arm and moved him along the narrow, dingy hallway.

He guided Jack into a stuffy, windowless room the pair they'd passed had just vacated. The place smelled of stale coffee and some kind of antiseptic cleaner. He assumed the others had already been questioned. Now it was his turn, and damn it, it was their word against his.

"Have a seat, Mr. LeFavor," the uniformed cop who'd escorted him said, indicating a long beat-up table.

Mr. LeFavor? What the fuck is up with that?

The door swung open, and another man entered. His bulk strained the seams of his ill-fitting suit, and he identified himself as Detective Tony Ciminisi. His clenched jaw and fierce, deep-set eyes sent a clear message.

Don't bullshit me.

Jack didn't blink. He could be just as hard-nosed.

Two men followed close on Ciminisi's heels and were curtly identified as Detectives Samuels and Conners from Ohio.

Jack's stomach dropped. What the fuck had brought these two flunkies here from Ohio?

Ciminisi circled the table, stopping by his side, while Conners took a seat across from him. Samuels propped one shoulder against the wall, shoved his hands into his pockets, and studied Jack. His hard stare revealed nothing.

The thickset Erie detective slapped a file on the table and flipped it open. "LeFavor, I want you to take a good look at this picture. Take your time; nobody's goin' anywhere."

Jack stared down at the picture. He stalled, looking from one detective to the other, purposely delaying to mask the shock coursing through him. Before he opened his trap, he wanted to get a handle on the situation and deal with the knot twisting in his empty gut.

This isn't about the drugs.

"Does the name Cassandra Burke ring a bell?" Ciminisi tapped a blunt finger on the open file.

Shit. Who the hell was Cassandra Burke?

Mind racing, he forced his eyes back to the picture. He wasn't sure why, but Jack suspected -- no, he knew damn straight -- this wasn't Sadie. Those were her eyes, but there was something different about her. Her face was softer. Clearer, maybe?

Sure, Sadie used drugs, yet he'd never known her to deal. But holy shit... who was this?

Cooperating might take the heat off him, but he had to feel his way. If they wanted to find Sadie, or Cassandra, or whoever the fuck this was, he'd point them in that direction. But damned if he wouldn't clam up and demand council if he smelled a trap

At last, hedging, he said, "I might. What'd she do?"

Samuels pushed away from the wall. A look passed between him and Conners. He approached Jack and slid one hip onto the table beside him, then casually leaned in to view the picture. "She might be a murder suspect."

Jack came close to pissing his pants. He swept the room with his gaze. The stone-faced men waited in silence. They hadn't mentioned Bob Morelli, but sure as hell, his gut told him, that's who they were talking about. Morelli was dead; he'd seen to that. But they must think Sadie had something to do with his murder.

Sweat beaded on his forehead. Forcing a cough, he asked, "Could I have a drink?"

Samuels picked up the picture and studied it. A nod from the detective sent the uniform for water. Jack drank deeply. Then, without batting an eye, he pointed to the picture.

"Can I see that again?"

He studied the woman's smiling face. Whoever this was, she was a dead ringer for Sadie. And Sadie hadn't had anything to do with Morelli's murder -- if, in fact, that's what they were talking about.

Christ Almighty, he could use a drink -- and something a hell of a lot stronger than water. He polished it off and wiped his mouth. All right, they could connect him to Sadie. Fuck, he'd spent all day with her yesterday. But that didn't mean crap.

He wasn't about to tell these yahoos what he suspected. For whatever reason, they wanted to find the woman in the picture, so why not throw the gentlemen from Ohio a bone? Jack LeFavor knew a bargaining chip when he saw one.

Forcing a smile, he tugged at his shirt collar. "How can I help you gentlemen?"

Chapter Twenty

Nick stepped outside at the sound of Cassi's CRV, and goose bumps prickled his skin. He could blame the cool breeze ruffling his hair, still damp from his shower, but more than likely Cassi's arrival had tripped that trigger.

As she approached, he admired her loose-jointed stride. Each step showcased her sculpted, alluring curves and those long, long, legs. Her eyes focused directly on him and held a promise.

Right off the bat, Nick knew he was in deep trouble.

Buttoning his shirt, he clamored down the steps. A hot, spicy scent wafted from the crock she carried, and he lifted it from her hands. After several trips carting various bags and an overflowing basket inside, he gaped at the delicious assortment that even included a nice cabernet sauvignon.

"I'm impressed," he said, opening the wine with a subtle pop. "You've brought one of my favorite dishes and paired it with a wine close to number one on my list of reds."

Using one hand, Cassi shook a bottle of salad dressing. "Just paving the way to paradise," she remarked, pouring the tangy herb dressing over the crisp greens.

His head shot up and his hand jerked, almost making him spill the precious cabernet. Cassi didn't blink an eye. He filled the wine glasses while stealing glances at the long, lean line of her back right down to the sweet curve of her hip.

A teasing, elusive scent hit him when she absently pushed her hair aside and picked up her wine. She swirled the deep red liquid gently and inhaled before taking a slow sip. She arched one brow in approval. Then her dark eyes met his, sending a hot jolt to his midsection. The heat spread, and every nerve in his body sparked like a damn Bic lighter.

On one hand, he wanted to grab her, lock the door, and take her fast and hard. On the other, however, he wanted to savor her like he did the rich cab. His heart rate damn near doubled just thinking about doing either. Where would acting on that lead him, and would it be somewhere he wanted to go?

She set her glass aside and tossed the greens. He took a sip, put down his glass, and settled his hands on her waist. Laying the salad tongs alongside the bowl, Cassi turned, twined her arms around his neck, and gave a gentle tug. Her warm breath, rich with cabernet, fanned his lips. Then she kissed him.

She teased him, taking small, nibbling bites. Her lips and the tiny thrusts of her tongue drove him wild. He pinned her against the kitchen counter with his body. The kiss she'd started, warm and slow, took on heat.

He broke off the kiss, coming up for air.

Time out.

He needed to breathe, to think about something besides the way their bodies fit together so perfectly, or how her wine-moistened lips moved beneath his.

"Nick?" she murmured against his mouth.

"Hmm?"

"I hope you told your cousin to get a date tonight so he won't bother us."

He burst into laughter, the perfect spell-breaker.

"Let's drink this great cab and enjoy the delicious food I brought." She wriggled free, reached into the basket, and produced a box of chocolates. "Then we can be decadent. No interruptions this time."

He picked up his wine, handed Cassi hers, and brought their glasses together with a clink. "Let's get started. I have a voracious appetite."

They drank to the evening ahead and sealed the toast with a kiss.

Nick fished his cell phone from his pocket.

"Hey, TJ," he said, reaching TJ's voice mail. "I'm unavailable tonight. If you need something, catch me tomorrow." He snapped the phone shut. "He'll get the message."

They devoured beef barbeque dripping in dark sauce and speared crisp greens coated with homemade dressing. Then Nick lit the fire. Bringing Cassi's decadent desert with them, they settled before the dancing flames and, between sips of wine, fed one another the luscious chocolate truffles.

Along with the heady combination of chocolates and wine, Nick feasted on Cassi. He sampled her lips, her neck, and the soft skin beneath her chin, until their goblets were empty and the truffles forgotten. Nothing remained but Cassi.

She raised her arms in silent invitation. Without hesitation he peeled the slinky top from her body and tossed it aside. He forgot about chocolate, and wine, and even the whole damned world, for that matter.

Nick wanted to go slow, to curb his aching, demanding body and delay the final plunge. But when his lips settled on the swell of Cassi's breast and a deep, throaty moan escaped her lips, he failed. She arched her back and cried out when he trailed his fingertips, very lightly, over her smooth belly.

He fumbled the snap on her slacks, and she laughed softly.

"Butterfingers," she murmured, her breath cool against his overheated skin. Then she gasped as he met success and yanked them down, revealing her sleek, toned thighs.

He took a moment to admire the wisps of delicate fabric barely concealing her lush breasts and other soft, secret places he craved to touch, stroke, and explore.

An avalanche of cushions followed the thick quilt he dragged from the sofa to the floor. She stretched out beside him, rested on her bent forearms, and lifted her hips when he hooked both hands in the delicate scrap of lace covering her and pulled. He trailed one finger lightly over her silky thigh, satisfied when he found her hot and wet.

Moving higher, he unclasped her bra and tossed it aside. Her breasts thrust out, and the firelight outlined her rigid nipples.

Good Lord. His heart nearly stopped. He stroked each one and cupped them in turn. Then he tasted them.

She collapsed onto the soft bed of cushions and fumbled blindly for his shirt. They rolled like playful, frantic puppies, their fingers tangling together as she helped him strip until their naked bodies glistened in the firelight.

"Cassi." He raked shaking hands through her tangled mass of golden hair, brushed it aside gently, and cupped her face. "My want... my *need* for you stuns me."

"Don't stop, Nick." Her eyes, luminous and soaked with passion, searched his face. "I couldn't stand it if you stopped."

He ravished her willing mouth. Plunging his tongue deep, invading, demanding, and taking from her. He shifted, moving over her. She rose to meet his quivering body, and he reached between them, searching and finding the soft nest between her thighs. Her breath caught, and her hips thrust against his bold, caressing hand.

The air thickened with the scent of her need.

With her lips pressed to his neck, she released a long, whimpering sigh. He pulled back, fumbling in the pocket of his discarded pants. His body throbbed and burned as he swiftly covered himself with protection.

"Nick?" Cassi reached for him, her questioning plea husky.

He came back to her, spread her thighs, and guided himself into her velvet warmth, inch by torturous inch. Her tender flesh closed around him. She sobbed his name and clamped her legs over his, pulling him deep inside her and tightening around him.

He drove into her slick heat. Pulling out, then returning time and time again, trying to hold off the plunge, teetering on the brink.

Cassi matched his passion, thrusting to meet him stroke for stroke until at last she cried out, "Oh, oh, Nick! Now, now!"

He held himself back for her pleasure, and as the pulsing grip around him eased, he moved fiercely. At last, on a long, low moan, he came. A blinding jolt of lightening in a lusty storm. His release left him trembling.

When the pounding in his ears softened and his desire was finally spent, he withdrew and settled over her like a gently shaken blanket. Eyes half closed, he savored the feel of her beneath him. After a long moment of recovery, he propped himself on his bent elbows and gazed down at her. Her eyes remained closed, and a relaxed smile spread over her gorgeous face.

"You look... blissful," he said, nudging her with a teasing push of his hips.

"And why wouldn't I?" she countered, returning the move. Her eyes opened and connected with Nick's, sending another lightening-like jolt though him. "The day's been perfect; the food and wine, unmatched."

He returned her smile.

"I look so blissful," she said, reaching up to cup his face, "due to a great encounter with a handsome man."

"Encounter?"

"I'm a romantic," she said, caressing his cheek. "I could have said, 'great sex'. I split the difference and called you a handsome man instead of a prince."

"I'm no prince, Cassi." Nick turned his head and placed a kiss on her palm. And with that, he rolled onto his side and faced her. His gaze drifted down her body. A fine coat of moisture covered her, and her skin glistened in the firelight. She shivered, a tiny tremor running from head to toe, and he pulled her against him. Resting his chin atop the silky strands of her hair, he breathed in its fresh, sweet scent. "I'm just a man, one who got unbelievably lucky with a very special lady today."

Tangled together, they rested in silence.

Cassi eased her body from his embrace. "I'll cherish this day, Nick," she said, pushing herself to her feet. Then she left the room.

Her supple curves flowed in the flickering fire as she disappeared down the hallway. She was beautiful. Slim, but not delicate. A chill surrounded Nick in her absence.

He took care of the used condom by tossing it into the fire. The action caused a spit of flames, and he smiled. The tiny eruptions seemed appropriate. Creating a stack of colorful cushions, he leaned back, hands linked behind his head, and stared into the fire.

Where would they go from here? He'd known all along Cassi wasn't a one-night stand. Nor would she take kindly to being one. On the other hand, she'd been the one with wine, chocolate, and a plan. "Paving the way to paradise," she'd said, clearly setting out to seduce him. And boy, had she ever.

He glanced down the hall. Paradise in Nick's book was synonymous with great sex. Being with Cassi had been both paradise *and* great sex.

But... had it been romantic?

The term alone scared him. Yet here he was anticipating her return, causing a familiar tightening low in his belly. But it was the unfamiliar, totally new tightening around his heart that he found most disconcerting.

A log crashed down, scattering the hot coals. He gathered more wood, slid the screen aside, and placed several pieces on the simmering embers. He settled back against the cushions just as Cassi emerged from the shadows.

The rekindled fire flared, and she glided from darkness into its glow and walked straight toward him. Totally naked. Something wrapped around Nick McGraw's heart and squeezed.

*****

Half naked, lounging in flickering firelight, Nick waited for her. When had she ever felt so loose, so limber, and so *alive*?

She pushed a persistent sliver of doubt away and allowed herself to simply enjoy the present. Nothing would spoil this night. Not this exciting, unforgettable, romantic night.

She stopped, standing over him, and he slid his gaze up her body. What woman wouldn't welcome the hot, appreciative gleam in those eyes?

Clasping her ankle, he gave her a gentle tug, and she tumbled into his lap. He'd draped the quilt across himself and he gathered her in, settling her against him. Heat radiated from his body, and her nipples tightened when her breasts brushed the swirls of dark hair covering his chest. He smelled of earthy spices, man, and sex.

He closed his warm hand over her naked breast and circled it gently as he kissed her. Then he lifted his head and met her eyes.

She smiled and murmured, "Remember the last time you grabbed my leg? I was covered with mud and trying to escape."

Wearing a devilish grin, he traced a line up her leg with one finger, trailing over her body to the peak of her breast.

"I found you holding a knife over a dead man, but these sweet things," he whispered, the tip of his finger circling and teasing, "kept catching my eye."

"You could have fooled me." Cassi covered his hand with hers and stilled the movement. "You had fire in your eyes. I was paralyzed with fear."

She shivered.

Nick slid the quilt from beneath her and covered her with it, tucking the warm cloth snugly around her legs and feet. His skin was fiery hot, and his muscles tensed and flexed as she settled in. He rested his cheek against hers and wrapped his arms around her.

"The hot body wriggling beneath me was what caused the fire in my eyes, and I had to call for backup."

"Speaking of which," she said, "do you think TJ has finally decided I'm not involved?"

Her eyes followed the dancing flames. A long moment passed. The banished sliver of doubt threatened to creep back into her mind.

"I have to let TJ work his case. He's well aware I have conflicting interest in his suspect." Nick shifted, making her acutely aware of his *conflicting interest* hardening and pressing against her.

She waited. Did he mean he was interested? Was his interest in *her*, or just her body? Her thoughts raced up, then down like a wild amusement park ride. The high points were rooted in the intimacy they'd shared, and the low points could mean his attraction was purely physical, and that's all it would ever be.

"Hey." He gave her a quick hug. "Penny for your thoughts."

His words melted her. She slid down, molding their bodies together and rekindling *their* fire while the embers on the hearth simmered.

How would she survive if she trusted Nick with her heart and he walked away?

Hours later, Cassi made her way back to Ada's. She could still taste him. His parting kiss had been deep and thorough. As she drove away, he'd stood hunched against the morning chill with his hands thrust deep into his pockets.

Fog rolled across the road, and frost lay heavy on the ground. Her headlights pierced the dawn, spotlighting a sporty red car parked in Ada's driveway. Taken by surprise, her heart pounded a fast, breathless rhythm, and every muscle in her body tensed.

Lanie's Miata.

Cassi jammed on the brakes and leapt out of the CRV, stumbling in her haste. She burst into the light and warmth of the kitchen. Ada looked up, a steaming teakettle in her hand, and Lanie turned from gazing out at the mist-shrouded lake.

"Hi," her friend said.

Lanie's simple, subdued greeting terrified Cassi. Why was she here? Those brilliant green eyes, always sparkling with life, had turned dark and intense.

Cassi rushed forward and embraced her. "Lanie, why…"

"Shh, it's going to be all right." She cupped Cassi's face with both hands, looked directly into her eyes, and took a deep breath. "Sit. Have some tea, and I'll explain why I'm here."

"I don't understand. Why can't you--"

"It's not good," Lanie added, shaking her head and guiding Cassi to a chair.

Ada brought the steeping tea to the table and placed her hand on Cassi's shoulder.

"There's been a fire," Lanie said.

Chapter Twenty-One

Sadie groaned aloud and slapped the shrieking alarm clock repeatedly. Blessed silence finally prevailed, and she dropped her arm. Her limp fingers brushed the floor. She'd driven like a maniac from Fox Chapel to Brecksville, arriving home near dawn.

Had it only been two days since her tryst with Jack LeFavor? Time had blurred her memory. Everything seemed different, as if something had shifted; as if something had tilted in her world, or was about to.

She rubbed her eyes and reached blindly for a cigarette. After lighting up, she drew deeply. The nicotine's harsh burn spread down her throat, making her insides twist. She bunched a shapeless pillow behind her head and leaned back, squinting through the spiraling smoke.

She'd hooked up with Jack in Cleveland. The man had liked the way she looked. He'd told her over and over. "You're gorgeous," he'd said. "Absolutely gorgeous."

They'd bar-hopped through a series of fancy bars downtown before checking into a room high above the city. He'd surprised the shit out of her by producing a hefty bag filled with fine white powder.

She pulled the ratty quilt tighter as the never-ending chills came and went. She'd been foolish to do coke, but he'd been generous with it. He'd also been stupid. She'd taken one hit while he watched impatiently, then he'd jumped her, huffing and puffing his way through a disgusting charade of sex.

Good thing I can act. With a smirk, she stubbed out the half smoked butt. He'd passed out cold after his pitiful workout and hadn't seen her slip a hefty amount of cocaine into her bag. Later, after he'd dropped her off in Cleveland, Sadie had headed southeast out of the city and driven for hours. Night had fallen by the time she strolled into a seedy bar along the river near Fox Chapel, Pennsylvania. Here she knew the white powder in her bag would be better than cold, hard cash.

Her plan had come out of nowhere. Jack and the cocaine had fallen into place without her having to lift a damn finger. Unless you counted that quick fuck. She smiled. Everything else had worked like a charm, and today she'd get her ass moving and finish what had to be done.

Sadie got up and draped the limp quilt around her to ward off the constant chills. Then it hit her.

Rick was gone. She peered at the bedside clock and the empty, rumpled bed. Cold from fear, and not just from the hit she'd taken, crept over her. He'd never come home from work.

She was alone.

"That son of a bitch," she muttered, glancing around. Her eyes itched and stung, and she craved more nicotine. She stumbled to the closet and swung open the door. His clothes were gone, every stinkin' ratty shirt he owned.

Shit. Shit. Shit.

One after another, she yanked open the drawers of the battered chest of drawers. Empty. Every friggin' drawer was empty. Rick Andrews hadn't left a thing.

Hot tears sprang to her eyes. At first, overwhelming loneliness crushed her. Then something inside her exploded. She hurled a bottle against the door, smashing it to bits, and the smell of cheap perfume filled the air.

"Fuck you, Rick Andrews!" she shouted.

Her temperature soared. With trembling hands she stripped and left a trail of crumpled, sweat soaked clothes behind as she stumbled into the shower. The cool, needle-like spray beat down on her, and her mind churned. She was alone now, but that was going to change.

News reports claimed Ms. Burke had denied knowing Bob Morelli. *Denied,* Sadie's ass. She would fix that woman's fuckin' wagon, by God. She'd show them the photo taken in Cleveland, and then the police, Ms. Burke's aunt, and that Philly cop she was screwing would think she was a damn liar.

When they saw that Sadie's face was so much like Miss Fancy Pants Burke's, smiling up at Bob in that picture, they'd freaking flip out. Maybe then good ol' Aunt Ada wouldn't be so proud of her lying bitch of a niece.

Sadie rubbed a rough towel over her skin, tossed it aside, and went to search through her new wardrobe. These were the kinds of clothes Ms. Burke wore. She studied herself in the mirror. Dull, boring clothes that made her want to gag. She'd add a little flash. God knew the outfit needed flash.

She swiped on some lipstick from her own stash. A bright, coral slash of color. The clothes still looked dull as dirt, and she grimaced into the mirror. It'd have to do.

When she jerked a suitcase from inside the closet, a tattered shoebox crashed to the floor. The box flew open, spilling its contents at her feet. She tossed the suitcase aside, dropped to her knees, and seized the snapshot.

After sliding the picture into an envelope, she placed it in the suitcase along with her clothes. Then she scanned the room and lit on a beat up leather handbag draped over a broken down chair. She dashed across the room and shoved her hand deep into the bag.

When her fingers wrapped around the solid, compact handle of a .25 semi-automatic, she heaved a sigh of relief.

She drew out the gun, checked the safety, and cradled the silver weapon in the palm of her hand like a precious jewel and admired its white pearl handle.

"Always check the safety," Jack had said, after she'd told him she was scared to go home from the bar alone at night and he'd given her the gun. No, she remembered. He hadn't given it to her. She'd paid dearly for that gun with her body and her soul.

"Stupid man," she scoffed, placing the pistol against her flushed face. She rubbed its cold, hard, stubby barrel against her skin, just like she'd rubbed herself against Jack.

Only this is a hard-on I can use.

She jammed the gun back into her bag, picked it up, and rushed out of the bedroom and down the short hallway. The silent TV caught her attention.

"How in the hell will he live without that dumb boob-tube?" She sneered at it.

Her eyes landed on a heavy, butt-filled ashtray. She picked it up, and with a mighty heave, threw it through the blank screen. Staring at the ragged hole it left, she dragged in raspy gulps of air.

"Good riddance, shithead," she muttered, stalking out the door.

She tossed her suitcase into the trunk, slammed it shut, and got into her car. Vowing not to look back, she tramped the pedal to the floor and shot down the street. Giddy with the certainty that this was the beginning of her new life, Sadie smiled.

Her life would really begin as soon as Cassandra Burke's life ended.

*****

"Should we stop her now?" Easily maintaining the tail, Fred glanced at his partner. His battered Chevy was an eyesore, but the engine purred as they sped along.

"No. Not yet. I'm still wondering why LeFavor gave her up so quickly. Something's haywire about the whole set up." Raife rubbed his hands over the stubble on his face, blinking hard to clear sleep-deprived eyes.

In the past twenty-four hours, they'd been forced to switch from sleazy looking characters to detective attire. They were back to sleaze. Erie PD had called when LeFavor had been rounded up during a bold daytime raid. Since he'd been working hand in hand with Ciminisi from Erie, Raife had welcomed the call.

Neither he nor Fred were thrilled to learn Erie did not have facilities where they could observe Lefavor being questioned and remain out of sight. So they'd cleaned up and hustled over to Pennsylvania just in time to sit in while detectives questioned the illusive drug trafficker. Now, in order to tail the woman in question, the two men were back in the street clothes that had so far served them well.

Jack LeFavor had provided them with an address in Ohio, a strange turn of events, but it was the only lead they had so they'd jumped on it. They'd driven to Brecksville and waited. The woman in question had returned just before dawn, surprising the hell out of them.

Raife flipped open a folder on the seat between them. He squinted at the dark-eyed woman pictured with LeFavor. Fred had taken the shots just days ago in Cleveland, and they'd had the girl's image cropped and blown up.

His cell phone rang.

He glanced at the screen and then answered, "Samuels."

"Raife, its Ciminisi."

"Yeah, Tony, what's up?"

"Christ, I must be gettin' old. Cassandra Burke's from near Pittsburgh. I still can't figure out why in hell LeFavor sent you to Ohio, so I double-checked. What I told you was right. She claimed to have stumbled across Morelli's body near here. Also claimed she's never met the man."

Raife lifted the picture. "Obviously, she lied."

Ciminisi grunted in agreement. "However, if she was recently in Cleveland with LeFavor, she might be a connection, one that might tie him to the murder. We all know Morelli was ass deep in drug traffic."

"No shit." Raife's mind refocused. Now he remembered. Burke had been all over the news recently. But he agreed with Ciminisi. What the hell was she doing in Ohio? "If she was connected to the murder and knew LeFavor, we just might get lucky. Where was Morelli found? Whose jurisdiction?"

"Pine Bluffs. The local PD there is handling the case. How about I give them a call? I'll tell them you might be in touch."

"Sounds good." Raife glanced up. "But there's no rush. From the looks of things, we could be heading their way. We're tailin' Ms. Burke, and she's traveling east on I-90."

Raife broke the connection. Holy shit. Maybe that was the answer, a connection in an out-of-the-way town near Erie. She might be the thread that pulled it all together. The damn woman seemed to be bouncing all over the place, but following her might lead them to a vital link in the drug trade.

Chapter Twenty-Two

Silent tears traced down Cassi's face and dropped unheeded onto her tightly clasped hands. Her nails bit deep into her skin. If she relaxed, unclasped her grip, she might shatter to pieces. Ada and Lanie's voices floated around her, faint, distant, and muted, as if she were underwater.

Fox Chapel Fitness was gone. Damaged almost beyond repair. They said the basic structure had been saved, but the interior -- workout fixtures, running track, sauna -- was a complete loss.

"Aw, honey," Ada murmured, "I wish there was more I could do for you." She lifted Cassi's ice-cold hands and warmed them between her palms.

Cassi raised her eyes and tried to focus on Ada's. They were dark with compassion, and Lanie's were luminous with unshed tears. Light-headed, Cassi failed when she tried to sort through a million thoughts crashing around in her head.

Someone pressed a steaming cup of tea into her hands.

"Drink some, honey." Ada's voice prompted her to mechanically lift the cup to her lips. The warm liquid burned a trail down her throat, and she bit her lip to keep it from trembling. Lanie moved in and smoothed back the strands of hair clinging to her tear-streaked face.

Cassi took another sip and drew in a shaky breath. "Tell me the details again, please." Her pleas came out raspy. "I'm afraid I blanked out most of what you said."

Lanie drew up a chair. "There's not much to tell. I got the call after midnight, and by the time I arrived at the club, flames were shooting through the roof."

Cassi hugged herself and rocked in place.

"The smoke was overpowering. I located a policeman who directed me to the officer in charge, the one who'd called me." She placed her hand on Cassi's arm. "Cass, they suspect the fire was deliberately set."

Cassi froze.

"Why?" she gasped. The suggestion was insane, senseless. "Why would someone burn down my place?"

"The men at the scene felt the job wasn't professional. They said arson is easier to detect when it's done hastily, or bungled. A witness gave them a lead to follow." Lanie glanced at her watch. "We can call. Maybe they know more by now."

Cassi barely heard the suggestion. She shot to her feet.

"I have to go there. They'll need to talk with me, and I want to see..."

She swayed unsteadily. "I want to see my club."

"Cassi, wait. Please." Ada steadied her. "You're tired and in shock. We'll call first, and then decide."

She slumped against her aunt. Tears choked her, and she shivered violently. Her life was once more spiraling out of control.

*****

"Shit," TJ flipped a pen onto his desk.

Nick paused in the doorway. He leaned against the frame, arms folded, and raised an amused brow at TJ's display of frustration.

"Bad day already?"

"Aw, shit," TJ repeated. He didn't look thrilled to see anyone, much less Nick. "Come on in and grab a chair."

Nick sobered. Stepping inside, he closed the door. He crossed to the coffee pot by the window and helped himself, then pulled a chair up to TJ's desk. He sat and took a careful sip, all the while observing TJ over the rim of his cup. Waiting.

Something had happened. His gut reaction was *not* from the bitter brew hitting the pit of his stomach.

"Cassandra Burke's business burned down last night."

Nick set his cup on TJ's desk with a smack. "What?"

He ignored the hot liquid that splashed over his hand. He'd been expecting a police matter. Something he could relate to, and maybe help with by talking through the day to day frustration every cop inevitably faced.

But not this. Not another blow that would slam into Cassi like a freight train. His chair scraped the floor, and seconds later, he yanked the door open.

"Nick, wait!"

He stopped, placing one hand on the doorframe above his head and gripping the wood with white-knuckled tightness.

"I haven't contacted her," TJ said. "I just got a call from Fox Chapel PD, and they relayed the news."

Puzzled, Nick dropped his hand and turned stiffly to face TJ. "Why? Why the hell would they call you about a fire near Pittsburgh?" TJ's pained expression twisted Nick's insides. "You're still checking up on her, aren't you?"

TJ pushed away from his desk and stood. "Go see if she's okay. Believe it or not, I'm concerned, too. Something isn't right, and I've got to find out what that something is."

"Son of a fuckin' bitch." Nick smacked his hand against the wall with a resounding crack. Two of the people he cared about most were pulling him apart. He ignored his smarting palm, turned, and stalked away.

Within moments, he'd arrived at Ada's and swung in behind a red compact in her driveway. Striding past the car, he noted empty cups, a sweater, and a tattered notebook tossed onto the passenger seat. The sweater was undoubtedly a woman's; the cups, definitely from Starbucks. The notebook was a vibrant purple. The car must belong to Cassi's manager, Lanie Delacor.

He ran his hand over the hood. Stone cold. She'd been here a while. Meaning Cassi already knew about the fire. He took the steps two at a time and rapped on the door.

Ada answered, and Rufus bounded outside.

Nick absorbed the dog's frenzied greeting and knelt down, rubbing his hands over the animal's silky coat. He gave Rufus a quick hug, stood, and backed the squirming canine into the kitchen.

"Ada, how is…"

Ada softly closed the door behind him.

From across the room, Cassi met his gaze. He glanced at the dark-haired beauty beside her, then back at Cassi. The soft, blissfully sated look she'd had when she'd left him early this morning was gone. Her face was void of color, making her eyes appear dark and wide, like a doe frozen with fear. Moisture flooded them when she saw him.

Two long strides brought him to her side, and she rose to meet him. He gathered her close. Her hands clasped the front of his jacket in a tight-fisted hold, and a ragged sob escaped her. Over Cassi's head he met the greenest eyes he'd ever seen.

"Hi. I'm Lanie, Cassi's manager. You must be Nick McGraw."

Her sultry voice struck a chord within him, and those luminous, green eyes glowed with curiosity as she took in Cassi's reaction to his presence with undisguised interest.

After a moment, Cassi released his shirt. Her hands rested on his chest, and when he moved to comfort her, she stepped back and shook her head.

"I'm sorry." Giving a weak laugh, she swiped tears from her pale cheeks with the back of her hand. "I didn't mean to leak all over you."

"Not a problem." He cupped her cheek and brushed away a stray tear. "Are you all right?"

"You've heard?" she asked.

"I heard." Nick placed a kiss on her brow and repeated, "Are you sure you're all right?"

"I'm fine, but I need to freshen up," she said, taking a deep, shuddering breath. She turned to Lanie. "How about you? Need to clean up a bit?"

"Sure. I probably look like something the cat dragged in." Lanie grinned half-heartedly and gathered her overnight bag, then followed Cassi down the hall.

Ada scoffed when Nick asked for coffee. "Try going a day without all that caffeine swimming around inside you, Nicholas."

"Awww, Ada. What kind of cop would I be if I sipped tea all the time?"

Ada ignored his plea and placed a steaming cup of tea before him.

"She's ready to break," she declared, once the girls were out of earshot. She settled her narrow-eyed gaze on him. "How did you find out? Lanie was here before Cassi arrived."

Nick stared into his tea. He felt ten years old again. Only this time, he wasn't on Ada's land. Oh, no. This time it was personal. He'd spent the night with her niece.

"TJ told me. He got it through police channels." He hoped Ada would accept his generic explanation and not probe any deeper. At the moment he felt like shit, partly because he knew TJ was digging into Cassi's life, and partly because he was afraid of what his cousin might turn up.

Ada sank onto the chair opposite him, never averting her eyes. "So TJ's been keeping you abreast of the case. Nick, I'd be a fool to overlook the fact that Cassi spent most of last night with you. I'm not that old, or that naïve. I also realize you're on vacation and a casual... um, *encounter* between attractive, consenting adults is not unusual. I've seen the attraction. The very first night at Pine Bluffs PD you never took your eyes off her."

Nick gave a wry smile. Busted. The lady had sharp eyes.

Ada continued, "TJ is smart, fair, and tenacious. But if what you feel for my niece is not an honest to goodness attraction and you've been doing a little detective work for your cousin by using her attraction to you, then you're not the man I thought you were."

Nick pushed down a surge of anger. He lifted the tea and drank deeply, wishing like hell it was strong, black coffee. His eyes met Ada's across the table. He leaned back with a sigh and chose his words carefully before speaking.

"Ada, I've been a cop a good many years. I deal in facts. One glaring fact is that I haven't seen one thing linking Cassi to TJ's case. I believe Rufus here," he said, placing his hand on the silken head resting on his thigh, "was responsible for dragging Cassi to that body, just like she said. Evidence supports that scenario, and what you're accusing me of, quite frankly, offends me."

He raised a hand, palm out, when she stiffened. "But I understand. You love her. I care for her too, Ada. Very much."

Ada averted her eyes. She was caught in the middle, too. Nick reached across the table and pried her tightly clasped hands apart. He sandwiched one between his and gently massaged her resisting fingers.

"TJ has a job to do. I'm going to stand aside while he does it, regardless of my personal feelings. Getting intimately involved with Cassi at this point probably wasn't too smart." He gave her hand a pat and released his grip. "I'm between a rock and a hard place, Ada. That's exactly where I am."

Rufus sprang up. The ladies returned, and much to his relief, Nick's conversation with Ada was over. For now.

*****

TJ's head pounded. While waiting to hear from Fox Chapel and Erie PD, he'd continued to dig for background info on Cassi Burke. He felt driven to do so, and for the life of him could not pinpoint any one reason. But here he was.

He knew Ada's deceased sister was Cassi's mother. Yet Cassi's birth certificate had been generated by the court when she was adopted by the Burkes in Erie. Her mother had died in an Erie hospital, but the official documents didn't state that Cassi had been born there. They only verified she was adopted from there.

"Crap," he muttered, raking fingers through his hair. Fragments, that's all he had, and he felt as if he were going in circles. He glared at the phone and silently willed it to ring.

After checking the Erie area and coming up empty, he'd widened the circle by placing calls to several inner-city free clinics in the Pittsburgh area. If any returned his calls, maybe something would click.

Did clinics keep records for twenty some-odd years? If Cassi had been born at one of them, what would that reveal? His need to know more about the beginning of her life compelled him to learn more, and that compulsion came from deep in his gut, not from any textbook.

Still chasing my tail. He lifted a stack of notes and tapped them on his desk.

The phone shrilled.

"McGraw."

"Mr. McGraw, I'm Ruby Gilliam, executive director of the Duquesne Clinic. I'm returning your call." Her voice was clipped, definitely Pittsburgh.

TJ grabbed a pen. "Thank you, Ms. Gilliam. I appreciate your promptness."

"It's *Mrs.* Gilliam, and you're welcome." Without pause, she continued. "I understand you're trying to locate someone who may have been born here twenty-five or thirty years ago?"

"Is that possible?"

"Anything's possible Mr. McGraw, but I'll need some information."

TJ had to smile. The clipped-speaking *Mrs.* Ruby Gilliam just might be tenacious enough to help him do the impossible.

He told her what he had, encouraged by her strong "umm hum's" following each fact he revealed.

"I'll check into your inquiry when time allows," she informed him in her no-nonsense voice. "Then I'll get back to you."

He'd barely disconnected when the phone rang again. An officer from Fox Chapel PD reported there was nothing new at their end in regard to the fire. However, the state fire marshal had confirmed their suspicions. The fire had been deliberately set. They had questioned several witnesses, but unless lives had been lost or they could tie the event to a high profile case, the investigation would be shoved to the bottom of the pile. The tired officer seemed relieved when TJ offered to relay a progress report to Miss Burke.

A short time later, when Erie still hadn't called, TJ decided to deliver the update to Cassi in person. He left instructions at the front desk for them to notify him right away if a call came in and grabbed his jacket on his way out the door.

Clouds hid the sun, and a light breeze sprang up. Dry, brown leaves rattled down the street. Tipping up his collar, TJ slid into his patrol car. When his destination came into view, he was not surprised to see Nick's truck parked at Ada's. But who owned a red Mazda? He pulled into the driveway. Noting the Pennsylvania tags on the unfamiliar sports car, he climbed the steps to the porch and knocked.

"TJ, come in." Ada seemed subdued when she opened the door. As he stepped inside, he met Nick's steely gaze before looking at Cassi. Nick still seemed pissed, and both he and Cassi appeared tired, wrung out. This new development was taking a toll on all of them. Even Rufus lacked his usual exuberance.

TJ moved forward, then stopped. His insides tightened. Another pair of eyes -- riveting green eyes -- met his. The door closed behind him, and for a long moment no one spoke.

"What do you want, TJ?" Nick's voice startled him.

"I stopped by to give Cassi an update."

Cassi's head came up.

"A short time ago, I spoke with Fox Chapel PD. They're still talking with witnesses. When they finish, they'll go over the Fire Marshal's report and contact you with their findings."

"Who are the witnesses? Do they work for me?" Cassi's voice faltered. Her pupils had gone wide and dark, as if she were in shock.

TJ shook his head. "They didn't say. Unfortunately, these things take time. I'm sorry, that's all I have for now." His attention returned to the dark-haired beauty beside Cassi.

"Oh," Cassi said. "TJ, this is Elaine Delacor, my manager. She drove here to tell me about the fire."

Reluctant to look away from the unwavering green gaze, he nodded. "We spoke on the phone. Is that your Miata, Miss Delacor?"

"Yes, it's mine," Lanie drawled. The roll of her low, smoky, voice undulated across the room, wrapped itself around his senses, and squeezed.

Cassi reached for Lanie's hand. "Lanie's been here since dawn. She didn't want to tell me about the fire by phone."

"Do you have time for tea, TJ?" Ada asked.

TJ pulled his gaze from Lanie. "No, thanks, Ada. I've got to get back to the station. I'll be in touch when I know more. Nick, walk out with me?"

He said polite good-byes to the ladies, and then left the cottage with Nick on his heels.

Squinting skyward at the ominous gathering clouds, TJ zipped up his jacket. "Cassi looks beat up."

"What did you expect?" Nick jammed both fists into his pockets. "She lost her parents less than six months ago, and now this. I think she's holding up well under the circumstances. Hell, TJ, how much more do you think she can take?"

TJ decided his questions could wait and slid into his car. Nick didn't seem ready to talk reasonably. He was way too close to the situation. He didn't envy Nick's position, but he did understand.

"You're right. She's a strong woman, though, and from the looks of things, she has lots of support." A long moment passed. "I've got some calls out. Gotta go."

He closed the door and started to back up, then braked, cracked the window, and looked up at Nick. Despite everything, he had to ask.

"So, what do you think of Cassi's manager, Miss Delacor?"

"So that's what you wanted to ask me?" Nick's hard look turned into a crooked smile. Welcome, but irritating. "Noticed the green eyes, huh?"

"Go to hell, McGraw." TJ shook his head and flashed his cousin a quick grin.

Then he surged backward, shifted the car into gear, and with a brief wave, roared off down the road. He was relieved to be back on even, albeit shaky, ground with Nick. But as he sped back toward the station he couldn't help but think about Lanie Delocor's eyes. They sure hadn't looked that green in her picture.

Too bad she had *attitude* written all over her pretty face.

Chapter Twenty-Three

Cassi needed to clear her head, to run until she ached. Maybe then her mind would settle, and she could put everything behind her and face what she must do.

Nick waited up ahead, hunched over, hands on his thighs, gulping air. He locked his gaze on her as she closed the distance between them. He'd insisted on joining her, stating he could use the exercise, too, and they'd agreed to meet where the trail along Pine Shadow Lake split.

There he was, standing tall and straight while the wind whipped his thick auburn hair into messy disarray. His tee shirt bore a faded Philadelphia Police Department emblem, and the same large white letters ran from waist to ankle on his faded navy pants. Despite his beard-roughened cheeks and ratty, well-worn sweats, the sight of him took her breath away.

By the time she reached him, he'd recovered and his breathing was strong and steady. His pushed-up sleeves revealed hard, strong, sinewy forearms. She'd wanted a diversion from her troubles, and the man could certainly provide one.

But was she simply trading one form of pain for another?

For now, he anchored her escalating turbulent life. She admired his vitality, and the calm, confident way he did things. Like introducing her to a well aged cabernet, or making sweet, sweet love before a crackling fire.

"What took you so long?" He grinned, eyeing her from head to toe. Goose bumps erupted beneath her running gear. With just a look he sent her inhibitions flying, but her raging lust wasn't only physical. Deep inside, her heart had opened to him as readily as her body.

Cassi loosened the sweatshirt knotted at her waist and retied it. Strands of wind-blown hair whipped across her eyes. She shoved them back and looked skyward. Thick clouds raced along, and dry leaves smacked against their legs.

"I'm just warming up," she said, ignoring him as she aligned her body and leaned forward, stretching her warmed muscles. "Then I'll do some serious running."

"Okay, teacher." He teased gently, leaning to one side and stretching his hard-muscled inner thighs. Cassi smiled and sneaked a look as his wind-whipped clothes outlined his superb body. His simple, lighthearted remark helped to ease her tension.

She concentrated on stretching, aware the lake had begun to roll in the wind. Tiny white caps broke the surface, and the sun disappeared behind the fast moving clouds, turning the water a flat gray.

Like the jagged whitecaps erupting on the lake, Cassi's swirling emotions threatened to break through. Mesmerized by the choppy water, she paused, crossed her arms, and hugged herself.

"Hey," Nick ran his hand down her arm. "I was kidding. Are you all right?"

"I'm fine," she said, covering his hand with hers. Then she executed a neat sidestep and moved away. That morning when Nick had arrived at Ada's, she'd summoned her ironclad willpower to clamp down on the impulse to let his strength shield her. The fire had come close on the heels of losing her parents, and the course of her life was now forever altered. But before long, Nick would be gone and she would have to face life alone.

"Let's go," she shouted over the rising wind. "From the looks of that sky, I'd say we're going to get wet."

Nick fell in beside her as the first fat drops of rain began to fall. Within moments, the downpour became a driving wall of water.

She forged ahead. Facing the storm head on proved she could handle anything.

*****

A deluge of pounding rain and strong wind gusts overtook Sadie as she headed east. She'd crossed into Pennsylvania a short time ago and now, bleary-eyed from straining to see through the driving rain, she pulled off the highway. Tired to the bone, she squinted at the outdated truck stop.

"Hell, I gotta' get some food and crash for a while."

Hunched beneath her skimpy jacket, she dashed from the car. A beat up sign above the weathered door advertised *G od Fo d*.

Wind pushed the door shut behind Sadie with a slam. She shed her jacket and gave it a shake, sending a shower of raindrops flying. She glanced around the stale-smelling room, and her hopes for *Good Food* faded.

Just like the pitiful sign outside above the door.

*****

Raife braced his hand on the dashboard as his partner did automotive acrobatics to exit I-90. The rain all but obscured Sadie's ancient compact, and the low ground fog swallowed up its taillights.

"Fuck, Conners. Where'd you learn to drive?" Raife growled, straining to see which way the car they'd been tailing had turned.

Fred chuckled and rolled to a stop. He glanced right to left. "I'd say she headed to the truck stop. It's the only sign of life I can see from here."

"Let's hope so. If we lose her in this mess, we'll be shit outta luck. I'm surprised she's managed to get this far. If there's a motel nearby, she'll crash there. I'd put money on it."

Fred nodded and turned right, edging into the poorly lit parking lot. They spotted Sadie's car parked near the door. Two pick-ups were parked out front, and several semis sat off to their left. An arrow painted at the corner of the building displayed the word *Rooms* in peeling white paint.

They parked beside Sadie's car. Rain pounded a deafening rhythm on the roof after Fred cut the engine.

He leaned back and stretched. "What now?"

"She won't recognize us. Let's go inside and see what she's up to." Raife leaned forward to see the partially lit sign over the door. "I'm so hungry my backbone and ribs are scraping together."

"Mine, too. If we order food, though, let's make sure it's deep-fried. Hot grease can kill anything," Fred announced wryly.

Raife turned up the collar of his jacket and reached for the door. "Shit, I hope you're right about that."

Chapter Twenty-Four

Nick flicked the useless switch several times. "No power. Wait here. I'm sure there are candles somewhere."

He crossed the room, leaving a trail of puddles. Pale light seeped through the rain-drenched windows, and flashes of lightning illuminated the room as he skirted around dimly outlined furniture. Utensils rattled when he searched a drawer for candles. Waiting just inside the door, Cassi shivered. Driven by ear-splitting thunder and vivid lightening, they'd gotten soaked dashing through the pelting rain to Nick's cabin.

"I'll be right back," he said, moving down a dark hallway. He returned with several large towels, handed one to Cassi, and briskly dried his soaking wet hair. He'd removed his shirt and sweatpants and put on dry jeans. His taut skin glistened in the semi-darkness. Cassi clenched her hands and fought the urge to run them over his naked torso.

He set out several candles he'd found and lit them. She moved closer, as if their wavering circles of light provided warmth. With a towel wrapped around her head turban style, she blotted moisture trickling down her neck.

"I laid out some dry things on the bed for you," he said. "They'll be way too big, but will keep you warm and dry until the power comes back on and we can use the dryer."

By the time she'd changed, Nick had a fire going. Licking flames crackled and spit to life, and the smoky tang of burning wood filled the room.

Cassi felt ridiculous in Nick's faded blue sweats. She'd pulled the drawstring on the pants as tightly as possible, and the man-sized sweatshirt reached her upper thighs. Even after rolling up the sleeves and cuffing the pants, the outfit swallowed her.

She rubbed her cheek against her sleeve. The cotton, soft from many launderings, smelled like Nick.

"Very chic," he remarked. "Give me those wet things. I'll put them in the dryer."

She handed over her wet clothes. He unfolded the sodden garments. Separating her bra and panties from the tangled mess, he held them up for inspection. Then with a lopsided grin, he casually tossed them into the dryer.

Her cheeks warmed. It wasn't as if he hadn't seen her underpants before. Last night had been quite revealing. But intimacy with Nick was still new, and the easy way he had handled her most personal items made her blush.

He joined her near the fire. A mat of dark, tightly curled hair covered his chest, and his well-defined shoulder muscles gleamed in the flickering light. Cassi turned away.

Methodically she squeezed moisture from her hair. A raging storm of bottled up feelings swirled inside her. At the center of the storm grew a hefty helping of guilt. She should be able to cope, to be strong and face this new disaster. Yet she wanted Nick's arms around her, holding her, erasing the fire's reality from her mind. But if he touched her, she would crumble.

"Are you feeling better?" He moved closer. His warm breath caressed her neck, and heat radiated from his body. She froze, clutching the towel against her.

"Cassi, look at me." He placed gentle hands on her rigid shoulders and gave them a little rub.

"Nick, please," she protested, hating that her voice was weak and shaky. His fingers contracted in a gentle squeeze, and with a strangled cry she turned to him. She looped her arms around him and clung as if she were drowning.

Her emotional dam had burst.

Deep, racking sobs shook her, and she pressed her face against his heated skin. Nick did what she so desperately needed. He held her. With his strong arms clamped around her, he rocked her from side to side, soothing her and letting her tears flow unchecked.

Her knees gave out and she surrendered, sagging against him. He scooped her up, enfolding her in his arms with ease, and then moved to the sofa. She needed him, now more than ever. So she held on fast.

Her towel came undone, releasing a cascade of damp, tangled hair. Nick smoothed the dripping strands away from her face. He sat, cradling her tenderly, and settled her on his lap.

"I wondered how long you could hold out," he murmured. The fire's reflection danced in his somber eyes, and desire smoldered between them.

She curled against him and buried her face in the curve of his neck. "Nick, hold me. I'm spinning out of control, and I want it all to go away. Please, make it all go away."

His damp, musky scent surrounded her, and pleasure speared through her when he tipped her face up and kissed her. She was on fire, frantic with need. And she wanted more.

He cupped her breast and rubbed, creating delicious friction against her nipple. Gathering her shirt's thick, bulky fabric, he lifted it, exposing her upper body. His hot mouth replaced his hand and she arched up, crying out from sheer pleasure.

Threading eager fingers through damp silky strands at the nape of his neck, she held him there, and he drew deeply on her. She squirmed, about to slide from his lap until he grasped her wriggling hips, lifted, and twisted her until they lay side by side, facing one another.

An exploding log created a burst of heat, and a shower of sparks disappeared up the chimney. Nick's insistent lips nibbled the sensitive spot beneath her ear and trailed heat down her neck like liquid fire. He pulled her sweatshirt off all the way, leaving her tender flesh unprotected, allowing him to nip and tease his way up her body. Her eyelids drooped, and the dancing flames blurred. With an explosion of movement he stripped her, removing the clothes she'd barely had time to warm from within.

Cassi submitted without a qualm. Lost in sensation, she encouraged those strong, lean-fingered hands as they traced a path for his hungry lips, and gasped aloud when he laved her sensitive nipples. He slid his hand down and touched her between her legs, rolling his fingertips, making her wet.

"Nick, please," she whimpered, clamping her legs on his questing hand. She was primed, ready. Rubbing against him, begging, offering. She reached down, her frantic fingers grappling with the snap on his jeans, unable to ignore the telltale bulge behind the taunt denim.

Pushing her hands aside, he unsnapped and unzipped them with record speed. He slid them down and kicked them away.

At last, he rolled on top of her. Hot and pulsing, he pressed against her naked belly. Cassi clamped her legs around him. Surging, seeking.

Needing.

He levered himself up and braced himself above her, his eyes like charcoal smoke, his jaw rigid. Confused, she pushed the wet, tangled hair from her eyes.

"Cassi," he rasped. "I need to protect you, honey."

"Hurry," she urged. "Oh, God. Hurry."

He fumbled and cursed in his blind search. Her body ached for him. He'd left her hot and throbbing, and she wanted him. Wanted him *now*.

Then he was back, straddling her, pinning her with his body and a heavy lidded, burning gaze. Hot coals hissed beneath the flaming logs, and she ran her trembling fingertips along his rigid thighs. He eased her legs apart, and she trembled. Unable to wait, she lifted her hips, a blatant invitation for Nick to ignite the tiny tremors building deep inside her.

Ah, at last. That first probing touch, gentle, yet searing, made her writhe beneath him. He slowly entered her. Impatient, smoldering, on fire, she grasped his hips and brought him tight against her.

She met him thrust for thrust. Until Nick took control, gripping her insistent hips, setting the pace. His tight, hard belly moved against her, driving her wild. Then he paused, lifting away and lacing his fingers through hers. Air chilled the moist skin of her breasts and belly.

"Nick?"

"Easy, Cass. Lie still." He curved his lips, smiling wickedly as he reentered her. "Umm... enjoy, baby."

"I can't. I'm so close..."

"Stay with me," he soothed, moving in and out, keeping his weight from her, sliding against her. Heels pressed down, she lifted her hips. There. Ah yes, right *there.*

Her inner muscles clenched harder, faster, until she screamed, "Oh, Nick. Oh, Nick. Please, please. Nick!"

He surged into her, his hips moving like a piston, fast and hard. Until he froze and held himself inside her, shuddering as he came. Then, with a groan, he collapsed.

Rolling to one side, he gathered her close, still buried deep within her. He cupped her face with gentle hands. "Oh, Cass."

She touched his face, waiting. "Hmm?"

"Nothing," he said. "Just... Cass."

The words she longed for never came. He was tender. He was gentle. His lovemaking made her quake. Between murmured words of passion, he brushed his lips across her cheek. Yet nothing crossed those sexy lips to suggest he felt anything for her besides hearty lust.

Her heart wept.

A sharp snap from the fireplace broke the hazy spell. Nick withdrew and eased to one side. The simmering flames burned low, and rain drummed on the skylights high above them. Thunder no longer shook the windowpanes, and the flashes of lightening that had driven them into this cozy shelter had ceased.

She skimmed her hand down the long, hard length of his back. His deep hum of contentment made her smile. He repositioned them and pressed his face to hers. The heavy musk of spent passion rose around them and she nuzzled his hair, inhaling the intimate scent combined with the spice and tanginess that was Nick.

"The storm is over."

"Are you sure?" he murmured.

Cassi trailed her hand lower. She lifted her leg between his thighs. His eyes darkened and he returned the pressure, letting her know a new storm was brewing.

Much later, Nick slipped Cassi's pliant arms into the sweatshirt he'd loaned her and slipped it over her head. He pulled on his jeans and knelt to stoke the fire.

When he turned back, Cassi was sound asleep, her rain-dampened hair spread in wild disarray on the cushion beneath her head. He skimmed his knuckles over her face. Her soft skin glowed in the aftermath of their frantic coupling. He'd taken her multiple times, and as he watched her sleep his body tightened with need again.

Ever since he'd found her clutching that knife, standing over a dead man, he'd been attracted to her. Now he'd gone and done it. He was not only involved with a murder case four hundred miles from his jurisdiction, but with an on-again off-again suspect. Not a brilliant move for a seasoned criminal investigator.

He'd peeled back her intriguing layers and found a smart, sensitive, funny, passionate woman. She'd surprised him, seducing him with food, wine, and a look in those cocoa brown eyes he'd never forget.

He wanted her.

Reluctantly he tore his lingering gaze from her and made his way to the kitchen for a beer. The dark interior of the refrigerator reminded him they still lacked power. Heavy rivulets of rain coated the window, and by his calculations it had to be midday. Yet the sky was as dark as midnight. Twisting off the cap, he downed half the bottle. Still clutching the beer, he returned to Cassi. She hadn't stirred. Standing there, he studied her.

Something had shifted in his life. He felt vulnerable, exposed. Much akin to the feeling he got when some overlooked detail on the job came back to bite him on the ass. Wasn't that a hell of a comparison for a romantic interlude with a beautiful woman?

In the throes of passion, that beautiful woman had begged him to make her forget the pain, to keep her safe -- and for the time being, he had succeeded.

One question kept circling him like a vulture, however. Could he sustain such a commitment and live up to Cassi's needs?

*****

The rhythmic slap of windshield wipers synchronized with Dean Martin's lazy voice. Water hitting the truck's underside created wide, arching sprays in sharp contrast to Dino's soothing assurance that *Memories Are Made of This*.

Nick's driving skills impressed Cassi. He dodged fallen branches and steered around heaps of debris left by the storm. She still wore the oversized sweats he'd lent her. After pulling her wet running clothes from his lifeless dryer, she'd stuffed them into a plastic bag. They now lay at her feet in a soggy lump.

"Whoa!" Nick shouted as he swerved to avoid a low-hanging wire. "This is one hell of a storm."

"No argument here." Cassi turned from Nick to peer through the rain-washed windshield. Torrents of water pounded down with blinding intensity.

They'd laughed like a couple of kids when Nick had swept her up in his arms and sprinted through the downpour to his truck. She'd clung to him and giggled.

Giggled. For Pete's sake. What was wrong with her?

The police thought she was a knife-wielding killer, her life was in turmoil, and her business was gone. Yet she'd giggled. Actually, she'd laughed out loud as they'd dashed from the porch.

Her eyes returned to Nick's strong profile highlighted in the dash lights. His dense mahogany hair was damp and wildly disheveled. The rough stubble darkening his jaw enhanced his appeal, and despite all her troubles, everything paled when she was with this handsome, enigmatic man.

He slowed to negotiate a wicked curve. Upon completing the move to perfection, he gave her a quick wink. He was so smug, so fearless, and so sure of himself. He was also risking his life to make sure her aunt and Lanie, whom they'd tried to reach unsuccessfully by cell phone, would not worry about her.

Ada's cottage came into view through the fog. Nick turned from the highway and parked. Loosening his seatbelt, he slid across and pinned Cassi against the door. "I'll kiss you good-bye now so I can do it the way I want."

She caught her breath and her stomach doubled-dipped like a roller coaster. With heat and hunger, his lips covered hers. At that moment, that crazy, crazy moment, being kissed breathless while sitting in Nick's truck with rain pounding down, Cassi knew she was hopelessly in love with Nick McGraw.

He slid his warm hand beneath the baggy sweatshirt, boldly cupping one unfettered breast.

"Nick." She groaned, reluctant to stop his advances.

"Umm?" His hazel eyes burned with desire, and his fingers teased her eager flesh.

"By now they've noticed we're here. Unless we go inside soon, they're going to wonder what we're doing. Nick, I don't want my aunt to catch us naked in your truck."

"Naked, huh?" His hands started to ease her shirt -- already hiked halfway to her armpits -- up her body.

"Nick!"

He laughed, and after sneaking in one last lingering caress, pulled the shirt down. "We'll have to run for it. Wait, I'll come around and get you."

He sloshed through deep puddles to her door, lifted her into his arms, and hurried through the downpour to Ada's porch.

They slid to an unsteady stop just short of the doorway. Cassi was laughing, swiping rain from her eyes, when Nick stiffened. With water pooling at their feet, he shifted her in his arms and directed his unwavering gaze at the cabin door.

Lanie filled the doorway, holding the screen door wide. Her sharp green eyes looked over them, and one delicately arched brow rose sharply.

"Nick. Nick, put me down." Cassi wriggled against him and gave him a quick nudge. She shot him a look and he released her, holding her steady until her feet hit the floor.

Groaning inwardly, Cassi moved past Lanie and into Ada's kitchen. Nick followed. She recognized the look on Lanie's face, knew it like the back of her hand. Blatant curiosity mixed with pure glee from seeing Cassi so comfortable in a man's arms.

Flaming candles on the table danced and sputtered in the stiff breeze until Nick closed the door.

"We were hoping you'd made it to Nick's cabin before the storm broke," Lanie drawled, handing them one paper towel after another. "What made you leave there and drive through this God-awful mess?"

"I tried to reach you by cell," Cassi explained, using the towels to blot moisture from the back of her neck. "But the call wouldn't go through. So we decided to drive here. The power is off all over town and along the lakeshore. Where's Aunt Ada? Are you two okay?"

"We're fine." Ada approached from the hallway, Rufus clicking at her heels. "Well, most of us." She gave the head pressed against her leg a brief pat. "Rufus here has a little problem with storms."

Cassi knelt and called softly. Rufus slunk across the floor and tried to crawl into her lap. She wrapped her arms around him and nuzzled his soft fur.

"Hey, big guy." Nick hunkered down beside them. "Thunder's got you spooked, huh?" Wriggling with emotion, Rufus circled between Nick and Cassi whining his anguish.

"There's a fire in the fireplace," Ada said. "Go take the chill off and get dry."

Nick straightened. "Thanks, but I've got to get back."

"Are you sure you don't want to wait until the rain lets up?" Cassi stood, keeping a comforting hand on Rufus. "I appreciate you driving me here, but it's still dangerous out there."

Her eyes searched his face. She really didn't want him to leave.

He assured her he'd be fine and bid the others good-bye. Cassi accompanied him to the porch. Turning up the collar of his jacket, he squinted into the night. The rain was more of a steady shower now, trickling from the eaves. Runoff gurgled and rushed through downspouts.

"Sure you don't want to hang out with us girls and wait out the storm?" she asked, lifting a hand to straighten the tip of his turned-up collar.

He covered her hand with his and turned his head, bringing her fingers to his lips.

"Tempting, but I think the worst is over." He pulled her against him and ran a casual hand down her back. "Before long everyone is going to want to crawl into bed and get a good night's sleep."

"I must be an appealing picture." She pushed tangled hair aside. "A real fashion statement."

Lifting an overabundance of shirt away from her side, she looked up at Nick. In the semi-darkness, his hazel eyes were greenish gold and framed by thick, spiky lashes. For a long moment, she stared into their depths.

Nick broke the enigmatic spell with a kiss, grazing along her sensitive jaw line.

"See you tomorrow," he whispered, his lips warm against her ear. "Promise."

Then, hunching against the rain, he hurried to his truck.

Her fingertips traced the path his lips had taken. She shivered, remembering his whispered promise.

Upon reentering the cottage, Cassi detected a familiar scent. The smell drew her into the next room where a crackling fire and burning candles created a cozy setting.

Lanie, curled in an overstuffed chair, and Ada, feet propped on a well-worn ottoman, had their hands wrapped around steaming cups. Ah, freshly brewed tea, but how...

Cassi spied an ancient kettle balanced on a heavy grate over the flames. Steam rolled from the quaint little pot.

"Comes in handy now and then." Ada took a careful sip, her smug smile visible in the dancing firelight. "Have a cup."

She angled a glance at Rufus, sprawled on the hearth sound asleep. "The storm is over. There's the proof."

Before long, Cassi's eyelids drooped. She snuggled beneath the afghan her aunt had tucked around her before heading off to bed. Tilting her head, she lifted the worn fabric of Nick's sweatshirt to her face and inhaled.

"Smells like him, doesn't it?" Lanie's voice cut into her thoughts. Her friend took a last sip of tea, grimaced, and set the cup aside. "It's cold."

She pushed upright in her chair and studied Cassi.

"Nick McGraw," she drawled in her throaty voice. "I'd say he's not cold at all. In fact, I'd say he's pretty freakin' hot."

Under Lanie's shrewd perusal, Cassi remained silent.

"You're ass over elbow about the man, aren't you?"

"No, not at all," Cassi huffed. She flipped her hand with dismissive dignity. "I don't have time for this. For love. No way. He's just... well, he's handsome and, and... damn it. Damn it, Lanie. You're right. So freakin' right. How'd you know?"

"How did *I* know?" Lanie scoffed. "Geez Louise woman, he had you locked in his arms like he'd never let go when I opened that door tonight. But I had my suspicions this morning when he walked in and you almost collapsed. And now you're sitting here sniffin' his shirt? I'd bet my pitiful savings account you two had some mutual nakedness going on between the time you removed your wet clothes and slipped into those manly smelling sweats."

As per her usual, Lanie's observations were right on. She'd always said that one of these days some guy would come along and knock Cassi on her ass.

Looked like that day had arrived.

Staring into the dying embers, Cassi picked flecks of lint from the soft afghan.

"What am I going to do, Lanie? He'll be gone in a few days, back to Philadelphia and his life. He's a detective, you know, and from what I'm told, he's a darned good one. But right now, my life is a wreck. That complicates things."

"Don't overthink everything," Lanie admonished. "You always do that. Nothing's ever that perfect, or without risk." The edge left her voice. "Tell me a little about him, and um... his family."

Cassi studied her friend's face. His family? Since when was Lanie interested in a man's heritage?

Aha. A smile tugged at her lips. She tapped one finger to them, as if considering. "Well, I've not met his parents, but Ada tells me he looks a lot like his dad. His uncle, Tom McGraw, is the chief of police here in town.

"Nice family. That's a plus," Lanie said.

"And, of course you met his cousin, TJ."

Bingo. That branch of the family tree got a response.

"Ah, yes. Officer McGraw. That's how he introduced himself to me, and yikes, all that red hair." Lanie picked up her empty cup. Toying with it, she shifted restlessly, mischief dancing in her eyes. "But I gotta admit he's got one great ass."

Cassi laughed aloud. "I knew it. I can always measure your interest when I catch you checking out a guy's butt. You're a shameless *ass checker.*"

"Makes me wonder, though," Lanie mused. She moistened her lips with the tip of her tongue. "Is the red hair an all over kind of thing?"

"Elaine!" Cassie choked out.

Smothering laughter, they banked the coals and blew out all but one of the candles. Cassi retrieved an extra pillow from her room and helped Lanie make up the deep-cushioned sofa.

"I should go back with you tomorrow." Cassi straightened the edge of the quilt. "Surely there's something I can do."

Lanie shook her head. "Before the storm hit I called Fox Chapel. Being that tomorrow is Friday, they don't expect anything new before next week. Stay here. Ada says there's some kind of Fall Festival event tomorrow night. Are you going?"

She patted a spot on the sofa.

"Yes." Cassi sat beside her. "It might be the last time I get to see Nick. He's never told me exactly when his vacation ends, but he's been here for over a week."

"Then stay. See where this thing with him is headed, honey." Lanie hugged her close.

Rufus gave a large yawn, stood, and shook himself. His tags jingled as he crossed the room. Cassi scratched one velvety ear.

"Need to go out before bedtime?" she asked, and the dog trotted to the door.

Snapping on his lead, she braced herself for one last trip outside. To her relief, the rain had ended. Heavy fog drifted up from the lake and water dripped from the eaves, plopping into lake-size puddles. She waited for Rufus to do his business, then hurried in from the bone-chilling dampness.

At the door, she toed off her wet shoes. Padding in sock clad feet with a lit candle gripped in her hand, Cassi made her way down the shadowed hallway to her room.

Not bothering to change, she blew out the flame and crawled between the soft sheets. Rufus circled briefly and dropped with a thud near the foot of the bed.

Eyes drifting shut as the night closed in around her, Cassi rested her cheek on one bent arm and inhaled the sexy scent of Nick McGraw.

Chapter Twenty-Five

Impenetrable fog settled over the parking lot, and huddled in his car beneath a musty-smelling blanket, Fred Conners waited. He and Raife had grabbed a bite to eat, all the while keeping an eye on the tired looking woman they'd been tailing.

After downing a burger, a monster plate of fries, and several soft drink refills, she'd paid her tab and returned to her car. She yanked a beat up suitcase from the trunk and disappeared into room number seven behind the truck stop.

Confident she wouldn't go anywhere for at least a couple of hours, they'd finished their surprisingly good omelets and secured a room for the remainder of the night.

Raife had won the toss, and Fred took the first watch. Just a precaution in case their subject decided to head out during the night. By now his partner was no doubt snoring away behind the door of room number nine. Fred glanced at his watch, pulled the blanket tighter, and scanned the shrouded parking lot. He'd been running the engine periodically to stave off the worst of the chill. Aside from that, the only sound in the darkness was the distant hiss of tires on the rain-slicked thruway.

A sharp rap on the window made him jump.

"Shit," he muttered, flipping the locks open. "I didn't see you through all this damn pea soup."

"Go get some sleep." Raife slid into the seat beside him, clutching a steaming cup of coffee. "I'll ring you on your cell in a couple of hours."

"How's the room?" Fred eyed the cup. The smell was potent, but he needed sleep and that ruled out slugging down caffeine laced coffee.

"Not as bad as I'd pictured. I even took a fast shower before I crashed. It's no Hampton, but it'll do." Raife handed over a key. "Any movement?"

"Nah, she must have gone out soon as she hit the bed. See you in a couple of hours." Fog clung to him as he made his way to the room. Once inside, he shucked his jacket and jeans, laid his cell on a bedside table, and fell into bed.

*****

Almost the moment her head had touched the lumpy, misshapen pillow, Sadie went out like the proverbial light. Just before dawn, an annoying rattle coming from the room's heater kept invading her much

153

needed rest.

Finally giving up, she stumbled across the room. After much cursing and fumbling with the unit's fan switch, she triumphed, and blessed silence filled the room.

Shivering, she pulled aside the heavy drape covering the window. Through the early morning mist cars and trucks appeared as ghostly outlines, and tall trees surrounding the lot created a dark, foreboding wall.

Crossing her arms, she scurried back and dove under the covers. But sleep was elusive. She lit a cigarette and drew deep, triggering a cough. As she gazed at the glowing tip in the darkness, determination simmered inside her, and the soothing nicotine embraced her senses. By her calculations, she had plenty of time. The day had barely begun, and Pine Bluffs was no more than a couple of hours away.

She tried to ignore the sudden onset of indigestion, probably the result of last night's fried feast, and reached for her purse. The lumpy, cumbersome bag thumped to the floor.

"Son of a bitch." She clamped her lips around the dangling cigarette, bent down, and hauled the fallen bag onto the bed. Then she delved inside it. With great care, she withdrew the compact silver gun. A feeling of power ripped through her. Fingering the safety, she cradled the cool, solid weapon in the palm of her not-so-steady hand.

Tremors returned in waves to wrack her body. Fighting them, she laid the gun aside and snapped on the bedside lamp. She scrunched her eyes against the sudden brightness and again dipped into her purse, searching for the bag of white courage she'd held back from the punks in that seedy Fox Chapel bar.

She controlled what happened today. Being in control was important. She needed a steady hand. A steady hand, and a focused mind.

The white powder shifted like fine beach sand when she rolled the bag and held it under the lamp's glare. Another chill shot through her. Damn it, she couldn't afford to screw this up.

She picked up the gun and shifted her gaze from one hand to the other. This would do it. The cocaine would calm her, give her courage.

The silver gun would take care of the rest.

Chapter Twenty-Six

What the hell!

Nick bolted upright and tossed aside the tangle of sheets. Light spilled from the bathroom, and a thumping whir echoed through the cabin. He flopped down and covered his eyes with a bent arm. With electricity restored, his wet clothes rotated in the dryer.

His sleep-fogged mind cleared, and he groped for his watch on the bedside stand. Blinking the luminous dial into focus, he discovered it was past six-thirty a.m. He bunched up his pillow, and after folding both arms behind his head, rested against the soft mound.

He'd been in Pine Bluffs over a week. During which time, several aspects of his life had done a serious about face.

Friggin' unbelievable.

Philadelphia seemed another world away. Yet he'd soon be heading back to that world. A cold, hard knot formed in Nick's gut. He had decisions to make.

Life-altering decisions.

He'd always known a part of him had stayed behind when his family had moved away from Pine Bluffs all those years ago. Shit, he'd risked his life -- and his parents' wrath -- hitching clear across the state in a defiant effort to hold on to the love and stability he'd left behind in this sleepy little town.

Not that his parents didn't love him. They did. He never wanted for anything, material or emotional. And their lives, their lives were full and complete. For that, he was glad.

He didn't regret the years in Philly. They were valuable years. Good years spent forming the foundation for a career he loved. But this short time in Pine Bluffs had been eye opening.

Checking the time again, he rolled out of bed. He wanted to track down Uncle Tom and talk to him. TJ, too, when his cousin wasn't so preoccupied. And he wanted -- no, *needed* to have a serious discussion with Cassi.

His physical attraction to her was off the scale. Powerful. Like nothing he'd ever experienced. But what drew him to her was more than sex. Much more, and that scared the hell out of him.

This past week, he'd rediscovered the heady aroma of ripening grapes and the thrill of Lake Erie sunsets. Those little pleasures always made his heart beat faster. He'd also discovered that, much like Erie sunsets, Cassi made his heart beat faster, too.

The midday sun broke through in the cloud-scudded sky as he made his way into town. According to news reports, the storm had left heavy damage throughout Ohio, Western Pennsylvania, and New York. Downed trees and scattered power outages still affected many areas.

Officer Peters had a phone pressed to his ear when Nick entered the station, and he glanced up.

"Is TJ in?" Nick mouthed. Lon gave him a thumbs-up, pointed to TJ's office, and went back to his call.

Ringing phones, accompanied by the drone of voices, followed Nick down the hall. Absent was the rhythmic clatter of keyboards. No doubt the storm had wreaked havoc on their Internet service.

TJ's door was open, and Nick paused on the threshold. His cousin, engrossed in a heated phone conversation, motioned him into the room.

"You do that." TJ concluded, slamming down the phone. "What a bunch of bullshit."

He zeroed in on Nick.

"When Philadelphia gets hit with a storm, does the friggin' police department have to sort out all the crap themselves?" he ranted, shooting to his feet, tipping his chair. "And then end up begging the assholes responsible for the entire communications system to make them a priority?"

He caught the tilting chair and slammed it back down on four legs. A brimming cup of coffee on his desk sloshed over.

Without comment, Nick walked to the coffee pot, helped himself, and waited for TJ to settle. Funny, he'd always figured local PD problems were comparably smaller than those faced by larger departments. But the frustrations, the inability of civilians to meet the needs of law enforcement in the aftermath of such an interruption, were apparently no different. Nor any less maddening.

TJ paced the room, pausing to drum a pencil rapidly on his desk. He dropped into his chair and blew out a long breath.

"I see you survived the storm," he said, blotting up his spilled coffee. "Any problems?"

"Nothing I couldn't handle," Nick replied, eyeing TJ over the rim of his cup. "Communications slow coming back up?"

"No shit." Another deep breath. "I know, I know. I shouldn't let it get to me, but I was this close," he said, displaying a tiny gap between his index finger and thumb, "to getting important info either faxed or scanned and sent to me when the damn storm shut us down. Son of a bitch." He rubbed the back of his neck. "Where were you when it hit?"

His question caught Nick by surprise. "Uh, Cassi and I were running along the lake. We got soaked, but made it to the cabin just as the power went out. I built a fire, and we waited."

TJ grunted. He reshuffled papers and repositioned things on his desk. "Ready for the festival?"

TJ seemed ready to explode, and Nick hesitated before countering, "Yeah, I'm looking forward to it. How about you?"

"I hope to hell I get there." TJ leaned back in his chair. "Assuming everything is back in order by then. Mom's a nervous wreck, worrying about how the storm might impact the festival. She's on the planning committee and wants every little detail to be perfect."

He shifted his gaze to the window where sunlight slanted through the rain-streaked glass. The pencil in his hand broke with a snap.

Nick started when his cousin slammed the broken pieces into the trash can.

"Is Miss Delacor staying for the celebration?"

"Cassi didn't say." Nick frowned, trying to follow TJ's jack rabbit train of thought. "But when I dropped her off at Ada's late yesterday, Lanie was still there."

"Hmm, maybe in a social setting little Miss Green Eyes won't be so prickly." TJ stood and swiped his hand through his hair. "Sorry, Nick, but I've got follow-ups on hold. I'm way behind." He gestured to several folders on his desk.

Nick finished his coffee. Considering the way TJ's thoughts were bouncing around, their talk could wait.

"I understand," he said. "I'll see you tonight."

TJ accompanied him to the front desk where they chatted a moment with Lon, commiserating about dealing with Mother Nature's wrath.

The sun warmed Nick's face as he walked to his truck, and he paused to slip on his sunglasses. He'd put the talk with TJ on hold for now, and Uncle Tom had been out of the station. He'd have time to catch up with them before he left town. Right now, he looked forward to the evening ahead with Cassi.

Talking with her might be the best place to start anyway. Especially if there was any chance in hell she would be part of his future. A future he was about to change.

*****

Rufus balanced on three legs. Using an old towel, Cassi blotted mud from his paw and soaked up moisture dripping from his underside. They'd run hard, splashing through puddles and slapping aside rain-soaked branches. She reached for a dog bone and he sat, tail sweeping the floor. His whiskery muzzle tickled her fingers when he took the offered treat.

She checked the time. Lanie should be back in Fox Chapel by now. They'd risen early, drawn by the tempting smell of Ada's blueberry pancakes, and Lanie had departed soon after breakfast. Until the very last minute, Cassi wanted to return with Lanie. Arguing against such a move, Lanie and her aunt had pointed out she had no reason to rush back to Fox Chapel.

On the surface, their reasoning made sense. The insurance adjusters wouldn't have access to the police report yet, so what could she possibly accomplish? Regardless, she should have insisted. The waiting would be torture.

She plucked one of Ada's oatmeal cookies from its glass-domed case and stepped outside. Nick had promised he'd pick her up, but had neglected to give her an exact time. She wished he'd call. Hours had passed since Ada had gone to help Mary at the social hall. Her aunt had been reluctant to leave, but Cassi had assured her Nick would be there soon, and said she didn't have a problem waiting alone until he arrived.

Though a million tangled thoughts kept surfacing, Cassi decided she was actually coping quite well. Her parents' deaths had left a gaping hole in her life, but somehow the emptiness that had followed their deaths had faded.

Finding a dead body and having one's livelihood go up in smoke were not small bumps in the road, yet a strange new balance was unfolding, and she attributed her newfound ability to cope to those around her.

She couldn't imagine her life now without Aunt Ada. In an amazingly short time, the warm, trusting woman had wrapped herself around Cassi's heart. The ladies in her Pine Bluffs' fitness class were friendly, eclectic, and fascinating. A far cry from the regular class participants at her club.

And Lanie. God, what would she do without Lanie? The woman was like a sister, best friend, and employee all wrapped into one. She was irreplaceable.

Cassi popped the last bite of cookie into her mouth and brushed the crumbs from her hands. Upon reentering Ada's cottage, she inhaled the spicy aroma of freshly baked cookies, exactly how mom's kitchen used to smell.

Her aunt, Lanie, her new friends, and even Rufus had made her roller-coaster life bearable. Then there was Nick. He made her want to continue the breathtaking ride.

Aside from her father, she had never trusted a man so completely. Nick didn't promise much, but she knew any promise he made was gold.

The past few days, he'd just *been there*.

There to show her wine country and teach her to kayak. There to make her ache with passion when he touched her. And there to hold her in his arms when disaster struck. She'd learned much about Nick McGraw in a very short time.

Yet... what about his life in Philadelphia? Did he go out to fancy restaurants? Did he like musicals or art shows? He'd mentioned living just outside the city, but only in passing, much like the casual references he'd made concerning his parents.

Was someone waiting for him back in the city?

Her newfound confidence faltered.

She slipped into the shower and cranked the spray to full force, as if to whisk away that last disconcerting thought and send it spiraling down the drain.

When she emerged, the phone rang. Wrapped in a towel she dashed to answer it, positive it would be Nick. But the line was dead. Ever since the storm, making or receiving calls had been impossible. Apparently, there was still a problem.

Belting her bathrobe, she searched out her cell phone. Damn it. Dead battery. Irritation simmered inside her as she set the phone to charge, then went to dry her hair.

*****

Nick snapped his phone shut and stuffed it into his pocket. He'd tried several times to reach Cassi. The phone would ring, then click and disconnect. She hadn't left any messages; he'd checked after showering and dressing.

Shadows crept across the clearing. He glanced at the time, then slipped on a sports jacket .Catching a glimpse of himself in the mirror, he ran a swift hand through his hair.

What the hell? He chuckled as he headed for the door. If he was late, she'd probably chew him out. Same deal if he was too early. He'd just go over now and hope his timing was close enough.

He stepped from the cabin, and moist, heavy air wrapped around him. Yesterday's storm had brought down mountains of leaves. They layered the ground and gave softly beneath his feet.

Nick settled behind the wheel and secured his off-duty handgun in the glove box. The gun was usually tucked into a holster beneath his arm, but having it close at hand in his truck would do for tonight.

Once inside, he turned the key and flicked on the wipers, clearing the windshield of moisture and stray debris. The lights illuminated several deer at the edge of the clearing. Their eyes glowed.

While passing Pine Bluffs PD, he was surprised to see TJ's Camry out front. He negotiated a smooth u-turn, pulled around the corner, and parked. Why the heck was TJ still here?

The station was unusually quiet, with most of the desks deserted. He made his way down the hall, drawn by voices coming from TJ's office. He

159

stopped in the doorway and braced both hands on the overhead jamb. When Marcy and TJ looked up, he frowned at them.

"Give it a rest, TJ," he declared. "What the hell is so important you can't even take a night off for some fun?"

TJ and Marcy exchanged a look. TJ had several papers gripped in his hand, and a nearby fax machine spewed out more. Nick dropped his arms and approached them. TJ's jaw was rigid; his eyes, like flint as he extended one of the papers toward Nick.

He mutely took the offered sheet and focused on a grainy picture. Fingers of ice skimmed up his spine. The photo showed Cassi being helped into a dark gray Mercedes Benz by a casually dressed man.

His eyes flew to TJ's, then back to the picture. He gave the limp paper a shake and brought it closer, tilting it toward the overhead light for a better view.

"Where'd this come from?" Nick's voice cracked, his throat slamming shut.

"A fax from Erie," Marcy said.

He shot her a cold, silencing glance, then turned to his cousin. "TJ? Son of a bitch, talk to me. What the hell's going on?"

TJ reached for the picture.

"No!" Nick shouted, holding it out of reach. His head pounded. Stepping back, he demanded, "Who is this with Cassi?"

"His name is Jack LeFavor." TJ's flat, tight voice revealed nothing. He turned away, gathering new pages as they emerged from the fax machine. "Erie PD recently picked him up for drug related activity. That picture was taken two days ago in Cleveland by a couple of detectives from the Ohio Investigative Unit."

Nick stared daggers at TJ's back. Two days ago? Any genius could figure out that was the day Cassi had gone to Erie.

Or had she?

He dropped the picture onto TJ's desk. Had he been that easy to fool? Was he losing his edge just because she felt so good in his arms and made his heart twist and pound? Damn it. This could *not* be happening again.

"Nick..."

Feeling as cold as ice, he met TJ's solemn look.

"This might not mean what you think. I still have more pieces to add to this puzzle. You need to calm down and--"

"And what?" Nick's words cut like a razor. "Dig a little deeper until we find out she's not only gorgeous and smart, but a damn crafty liar, too? Fuck." He rubbed his eyes with the heels of both hands, as if to blot the photo image from his spinning mind.

The phone on TJ's desk rang just as a familiar, hearty voice echoed behind Nick, "There you are. I've been looking all over town for you."

TJ's eyes widened. Nick looked over his shoulder to find his parents crowding into the doorway. Concern creased his father's brow, but his mother smiled openly at the assembled, tense little group in TJ's office.

"Nicholas."

As always, his mother looked stunning. Her deep auburn hair swung softly when she turned her head and reached behind her.

"Surprise," she exclaimed, pulling a laughing Michelle Norris -- of the Bryn Mawr Norris's -- into sight.

Shit.

Paralyzed, he stared at them blankly. Across the room, Marcy grabbed the ringing phone. She listened intently, but her dark eyes remained on the unfolding drama.

With his mind scrambling, Nick met his Dad's eyes for one anguished moment. A frown spread across Alan McGraw's face seconds before Nick's mother wrapped her arms around him. He breathed in her familiar scent and, after a second's hesitation, returned her hug.

"Hi, Mom," he murmured, letting her go and holding her away from him. He nodded to his father. "Dad."

Tongue-tied, he turned to Michelle. She tilted her head, and a look of concern gathered between her questioning blue eyes.

"Hello, Nicholas. We seem to have caught you unaware."

Nick gave himself a mental shake and stepped forward to place a rather awkward kiss on her soft, flawless cheek. Throughout the difficult greeting, Marcy's urgent voice rang out in the background. Lifting his head from the token kiss, he noted TJ had moved closer to Marcy, and that their attention was no longer focused on the strange, unexpected reunion.

"You look good, son." Alan placed a hand on Nick's shoulder. "Your vacation must be agreeing with you."

He took a deep breath and collected his thoughts. "I was overdue for time off, Dad, and it's been rather... interesting."

Alan's brow rose. The room throbbed with tension. His father had to know something was wrong.

Michelle moved in, sporting a pretty pout, and curved a possessive hand over Nick's arm. "I've been told ad nauseam how wonderful this part of the state is in the fall. So I flew into Erie Airport, if you call those paths in the field an airport, and your folks picked me up. To be truthful, on the drive from the airport I thought everything looked rather gray and damp."

Blindsided by her presence, Nick opened his mouth to speak and then just closed it and stared down at her. She formed that questioning frown between her eyes again.

"Sorry, folks." TJ's voice broke in, "I've got to take this call."

He held up the phone. "Why don't you all head on over to the festival? Mom and Dad are already there. I'll catch up later." His eyes flitted to the picture still lying on his desk. "Nick, I'll have more to tell you shortly." He indicated the phone in his hand with a quick tilt of his head.

Clamping down on the sick feeling crawling up his throat, Nick gave his cousin a curt nod and left the room with his parents and Michelle. For the time being, he'd trust TJ and hope he'd come up with some explanation for this madness.

He and his dad escorted the ladies through the station and out into the cool evening.

Once outside, his father held him back, "Nick, what's going on?"

After throwing a quick glance at his mom and Michelle, Nick rubbed a hand over his face. "TJ's working a tough case and I've gotten... too involved. I'll meet you at the festival, okay? It's not going to be a smooth evening, Dad. My involvement isn't only with the case; I'm involved with someone I've met."

"Ahh." His Dad's eyes lit with understanding. "I wanted to give you a heads up about our visit, but you know your mother. Always the romantic."

"Not your fault, Dad. I'm afraid this evening will turn out to be anything but romantic."

Alan looked around. "Where's your truck?"

"I parked around the corner. Please, take Michelle to the dance. I'll drive over myself. The phones have been screwy, and it's important that I reach someone. I've got to keep trying."

With his cell phone to his ear, Nick strode to his truck. His frantic call to Cassi went unanswered. He was about to climb inside when Michelle rounded the corner.

"Nick, wait. I'm riding to the dance, or whatever, with you," she said with a vague flip of her hand. "I didn't come all this way to spend time with your parents."

His hopes dashed, Nick watched the taillights of his parent's car disappear into the mist. He turned and silently helped Michelle into his truck.

*****

TJ glanced at Marcy. She hadn't taken her eyes off him since she'd relinquished the phone.

"Call me when you get into town," he said, shifting the phone from one ear to the other. "I'll try to hook up with you then." He gave the caller his cell phone number and hung up.

"Well?" Marcy looked ready to burst. She planted her hands on her hips and set her feet wide as she waited.

"This just gets weirder and weirder," TJ said. "That was an agent from

OIU."

She lifted a brow.

"The Ohio Investigative Unit," he explained. "He and his partner are following someone *he* claims is Miss Cassandra Burke." He glanced at his watch. "They just exited I-90 and are heading this way."

Marcy studied the picture on TJ's desk. "TJ, something about this doesn't look right. Maybe cell phone photos distort people or something. Take a look at this."

TJ stepped closer and stared at the photos.

"Right here." Marcy tapped the photo. "The face is right, especially this headshot, but look at this one where she's getting into the Benz. There's way to much flesh on that girl. She's too soft. The Cassi I know is shapely, but toned. Remember, I was there when she showered the day we found Morelli's body."

She was right. The girl with Jack LeFavor was stockier, more settled than Cassi.

"Okay, I see your point," TJ conceded. He tucked the photos into a folder. "There's got to be an explanation for all this, but I'll be damned if I know what it might be. I'm going home to change. Keep trying to reach Cassi. I've tried Ada's several times and can't get through."

She nodded.

"And if you do," he said, glancing at his watch, calculating the time. "Ask -- no, *tell* her to come here at seven o'clock."

He was on his way out the door when it hit him. "Marce, are you supposed to be here now? I thought Peters was on tonight."

"Lon had a root canal yesterday. He called about two hours ago and said something went wrong. He's in a lot of pain. I agreed to work his shift. I couldn't find a sitter for tonight, so Rob's home with the kids. I won't go to the festival without him. No point calling in someone else and ruining their evening. Go. I'll stay here. Chuck Long in on the desk tonight; we'll keep one another company."

"Thanks, Marce, I owe you," TJ said.

Marcy's smart comeback made him grin as he hurried away.

Chapter Twenty-Seven

Fred Conners stared at the sizable new dent in the side of his battered car. "That bastard came out of nowhere. Did you see where he went after he bounced off my door?"

Hunched against the chill, Raife stood by the side of the road. Fatigue burned his eyes, and the fine drizzle misted past the headlights piercing the darkness. The car rested at an angle, nose deep in the brush lining the berm.

Without warning, the deer had crashed into Fred's door and sent him skidding off the road. Raife circled the car and swept the ground with a flashlight. "He's gone. That son of a bitch just kept right on goin'."

He didn't see a drop of blood, just a big dent in the side of Fred's car. Clicking off the light, he squinted down the road in the direction the car they'd been tailing had disappeared.

"He's gone, and so is our girl," he stated, zipping his jacket and heading for the shelter of the car.

After one last damage check, Fred climbed behind the wheel. The engine turned over on the first try, and he eased the car back onto the pavement. They'd lost precious time, but less than a mile down the road a sign appeared through the hazy moisture.

It read, *Welcome to Pine Bluffs.*

*****

Chuck Long manned the desk while Marcy went for take-out. So far, the night had been uneventful. Rain and fog had moved in, and with most of the town at the Fall Festival, they might have a quiet Saturday night.

The door to the station opened.

"Hey, Marce, that didn't take long. I figured you'd--" He looked up and stopped in mid-sentence. "Miss Burke?"

The woman hurrying toward him looked like Cassandra Burke, but something about her was... different.

She wore a dark, hooded jacket dripping with moisture. As she approached him, the hood slid from her head. She appeared nervous and glanced around while digging into a bag slung over her shoulder and extracting a crumpled envelope. "I want to leave this for... uh... whoever's in charge of the Morelli murder."

"For TJ?" Chuck inquired, coming to his feet.

"Yeah. Can you give him this?" A lock of damp hair fell across her face. She swiped at the wet strands impatiently, then gave up and held the envelope out to Chuck.

"Yes, I can. He should be--"

"Great. Thanks." She thrust the envelope into his hand. Flipping the hood back into place, she was out the door before Chuck could react.

He studied the envelope and scratched the side of his head.

What the hell is this?

Minutes later, the door opened again and Marcy entered, hugging a take-out bag.

"Did you just see Cassandra Burke leaving here?"

"No." Marcy glanced behind her. "Why, was she here?"

"I'm not sure," Chuck responded.

Marcy gave him a sharp look as she placed their supper on the desk. She removed her wet jacket, dropped it onto a chair, and finger-combed her damp hair.

"What do you mean by that?"

"I mean a girl just blew in here, handed me this envelope, asked me to give it to TJ. Then she ran out the door. She looked like Cassandra Burke." He scratched his head again. "Don't ask me why, but I don't think that's who it was."

Marcy took the envelope and inspected it. Obviously something was inside it, but nothing was written on the outside and the flap was sealed.

Chuck figured Marcy might give him a bunch of grief about his crazy observation, but she seemed lost in thought. Serious thought.

"I don't like this at all." She tapped the envelope against the palm of her hand. "Try and reach TJ."

He nodded and reached for the phone.

"He went to his place to change. I want him to stop here before he goes anywhere else. I'll be in his office."

She picked up her wet jacket, paused to grab a sandwich from the bag, and hurried down the hallway.

*****

Cassi flipped on the kitchen light and went to the door. Where was Nick? She peered into the pitch black night, and tiny pricks of unease danced up her spine.

She turned back to the well lit kitchen and patted Rufus absently as he pressed against her. Her watch confirmed it was well past six. Ada had left early to help Mary, as they anticipated problems from the storm. Maybe Nick was helping his aunt, too, and had lost track of time. She'd wait ten more minutes and then go to the dance alone.

Before she left, she took the dog out one last time for a quick duty call.

Within minutes, he clattered up the steps anxious to go back inside. She secured him and locked the door behind her. Visibility was poor, and she used caution driving the short distance into town.

She found Nick's truck at the social hall. Her guess had been right; his aunt had roped him into taking care of last minute details. She parked along the street, relieved he'd be spared the dangerous drive along the lake to Ada's. She anticipated a good laugh when they connected after being unable to reach one another all day.

The warm, crowded hall hummed with activity. She removed her jacket and made her way toward the large, open ballroom. Stopping just inside an arched doorway, she searched the room.

Almost immediately she spotted Nick and was about to move in his direction when a slim, petite, dark-haired woman touched his arm. She looked exquisite. Refined, delicate, and, as Cassi painfully noted, the exact opposite of her tall athletic build. Nick bent down to his companion and listened intently.

Nearby voices faded into an incoherent, muted buzz, and for Cassi, time stood still. Nick's thick, slightly mussed hair glistened in the low light. He looked unbearably handsome in his sports coat and dark slacks. His hand rested in the small of the woman's back, and she leaned into him with a familiarity that was hard to mistake.

Cassi knew his touch, knew the heat and feel of his hand on *her*. That hand now rested on the body of another woman.

What was going on? Cassi fell mute, and her head spun. She blinked rapidly and glanced from Nick to the lady at his side, then back to Nick just as he turned to a tall, lean man nearby. The stranger had his arm draped around a slender woman with shoulder length hair, and his resemblance to Nick was striking.

Realization dawned. They were Nick's parents. Except for the russet McGraw hair, his dad was an older replica of Nick, and the auburn-haired beauty at his side left no doubt as to where Nick had gotten his thick, dark waves.

Nick glanced up and scanned the room. Fearing he would see her blatant stare, Cassi turned and fled blindly through the crowd. She yanked open the door to the ladies room and plunged inside. The door hissed closed behind her as she stumbled to the sink. Grasping the countertop, she willed her pounding heart to slow.

Her face burned. With trembling hands, she wet a paper towel and pressed its soothing coolness to her cheeks.

Before she regained her composure, the door to the ladies room opened, and in sauntered Nick's lady friend. Averting her eyes, Cassi continued to blot her feverish skin, praying the woman wouldn't linger.

Her cool blue eyes flicked over Cassi. When they met hers in the mirror, the woman flashed her a brittle smile and bent to search through her clutch bag. After producing an elegant looking lipstick, she concentrated on applying a thin layer and then blotted the gleaming finish. Caught staring, Cassi jerked her gaze away and clumsily smoothed her hair with shaky fingers.

"Are you all right?" Tiny lines marred Miss Slim and Petite's near-perfect face when her eyes met Cassi's in the mirror.

Cassi forced a smile.

"I was dancing and got a little overheated," she lied, struggling for composure.

Nick's friend nodded and primped the stylish hair framing her face.

"It is a rather stuffy old place," she confided. "I'm not from here, and trust me, I'll be more than happy to see Philadelphia again."

A frown appeared between her finely arched brows. "I hope I haven't offended you. Some people like this lifestyle." She shrugged and skimmed her eyes over Cassi. "I'm just not one of them."

Cassi's body grew rigid, and she narrowed her eyes as anger rapidly replaced the stinging hurt.

Casting a wary glance her way, the woman returned her lipstick to her purse and turned to leave.

"Wait!" Cassi called out. When the woman spun around, once more facing her, she asked, "Are you with Nick McGraw?"

"Why, yes." She hesitated. "Do you know Nicholas?"

Cassi ignored the question. She dipped into her purse, searched briefly, and then extended her hand toward the puzzled looking woman.

"Please, give this to *Nicholas*," she emphasized, placing a single penny in the flawlessly manicured hand.

Cassi bolted, somehow managing to control her emotions until she reached her car. Blinded by tears, she careened through the fog. She drove too fast, fueled by a volatile mixture of hurt, humiliation, and anger.

What was that woman to Nick? His girlfriend? A mistress? Or, heaven forbid... his fiancé?

The possibilities taunted her, made her want to just keep driving. To run and not face the humiliation of being the *casual fling* or maybe in this case, the *murder suspect*.

She turned from the highway and plowed through the heavy mist surrounding Ada's cottage. The blurry outline of a light in the window guided her to the door, and inside Rufus greeted her. She tossed her keys, jacket, and purse onto the table. Dropping to her knees, she hugged her dog fiercely.

"I'm an idiot, Rufus. A stupid, stupid, fool," She cried. Rufus gravely licked her damp cheeks, and she laughed through a fresh onslaught of tears. Pushing herself to her feet, she gathered her discarded belongings.

She'd fallen for Nick's smooth line when all the while he was using her. His loyalty to his family was no secret, yet she'd been sucked into his plot. He'd liked the intimacy. She'd been a nice perk while he played along with TJ.

She'd been used. She could think of no other explanation for tonight's disaster. Not only had *she* been used, but Aunt Ada, the woman she'd grown to love, had been used, too.

Cassi paused and smoothed the damp fabric of her jacket as she hung it up. Some things just didn't make sense, though. Why hadn't he made an excuse for tonight? Was he that cruel? Had he sent for his lady love knowing she'd see them together?

A sob caught in her throat. Rufus pressed against her legs and whined as if he felt her pain. But when Cassi moved to turn on a light, she suddenly sensed a change.

Rufus stiffened beside her.

"Rufus?"

A deep, savage growl rumbled low in the dog's chest, and she grabbed his collar.

*****

TJ burst into his office. He stopped to brush moisture from his sports coat and frowned at Marcy. She was sitting at *his* desk. That in itself annoyed him, but spread out before her was a crumpled sandwich wrapper and a half-eaten sub. She took a sizeable bite of it and stared down at his desktop.

His eyes followed hers to an unopened envelope beside the faxed photo. Scowling at the mess, TJ approached her.

"Lunch room too crowded?"

Marcy jumped. Choking, she reached for the oversized soft drink at her elbow. She took a huge swig, wiped her mouth, and blurted out, "This arrived while you were gone."

She lifted the envelope and shoved it at him. "Chuck said a girl who looked like Cassi Burke ran in, practically threw this at him and told him to give it to you, and then ran out."

"The girl *looked* like Cassi?" TJ lifted the envelope by one corner. Frowning, he turned it over and examined both sides.

"At first he thought it was her," Marcy explained, "but then, he said something wasn't right. You know, kind of the way I felt about the pictures."

TJ shoved the mess on his desk aside and located his letter opener. He made a neat slit in the envelope and tapped its contents onto his desktop. Marcy's dark eyes went wide as a photo dropped face up between them.

She reached for it.

"Don't." TJ grabbed her hand. "Don't touch it."

He gently lifted the photo with the tip of the letter opener and slid a clean napkin from the stack beside Marcy beneath it. Slipping his hand under the napkin, he brought the image close and stared at the couple captured on film.

Marcy rounded the desk for a better view.

"That's her again."

"Who," TJ said, scowling. "Cassi?"

"No, the girl. Her... twin, or whatever. Look here," she said, and pointed. "See how much heavier she is around the waist? Her face is fuller, too. And look at her hair. Cassi's is a natural honey blonde. That girl's is much lighter, and I'll bet my next paycheck her color comes from a bottle."

While TJ digested what Marcy had suggested, Chuck appeared in the doorway. "TJ, the two agents you spoke with from Ohio are here."

He stepped aside, making room for a couple of tired looking, rather scruffily dressed men in threadbare jeans. One was tall, thin, and sandy haired. He had on a brown jacket that was rolled at the sleeves, and a long-sleeved tan turtleneck.

The second man was shorter, though still over six feet, and unlike his partner, his hair was raven black. The crude logo *Bite Me* was prominently displayed on the faded tee shirt he wore beneath his well worn leather jacket. He stepped forward and offered his hand.

"Raife," he stated as TJ shook hands. "Raife Samuels. My partner here is Fred Conners."

TJ gestured to some chairs. "Have a seat."

Then with Marcy's help, he explained what they were dealing with so far.

"So you believe your suspect Cassandra Burke has what... a twin?" Raife said, studying the photos.

"I can't explain the situation any other way," TJ admitted. "You claim to have been tailing her for almost two days, and I know for a fact that Cassandra Burke has been in Pine Bluffs during that time. I was about to track her down and talk to her about the pictures Erie PD faxed me."

Raife slanted a look at Fred, who shrugged as he stuffed a stick of gum in his mouth and crumpled the wrapper.

"Mind if we go with you?" Raife asked.

"Not at all." TJ stood, checked his off duty weapon, and secured it beneath his jacket. "Marce, you take a marked car. I'll follow you to Ada Blaine's. These gentlemen can ride with you. I need to make a quick stop at the dance. I'm afraid Nick got trapped by circumstance, and I owe him an explanation."

They were approaching the door when Chuck called out, "TJ, wait a minute."

He turned, frowning when Chuck held up the phone. "I think maybe this is one you should handle."

"I'm sure you can handle it, Long." TJ shifted his keys impatiently. "I'm not on tonight, so--"

"TJ," Chuck broke in, "the caller insists you were awaiting her call and that her message is of primary importance. Her name is Mrs. Ruby Gilliam from the Duquesne Clinic."

TJ swung to face Marcy. "I have to take this. Go on to Ada's. If Cassi's there, wait for me before you go in."

Raife and Fred followed Marcy out the door, and TJ sprinted back to his office to take the call.

Chapter Twenty-Eight

Nick gaped at the single penny Michelle had dropped into his hand. Bolting away, he rushed to the ladies room and jerked the door open.

"Cassi!" His voice bounced off the tiled walls.

A woman inside whirled around, a damp paper towel clutched in her hand.

"Sorry, ma'am," he mumbled. The steely-eyed look she gave him barely registered.

Heart pounding, he burst out into the night. How could he have been such a damn idiot?

Cassi was nowhere in sight.

Why in hell had his parents shown up just when those faxed pictures arrived? And damn it... he'd let those photos screw with his mind.

He should have asked, no *demanded*, to know what the hell kind of info TJ and Marcy had gathered. His skyrocketing temper had clouded his judgment, but then, as if enough crap hadn't already hit the fan, he'd had to deal with Michelle.

Shit. Shit. Shit.

If he'd only been able to reach Cassi, but his calls would not go through. He'd been on the verge of taking off to find her when good old Ms. Norris changed her frigging mind, insisting she ride with *him* to the dance.

Figuring once he'd delivered her he'd find an excuse to slip away, he'd made record time getting to the hall. After they'd arrived, he'd taken a breather to come up with a plan, not wanting to rock the McGraw family boat.

Then Michelle's trip to the restroom had blown his stupid-assed scheme sky high. When she'd returned, she'd looked puzzled and had worn her perpetual frown. She'd dropped that penny into his hand, irritated with the "tall, athletic-looking woman" who'd instructed her to give it to him.

In his haste to catch Cassi, he'd rushed from the hall without stopping to explain. He'd deal with Michelle later.

Cursing a blue streak, Nick floored his truck and shot out of town, heading for Ada's through the treacherous fog. He had to find Cassi. Instead of doubting her, he should have helped her, stood by her.

Cassi was *not* Kat. Not even close.

His instincts had been whispering, but now, as he barreled through the cold, dark night, they screamed.

*****

Rufus quivered, and Cassi tightened her grip on his collar. A gust of damp air rushed into the room. The door closed with a muffled thud, and her head snapped up.

"Who's there?" she demanded.

A woman emerged from the shadows. Rufus snarled and charged at the stranger, jerking Cassi forward. She managed to stop him by gripping the edge of the counter and hanging onto him for dear life. She slapped a switch by the patio door. Light flooded the room.

"Hold on ta your fuckin' dog. Lock em' up, or I'll kill him." The disheveled, rain-soaked woman leveled a gun at Cassi.

Rufus lunged at her again, nearly jerking Cassi off her feet. Pain shot up her arm.

"Stop it, Rufus!" she ordered.

"I don't want to kill him." The intruder's harsh voice changed to a cajoling whine. "I like dogs."

Cassi dropped to one knee and placed a hand over his muzzle. She couldn't take her eyes off the compact silver gun in the woman's hand. She moved closer and aimed the gun at the snarling dog. Rufus bared his teeth.

"No, please," Cassi pleaded. Bile rose in her throat, and she drew in huge gulps of air. She had to think. If Rufus didn't stop, the woman would kill them both.

"I'll put him out," she said, starting for the door. "Then we can talk and--"

"No!" she shrieked, and Cassi ducked, expecting the gun to blast and a bullet to rip into her flesh. The woman's shout bounced off the walls.

Rufus went wild, from guard dog to Cujo in a split second. Cassi fought to control her furious pet, pinning him with her body. Frantic for a solution, she searched the room.

The pantry.

Cassi tightened her grip on Rufus, her hands burning like fire, and tugged him toward the narrow room. Her rain-soaked shoes made her skid on the hard floor when his sturdy canine legs locked, stiff and unyielding. Like a drawn bow, his body sprang taut.

At last she reached the open pantry door. Her quivering muscles screamed from dragging the dog across the room. Tears burned her eyes as she shoved her beloved Rufus inside and yanked the door shut.

He howled and threw himself against the barrier between them. Hands pressed against the shuddering wood, Cassi struggled for breath.

When she turned to face her captor, she went lightheaded, fell back against the door, and squeezed her eyes shut. She rubbed them with both hands and then opened them wide.

Was she hallucinating?

Staring at her -- like a *deadly reflection* -- were chocolate brown eyes exactly like hers.

The muffled panting, accompanied by the dog's low whines and persistent scratching, suddenly ceased. The room grew quiet.

She raised shaky fingers to her face, and the woman let out a shrill laugh. "Can't believe it, can you, bitch? Kinda like lookin' in a freakin' mirror."

"No, this can't be," Cassi whispered, shaking her head. Nothing made sense. "Who are you?"

"Who am I? *Who the hell am I?*" Using the gun to point, she aimed it at her own chest.

Did this insane woman plan to shoot herself? Cassi gasped, and without thinking, reached toward the hand holding the gun.

"Don't even think about touching me. Never touch me!"

Cassi snatched her hand back. She recognized pure madness in the woman's eyes, and trembled. The hand she'd been reaching for arced, and the gun's silver snout cracked against her jaw.

She sprawled across Ada's spotless countertop. Eyes closed, she fought waves of nausea. When her hand bumped something solid, and through a red haze she focused on one of her aunt's prized cookie jars.

Before she could think, the bleary outline of a hand shot past her and sent the precious cut glass container flying. It crashed to the floor and shattered on impact. Razor sharp pieces struck Cassi's legs, and when she reached down, her fingers came away covered with tiny fragments of glass. Hastily she wiped her hand against her leg, driving tiny slivers into her palm and leaving smears of blood on her slacks.

When the cookie jar hit the floor, Rufus broke into rapid fire barking behind the pantry door. He howled like a banshee between barks.

The woman took aim at the door. "Damn, stupid dog. I warned you.'

"No! For God's sake, don't." Cassi's knees buckled as she tried to move forward. "He won't hurt you. Oh, please!"

The crack of two rapid shots rang in Cassi's ears. The dog's piercing, painful wail ended abruptly, followed by silence.

"No. Oh, no," Cassi sobbed, sliding to the floor. Tears mixed with the blood trickling from her wounded cheek, and she stared numbly at the sparkling carpet of shattered glass surrounding her.

Two feet stopped in her line of vision, inches from where she cowered on the floor. She cringed, not daring to look up, when, almost gently, a hand smoothed her hair. "It's all right. Don't cry, I'm your sister, you know, and sisters look out for one another."

Once again, the woman's voice had changed.

Sister? Cassi didn't have a sister.

"Here, let me help you up."

The stranger grasped her arm and tugged. Cassi hesitated before pushing herself off the floor and rising unsteadily to her feet, well aware the woman still clutched the gun in her other hand. Her stomach pitched and rolled, her injured jaw throbbed, and she struggled to get enough oxygen.

Oh, God. Please don't let poor Rufus suffer.

Once on her feet, she edged away from her captor and tried to get her bearings. The woman moved closer. Her gaze, from wide, glassy eyes, roamed over Cassi's face. She smiled a strange, dreamlike smile, and murmured softly, "Look at you. You're my twin."

Then just like that, the madness returned. Her voice turned razor sharp. "You got it all," she said. "And I got screwed. I got nothing." Her voice rose, ending in a high pitched scream. "While the world unfolded at you fuckin' feet!"

She grabbed a handful of Cassi's hair and yanked. Their eyes met, inches apart, and she whispered, "That's all going to end right now. Tonight." She shoved Cassi away.

Cassi staggered back on rubbery legs. She was *not* going to faint. And dammit, she was not going to die.

Despite the churning in her belly, she drew in a deep breath and shifted her weight, testing for balance, and averted her gaze from the silent pantry door. A quick spurt of anger blocked a mental vision of her foolishly brave companion crumpled and bleeding. She'd deal with the painful loss later.

Maybe she'd die tonight, too. But she wouldn't go quietly or without leaving a mark on this woman who dared to claim they shared blood.

The woman lifted her gun. Using it to motion toward the door, she snapped out, "Open them doors. I think we've messed up Aunt Ada's fancy kitchen enough."

"Please, give me a minute, I'm dizzy." Cassi didn't wait for permission. She grabbed a paper towel from the rack by the sink and knelt on the floor. She pressed the folded towel against the wound on her cheek and closed her eyes.

The woman huffed in disgust, though she didn't stop Cassi, and her quick, ragged breathing pointed to a deteriorating emotional state.

Cassi fumbled on the floor with her free hand, keeping her movements to a minimum and out of her captor's sight. She finally found a sizeable chunk of the broken cookie jar and closed her fingers over it. Then she waited, breathing slow, even breaths, before struggling to her feet and tucking the makeshift weapon into the blood-soaked paper towel in her other hand.

She backed away from the stranger until she bumped the door. Reaching blindly, she fumbled with the latch. The door slid open. Determined to deal with the pain and terror shooting through her, she gritted her teeth and stepped out into the jet black night.

She could not afford to panic, and called on her years of disciplined physical training. A cold blast of air, heavy with the poignant smell of herbs, mingled with the dampness and sharpened her senses. She drew in deep breaths, filling her lungs, clearing her head.

What were her chances of escaping? Could she outrun the woman and hide until Nick came for her? And...

Nick's smile flashed in her mind, directed at his date's perfect, upturned face. The recollection sliced into Cassi like a knife. A sharp, painful stab to her heart, almost worse than the glass splinters digging into her flesh.

Cassi stiffened her spine and descended step by step from Ada's porch. She clutched the ragged chunk of glass, and with each step, mentally ticked off her options and plotted to survive. She had no choice. Nick McGraw wouldn't be coming to save her.

She tensed and released her muscles one at a time. In order to escape, to overpower this woman, she'd have to move fast and rip the gun from her captor's hand, then physically take her down.

The woman's haunting expression revealed her fragile state of mind. Pure insanity. Cassi *refused* to surrender to madness.

A vicious shove from behind sent her stumbling. She slipped on the wet grass and almost sprawled on her face. Regaining her footing, Cassi moved forward, shivering as cold drizzle trickled down her neck.

Twin headlights penetrated the fog, and tires crunched on loose gravel. Someone *was* coming.

The woman banded her arm around Cassi's neck from behind and snapped her head back. With her free hand, Cassi clawed at her neck. The move threw her off balance, and she clamped on to the arm cutting off her air.

Hot breath fanned her cheek, and the stranger shoved the gun hard against Cassi's back. She whispered harshly, "If you move, I'll blow your friggin' guts out."

"Please... I can't breathe."

The woman eased the pressure on Cassi's neck. She gulped in air and struggled to stay on her feet. Time had run out. Whoever had pulled into Ada's driveway would either be her backup, or become another victim.

She repositioned the ragged piece of glass in the palm of her hand. In a flash, she lifted her arm and brought down the crude weapon, stabbing blindly behind her. The sharp edges cut into her hand, but she dug in hard, driving the point into the woman's thigh.

"You bitch!" she shrieked. "I'll kill you right here!"

With surprising strength, the woman gave Cassi a mighty shove. She hit the ground hard, momentarily dazed and disoriented.

Blood gushed from her twin's wound and she doubled over, screaming, "You bitch! You fuckin' bitch!"

Bathed in the white glare of headlights, she ripped the broken shard of glass from her leg and tossed it aside. She'd dropped the gun, and tears streamed down her anguished face.

Apparently forgotten for the moment, Cassi hid in the shadows. The gun rested just a few feet from her shaking hand, but before she could react the woman dropped to her knees and grabbed up the weapon with her blood soaked hand.

She shoved herself to her feet, staggered, and looked around wildly.

Cassi couldn't move. Numbness settled in, and she fought to remain conscious. Then the woman settled her frantic gaze on her and raised the gun.

Cassi trembled, cowering beneath her twin's piercing stare. She had nothing left to give.

From inside Ada's cottage came a piercing, mournful, wail.

*****

Nick reached for his weapon almost before his truck rocked to a stop. He flung open the door. A misty, persistent rain swirled around the vehicle, and the blurry outline of a woman grabbed his attention. He crouched low, using the door as a shield as well as to support his gun.

Howls, one after another, came from the direction of Ada's cottage.

What the hell?

A woman lay on the ground curled in a tight ball, half in and half out of the beams piercing the night. Another woman swayed on her feet, clutching a gun in her hand. Nick's heart leapt into his throat when she took aim at the helpless figure huddled at her feet.

"Stop! Drop your weapon!" he shouted, sighting in with his Walther.

The woman with the gun whipped her head around. Her eyes were wide open and wild. Sick dread curled in Nick's gut.

For a second or two, his mind refused to acknowledge what he saw. Then the huddled figure rose into a crouch and lurched away.

The armed woman jerked around and fired wildly. The loud crack and spurt of flame sent Nick's heart hammering. The victim slumped over, face down and lifeless.

In all his years on the force, he'd never hesitated to use his weapon -- until now. This was Cassi. *His Cassi.*

Feeling oddly calm, he sighted in on the killer. The heart wrenching howls grew fainter. Rain pattered on his outstretched arm and ran in rivulets over the weapon clutched in his hand. He pointed it, dead center, at the woman he'd misread so totally that he didn't know if he'd ever get over the sick dread filling every thread of his being.

"Put down the gun, Cassi." His hollow, detached words sounded as if they came from someone else. Rain dripped from his hair into his eyes. He blinked and forced his gaze to meet the startlingly familiar face when she turned slowly. A strange smile crossed her face.

He steadied his hand, stepped from behind the door, and repeated, "Drop. Your. Weapon."

The scream of sirens transfixed the woman's calm, almost serene look into something so ugly, so evil it took Nick's breath away. With squealing tires and flashing lights, several cars converged on the scene.

"Nick?" The frail plea from the victim on the ground rocked him.

Confused, he hesitated.

Doors slammed. Running footsteps approached them.

"Nick, get down!" TJ bellowed. He hit Nick hard from behind, knocking him roughly aside before firing several shots in rapid succession.

In the split second Nick's attention had wavered, the woman fired again. The bullet went wild, bouncing off the Ridgeline's roof just before several rounds slammed into her. Nick caught a look of stunned surprise on her face as TJ's bullets hit home.

Stunned, Nick lay on the wet grass. His cousin seemed to be everywhere at once. Keeping his weapon aimed at the fallen shooter, he sent her gun skidding across the ground with a sure kick. More screaming sirens approached them, and brightly colored strobe lights pierced the mist.

TJ knelt beside the person the woman had shot.

"Cassi," he said, grasping her outstretched hand.

Oh, my God! Oh, God.

Nick scrambled forward. "TJ, my God, what the hell's going on?"

Strobe lights lit the scene, and the deadly tableau before him heightened the sick feeling in his stomach.

"Nick, come here," TJ ordered. He grabbed Nick's shaking hand and placed it on the victim's cold, limp arm. "She's alive. *This* is Cassi, and she's alive."

Nick ripped off his jacket and covered her, acting more on instinct and TJ's words than from any real comprehension as to what had just occurred. He'd seen the oozing wound on her upper back and automatically started basic first aid. He wanted to lift her, to cradle her in his arms, but he fought the urge.

Instinct kicked in instead. God, so much blood. He *had* to keep the pressure on her wound. He *had* to stop the blood.

The drizzle changed to a cold, steady rain, plastering Nick's shirt to his back. He shook so hard his teeth rattled. Out of the turmoil and shouting Marcy's calm, familiar voice brought a strange surge of relief.

Thank God, she was going to check on Rufus. He didn't want to think about what she'd find. The howling had stopped, and Nick feared the worst.

TJ placed a hand on his shoulder. "Come on, buddy. The EMTs are here. Let them help her."

"Sir?" An EMT stepped forward. "Move back, please."

Reluctant to leave Cassi's side, Nick inched away from her, and then collapsed. He sat, resting his arms on his bent knees and bracing his head with shaking hands while they worked on her. He had gone numb from the cold, the wet, and being unable to do one damn thing to help as they bent over her unmoving body.

Someone draped a coarse blanket over his shoulders. He glanced up as Marcy moved away.

TJ crouched beside him. "Are you all right?"

"I'm fine." He looked down at his hands. "This is Cassi's blood, not mine."

"Okay."

"Who is that other woman?" He met TJ's concerned gaze.

TJ glanced at the body behind them. A yellow blanket had been draped over her to protect the scene. "It's a long story. I'll fill you in later; now's not the time. I'm too concerned about Cassi, and you."

Nick grabbed TJ's arm as he started to get up. "I couldn't pull the trigger. I looked into her eyes and, by God, TJ, I couldn't do it."

"Come on." TJ extended his hand and pulled Nick to his feet. He placed both hands on Nick's shoulders and forced him to meet his steady gaze. "Any man in your position, not knowing the situation, would have reacted the same way. You had no way of knowing. None of us did."

Nick heaved a shaky sigh and attempted to pull himself together.

"Go," he said, gesturing to the chaos surrounding them. "It's your crime scene."

"Not anymore." TJ smiled grimly. "Montroy has secured the scene, and Dad's here. I'll go turn in my weapon. You know the drill."

"All too well," Nick responded.

Together they watched the ambulance carrying Cassi scream away into the night.

Chapter Twenty-Nine

A cold gust of wind accompanied Nick into the Pine Bluffs police station. Lon Peters paused in the act of shaking pills from a bottle.

Nick rubbed the dark stubble covering his face. "Mornin'."

"Root canal gone awry," Lon explained, gulping down water.

"Hmm. Care to share?"

Lon shook a couple more pills from the economy sized jar, spilling them onto the desk. "How is she?"

"She's alive. They'll move her from ICU today. She's got a long road to full recovery, but she'll make it." Nick scooped up the pills, crossed the room, and bent over the water fountain. Upon returning, he dropped into a chair, leaned back, and closed his eyes.

He felt like shit. The night Cassi had been shot, he'd been at Hamot Medical Center in Erie until dawn. Two days had passed since then, and he'd spent them running back and forth from Pine Bluffs to the hospital, getting little or no sleep.

On top of that, his supervisor in Philly was on his ass demanding that he return ASAP. He'd been given some leeway after explaining what had happened and asking for more time off, but cases were piling up and his boss's patience was running thin.

Taking a deep breath, he straightened and looked at Lon. "Is TJ busy?"

He'd seen his cousin's car out front and hoped to get help sorting out all the crap bouncing around in his head.

Lon lifted the phone and buzzed TJ's office. After a brief exchange, he hung up. "He said for me to send you on back."

"Thanks, Lon." He eyed the bottle of pills, "A few more of those and about two days sleep might help me feel human again." Lon chuckled, and Nick pushed himself out of the chair and headed for TJ's office.

He'd lied. A truckload of pain pills and a week in bed would not erase his deep-seated pain.

He discovered TJ was not alone.

"Nick, come on in. Grab some coffee and have a seat." TJ was clean shaven and wore a fresh, crisp uniform. Dark circles framed sleep-depraved eyes. "You remember Raife Samuels and Fred Conners. They're from Ohio's OIU."

Both men had been at Ada's that night, but for the life of him Nick couldn't remember them. Shaking their hands, Nick apologized. "Excuse my muddled brain, guys. I know you were at the scene, but I don't recall meeting either of you."

"Been there, pal," Raife responded in a deep voice. "Get some coffee. Caffeine rules."

Nick did so, and when he rejoined them, TJ asked, "How's Cassandra?"

Nick repeated what he'd told Lon. Somehow the words sounded like a standard news release, but they were all he had. Ada had relayed frequent updates during surgery. Upon waking, however, Cassi had refused to see him. No amount of pleading or threatening could get Ada Blaine to go against her injured niece's wishes.

"She's lucky," TJ said. "Had it been a twenty-two round instead of a twenty-five, there'd have been more damage."

Nick agreed. "Apparently the round tore through a couple of vital arteries and nicked her right lung. She was in surgery almost three hours. I'm told she's damn lucky to be alive."

"I have the round," TJ stated. "It's key evidence."

"What else have you got, TJ? I have some idea what transpired prior to that night, but the facts are jumbled, like a jigsaw puzzle."

TJ flipped open the folder on his desk and handed Nick a photo. "Recognize her?"

"Of course, that's the promo shot of Cassi the press used when Morelli's murder hit the news."

"Right. Now meet Sadie Mitchell." He handed over two pictures of Sadie; one with Jack Lefavor, the other with Robert Morelli.

"Holy shit." Nick's headache resurfaced. Grasping a picture in each hand, he compared the photos. The first time he'd seen them, Nick had assumed the woman was Cassi. Just as he'd wrongly assumed she could kill another human being. He'd been dead wrong on both counts.

"My sentiments exactly." Raife leaned in to view the photos. "She sure fooled us."

"Twins have identical DNA," TJ stated. "We're in the process of running samples from both women."

"How'd you pull it all together?" Nick asked.

"Persistence."

Tearing his eyes from the photos, Nick met TJ's steady gaze. He had to smile. His cousin had just tossed back advice Nick had drummed into TJ's head since the day he'd pinned on a badge. At that moment, he regretted all the grief he'd given TJ for doing exactly what he'd been trained to do.

"Despite your objections to my checking up on Cassandra, I never stopped," TJ admitted. "One thing led to another, and fortunately I connected with Mrs. Ruby Gilliam. A woman with a very sharp memory."

"The one from Duquesne Clinic?" Nick asked.

"The same." TJ nodded. "Her call the night Raife and Fred arrived in town sent us scrambling to find Cassi. After hearing from her, we knew Sadie Mitchell was in town and that Cassi's life was in danger."

Fighting fatigue, Nick lowered himself into a chair. "Put the pieces together for me."

"Apparently, Alice Melnor, Ada's sister, gave birth to twins at the clinic." TJ dug into the file for his notes. "Cassi was in a room with her mother, but Sadie developed problems and her doctor placed her in a medical observation unit."

"So Cassi's mom left the clinic and took Cassi with her," Nick deduced. "I'm aware her mom died shortly thereafter, and Cassi was adopted. What happened to Sadie?"

"According to Ada, her sister contacted her from the hospital in Erie. By then it was too late. Had Alice stayed in Pittsburgh at the clinic, the infection she'd developed would have been caught sooner. Maybe the twins wouldn't have been separated, maybe Alice would have lived, and maybe Sadie wouldn't have been dumped into a system that failed to recognize or treat mental illness.

"Hell." TJ threw up his hands. "Maybes and what ifs. The bottom line's this: There was no way to trace Alice. In Pittsburgh, she'd falsely given *Mitchell* instead of *Melnor* as her last name, and Mitchell stuck with *Sadie.*

"Cassi got lucky, and Sadie got shit-canned, eventually turning to drugs."

Nick leaned forward. "And when fate put Cassi's face all over the news, Sadie set out to settle the score for being abandoned by their mother."

"Amen." TJ slapped the folder closed and slumped in his chair. "In her twisted mind, Cassi was the enemy."

"Did she know Cassi was her twin?" Nick asked.

"We'll never know for sure. She'd dug deep enough to track Cassi almost from the time she was adopted. Sadie's birth date was authentic. Authorities guessed at Cassi's since Ada's sister had taken her and escaped to Erie." TJ shrugged. "But the dates were close, and after Sadie saw Cassi, well…"

Nick turned to Fred and Raife. "I heard about your history with LeFavor. Can you pin Morelli's murder on him?"

"Doubtful." Raife refilled his cup. "Although we have a tentative ID from an employee at the Erie Sport Store. A man matching LeFavor's description purchased a wooden-handled hunting knife the day before Morelli was killed."

"We may have gotten a print match from the scene if Rufus hadn't slobbered all over the knife handle." TJ smiled ruefully. "The prints we lifted were smudged, and all were Cassi's. We're combing the cabin where Morelli was killed, but so far we haven't found anything."

"We can't put him at the scene," Raife admitted. "And Erie had to release him when they didn't have anything concrete to hold him on. He's no doubt slithered away by now." He turned to Fred. "Hell, partner, looks like we've still got a job."

Shortly thereafter, Raife and Fred departed.

The day was raw, and the clouds overhead threatened more rain. Nick and TJ hustled the few blocks to the Pines Dinor. Over the first decent food he'd eaten in days, Nick revealed a plan that had formed in his mind.

He'd already talked to Uncle Tom, TJ's dad. Encouraged by the support he'd gotten on that front, he now forged ahead, hoping his idea would take hold. If TJ agreed, all three lives -- Uncle Tom's, TJ's, and his own -- would be altered forever.

Chapter Thirty

"Are you comfortable, honey?" Ada adjusted the throw covering Cassi's legs. "Here, I made fresh tea."

She placed a tray bearing tea and muffins on a nearby table. Steam curled from the teapot, and the aroma of fresh-baked cranberry muffins made Cassi's mouth water.

"You're responsible for these three pounds I can't lose." Cassi repositioned the cushions and chuckled at the look Ada tossed over her shoulder.

"Oh, look outside," Ada called from the kitchen.

Fat snowflakes drifted past the glass doors overlooking the garden. Already a thin coat covered the grass and Ada's dormant herbs. Cassi loved snow. These first flakes marked the passing of time, and her eyes were drawn to the spot where Sadie Mitchell had tried to kill her.

The night her world had changed.

Two months had passed, and she still had nightmares about white hot pain, Rufus howling, and Nick calling her name.

Rufus rose from his coveted spot on the hearth. He stretched and circled before resettling with a thump, causing his tags to jingle.

He'd had a rushed trip to the veterinarian that night. Thank goodness the bullet Sadie had put in him, meaning to silence him forever, had missed all of his vital organs and bones and lodged in his shoulder muscle.

"My hero," she said, giving a deep sigh. Her eyes were drawn to the crackling fire, and memories from that pivotal night in September came rushing back.

Thinking about Nick McGraw reopened a fresh wound. She'd experienced love completely for the fist time with him, and he had shredded her heart.

"How are the muffins?" Ada settled in a nearby chair with the morning paper and a steaming cup of tea.

Cassi glanced up. "I haven't tried them yet."

"Cassi..." Ada lifted her concerned eyes. "You feeling all right?"

"I'm fine." Cassi forced a smile. "The fire's relaxing, and my mind drifted."

Her aunt studied her for a long moment before returning to her paper. Unshed tears burned Cassi's eyes. Weeks of working through physical pain and the mental anguish of recurring nightmares always pushed to the surface when she relaxed her guard. Like the rising tide of a turbulent sea, vivid memories threatened to force open the tightly guarded floodgates in her mind.

Her physical strength had returned. In that respect, her healing was nearly complete. But sometimes, like now, deep, soul-wrenching mental pain crept into her thoughts.

Throughout her recovery, bit by bit, she'd learned about her twin sister. She'd be forever grateful for TJ's tenacity. A single phone call had sent him rushing through the night.

"I was scared shitless," he'd insisted, when describing his state of mind.

Thank God he'd arrived in time. He'd saved her life. But in doing so, Sadie Mitchell had died.

Cassi put aside her half-eaten muffin. Her tea had gone cold. Rufus rose and ambled over to her, eyeing the remnants on her plate with soulful eyes. Sneaking a glance at Ada, Cassi snuck him the remaining bits of muffin.

Satisfied, he limped to the patio door and stared out at the falling snow. Welcoming the distraction, Cassi bundled up and snapped on his lead. Invigorating frigid air greeted them as they stepped outside, and snow continued to fall as they made their way to the path along the lakeshore.

Cold, gray water lapped at the shoreline, and painful memories rolled over her. The autumn day she and Nick had kayaked through the crystal clear water seemed so long ago.

She'd been told he'd waited through the night at the hospital during her surgery. Cassi couldn't forget the look on his face when he'd used her name and demanded she drop the gun. Granted, he'd assumed Sadie was her and had concluded she was about to kill someone. He was a cop, wasn't he? And that's what cops did.

However, he'd known from the start he'd be leaving Pine Bluffs when his vacation ended, so she had instructed Ada to send him away. Her decision to do so might have been unfair. But she'd been weak and vulnerable at the time. She couldn't have faced a painful goodbye.

Apparently he hadn't forced the issue, for several days later she overheard TJ telling her aunt that Nick had returned to Philadelphia. He'd gone back to his dark-haired beauty, she'd surmised. Back to his life in the city.

During the Thanksgiving holiday, she'd returned to Fox Chapel and settled her parents' estate. While there, another shocking revelation had come to light.

Sadie had been responsible for the fire at Fox Chapel Fitness. Two young men had identified her from pictures TJ had forwarded to Fox Chapel PD. She'd paid them with cocaine to burn down Cassi's business.

Cassi decided to cut her losses and leave Fox Chapel. She worried about Lanie, though. What would she do? As usual, though, her friend had landed on both feet.

During Cassi's stay in the hospital and her recovery at Ada's, Lanie had been a frequent visitor. Whenever TJ's and Lanie's paths had inadvertently crossed, sparks had flown. Their strange personality clash amused Cassi. Lanie's attitude suggested she disliked TJ, but on several occasions she'd caught Lanie checking him out as he walked away.

The settlement from Cassi's parents' estate proved generous. So much to her aunt's delight, she'd decided to postpone any decisions regarding her future until the first of the year. She put her belongings in storage and moved in with Ada.

Rufus shook, sending a shower of snow flying.

"Come here, you," she said, and Rufus hobbled over, his tail whipping. She gave him an intense hug and ducked her head to avoid his avid kisses.

Several new inches of snow coated the ground as they retraced their path to the cottage. After stomping her boots and giving Rufus a vigorous rub to remove the clinging snow, she stepped into the warm, fragrant kitchen. The walk had lightened her spirits, and Ada stirred something on the stove that smelled delicious.

Despite the pain and heartache in the recent past, Cassi felt blessed.

Losing her parents had created a vast emptiness inside her. Losing Nick, after tumbling helplessly into love with him, left her standing on the edge of an unknown abyss.

Ada Blaine had made the emptiness less threatening, and her unconditional love had pulled Cassi back from the unknown brink.

Simple things cradled her fragile state of being. The first snow of winter, wet puppy kisses, and the warmth and love within the cottage by the lake would help her continue to heal.

Ada kept stirring. She glanced around and bestowed a tender smile on Cassi. That calm, simple gesture made Cassi feel loved and wanted.

"You look better, honey," Ada said, scooping up the hot soup with a tasting spoon. "Here, taste this and tell me what you think."

Cassi took the offered sample. Her eyes met Ada's, and she said. "I think it's good to be home."

Chapter Thirty-One

Nick hauled one last box into the cabin through the pelting snow. He kicked the door shut and added his burden to an accumulating stack. Scanning the room, he pulled off his thick gloves, mentally ticking off projects he'd planned for the coming months. For starters, he wanted to sand and refinish the mantel, followed by updating the ancient plumbing. Maybe he'd enlarge the bath next to his bedroom and install a walk-in shower. He could do whatever time and his money allowed, for the cabin in Pine Bluffs now belonged to him.

He shrugged out of his heavy parka, crossed the room, and with a long wooden matchstick, set the stacked kindling ablaze. The flickering flames conjured up past images, and a vision of Cassi's satiny skin glowing in the firelight teased his senses.

He'd never forget how she'd quivered and moistened in response to his bold exploration. Shoving clenched fists into his pockets, he watched the growing flames and absorbed the heat.

The jangle of his new phone chased away his pleasurable thoughts. Uttering a curse, he hurried across the room.

"McGraw," he answered gruffly.

"For Pete's sake, Nick." TJ laughed. "You're not in Philly anymore, and you're not working. A normal 'hello' or a nice seasonal greeting would suffice."

"Well, Happy Friggin' Holidays." Nick chuckled, dropping into a chair. "What's up, cousin? I've barely unpacked, and already you're buggin' me."

"Don't shoot the messenger. Mom insisted I check on you and invite you to dinner. I must advise you, though, before you decide to decline for any reason, that she's been baking up an avalanche of Christmas cookies."

Leaning back, Nick grinned foolishly at the ceiling. The unpacked boxes could wait. Outside, lazy snowflakes drifted down, making the season perfect. *Almost.*

The day he'd left Pine Bluffs in September, he'd set the course for his future. His first hurtle had been easier to cross than he had anticipated.

Tom McGraw had been considering retirement for quite some time. When Nick announced he wanted to apply for the position, his uncle had adjusted his time table and moved his retirement date ahead.

Next, he had a revealing talk with TJ. His cousin admitted that while he liked working for a small department, he'd applied for the State Police. This gave Nick a clear field to submit *his* application for chief.

A single nagging detail had yet to be dealt with, and Nick had a plan. He would be placing his heart in jeopardy, but nonetheless, he had to try. Past mistakes were behind him, where they belonged, and Nick was confident his decision to return to Pine Bluffs was the right one. He'd had plenty of time to reflect on that week in September, and he was betting the woman who'd shared herself so openly, so wantonly, with him in this cabin would eventually be his.

"Hey." TJ broke into his musings. "Are you coming or not?"

"I'll clean up and be right over."

"Great. See you soon." TJ broke the connection.

Nick showered, pulled on jeans and a sweater, and took time to bank the hot coals. After donning his coat, he paused.

A single lamp, along with the glow of simmering embers, enhanced the cabin's inviting atmosphere.

He was home, finally home.

*****

Despite the relentless snow, Cassi made one final trip to Erie and completed her holiday shopping. She hated the mall. Smaller shops west of the city offered items more to her taste.

Wild Birds Unlimited stocked a unique variety of garden accessories. A bronze sundial and a natural stone English hare would grace Ada's garden come spring. At Relish, a store specializing in beach glass jewelry, she purchased a pair of eye-catching earrings. The smooth green stones were perfect for Lanie.

As she reached the outskirts of Pine Bluffs, visibility diminished. Her trusty Honda never faltered, yet she was glad to see the welcome sign appear through the wall of white.

As she rounded the curve at the far end of the lake, something caught her eye. Foolishly, her heart fluttered. Easing to the berm, she stopped to study a tiny square of light barely visible through the trees.

A light gleamed in Nick's cabin. No, not *Nick's* cabin, she firmly corrected, the cabin where Nick had stayed. Lulled by the soft click of the wipers and a classic carol touting a blue Christmas, she stared through the veil of snow. There was no sign of life, no vehicle in sight. Fresh snow made it difficult to determine if anyone had been there recently. More than likely out-of-towners visiting relatives for the holidays were staying there, she rationalized, pulling back onto the snow-covered road.

Nick McGraw would be preparing for Christmas in the city, enjoying all the excitement and crowds rushing about. He certainly wouldn't find a tiny cabin in Pine Bluffs suitable for holiday celebrating. The disdainful comment about Pine Bluffs' *lifestyle* made by Nick's companion on that long ago night came to mind. No, an isolated cabin would certainly not have the *style* he'd want for his lady friend.

A welcoming glow came from Ada's windows. Setting thoughts of Nick aside, Cassi gathered her packages and tromped through the snow to the wreath-bedecked cottage door. Lights adorning their Christmas tree cast a colorful reflection on the snow through the corner window.

Ada glanced up as Cassi came through the door and skillfully slid cookies fresh from the oven onto a cooling rack. "My word, girl. Did you buy out the mall?"

"I wasn't near the mall," Cassi declared, removing her coat and toeing off her boots. "I did just fine, far, far away from Peach Street."

She snagged a warm cookie.

"Heavenly," she mumbled around the gooey concoction, juggling her purchases and maneuvering down the hallway to her room.

Later, enjoying hot chili, Cassi paused and tore off a chunk of crusty bread. "I saw a light in the McGraw's cabin, the one Nick rented last fall."

"Hmm, someone must be staying there." Ada's indifferent comment seemed odd. Whatever went on in Pine Bluffs rarely escaped her. Cassi chewed thoughtfully. Never breaking stride, her aunt continued to remove cookies from the oven.

"This is the last batch," Ada said, setting the hot pan aside. "We have more than enough for the Christmas Eve gathering at Tom and Mary's. You haven't forgotten about that, have you?"

"No, I haven't." Cassi carried her empty bowl to the sink. She'd become attached to the McGraws during her recovery. The family seldom mentioned Nick in her presence, and despite her curiosity, she stubbornly refused to ask about him.

"I'm sure the evening at the McGraws will be lovely. But what I'm most looking forward to is *our* first Christmas together." She crossed the room and wrapped her arms around Ada. "The holidays are for family, and I thank God every day that you came into my life."

Chapter Thirty-Two

Christmas Eve snow held magic for Cassi. As a child she'd creep from her bed, quiet as a mouse, and peek out her window to watch the sky for those first flakes.

Tonight was a mixed blessing. As if on cue, snowflakes started to drift down at dusk. They clung to exposed surfaces like festive garlands created by Mother Nature.

Her eyes filled, overflowing like the memories spilling from her heart. She longed for those no longer here to share this night with her.

The swish of fabric, accompanied by the subtle clicking of heels on tile, met her ears, and she blinked scenes of Christmases past into submission. Her eyes widened as Ada approached her. She wore a stunning outfit, part of her early Christmas gift from Cassi. A few days prior, they'd visited a spa in Erie together. Had the pampering not been a gift, Ada, no doubt, would have balked. But she'd loved every minute of it, and tonight she looked amazing.

Beneath a flowing cream-colored jacket her aunt wore a deep green shell with a scooped neck. Her wide-legged taupe pants moved gracefully as she walked, and her simple strappy low heeled shoes completed her outfit.

"Oh, Aunt Ada." Cassi held out her hand. "You're beautiful."

Ada smoothed a soft wave sweeping her cheek. "You don't think the hair is too much?"

"You'll knock em' dead." Cassi touched the small cluster of green stones dangling from one of Ada's ears and grinned. She did a little twirl with one finger. "Turn around."

Ada complied.

"You're quite a sight yourself," she said, looking Cassi over from head to toe. "I think it's the first time I've seen you in a dress. The simple shirtwaist style is classic, and brown velvet makes your eyes look like melted chocolate. The dress is you, honey. No doubt about it."

Cassi touched the open neckline of her dress. She'd left the top three buttons undone, and the wide collar framed her face. She'd added a pair of gold drop earrings for a touch of class. "You're sure I don't need anything around my neck? I feel kind of bare."

She fiddled with the buttons again.

Ada tilted her head and studied her. "Not unless you have something very simple, maybe a charm on a chain. Do you?"

"No, I don't have anything like that. This will have to do." Cassi moved to a nearby mirror and shrugged. She ran her hand over her newly-highlighted hair.

Ada glanced at her watch.

"We have plenty of time to enjoy our own little party here first," she said, crossing the room and switching on the multi-disc player.

Cassi had been pleased to discover they shared a love for holiday music, from classics to modern pop.

Ada brought out a tray of fruit, cheese, and crusty bread. Pouring them each a glass of Shiraz, she lifted her glass to toast their first Christmas Eve together.

Cassi's gaze swept the room. Festive natural touches adorned the tables and shelves. Off to one side, a small table held an array of glass vases filled with sprigs of dried herbs, and a basket of fresh cut holly sat near the fireplace. The nativity set placed beneath the tree was one she'd had since she was a child.

Balancing her wine glass, she knelt to examine the brightly wrapped gifts beneath the tinsel-laden branches. Like a curious child, she poked several bearing her name. She'd been sizing them up, making guesses as to what they might contain.

All of a sudden, she noticed a small square box wrapped in glossy red paper and tied with a delicate gold bow. She lifted the box and examined a tiny envelope tucked beneath the ribbon.

"Ada, I didn't see this earlier." She raised her eyes to Ada. "Is it from you?"

"No, dear." Ada sipped her wine and carefully selected a sugared green grape from the platter. "I'm not responsible for that lovely gift."

Cassi rose, bringing the box with her, and walked over to stand in front of her aunt. Ada selected another grape.

"Do you know who delivered it?" Cassi prodded.

Taking her time, Ada swallowed the succulent fruit she'd popped into her mouth. Then she turned her full attention to Cassi.

"Open the card, honey. I think you have a decision to make," she said quietly, and left Cassi alone.

Cassi's knees shook. She eased into a chair by the fireplace and slipped the card free. The front of the card read *Cassi,* and inside was a white, gold-edged gift card. With trembling hands, she unfolded the card.

"I'll be waiting," she read aloud. The note was signed, *Nick.*

She closed her eyes and swallowed hard. When she looked again, the message hadn't changed. Why would Nick get her a gift? And how had it gotten here? She glanced around, as if he might materialize before her eyes. The tree lights glowed, and the flames in the fireplace created shifting shadows. But no tall, handsome man with mesmerizing hazel eyes appeared.

With trembling fingers, she slipped the ribbon from the box. Her breath caught when she lifted the lid. Displayed on a simple bed of white velvet lay a shiny copper penny set in a delicate gold rope frame. The tiny medallion hung from a gold chain and shimmered in the firelight.

"He's at the cabin, Cassi." Ada's voice startled her. Overcome by the gift, she hadn't heard her aunt's approach.

Cassi snapped the lid of the box closed.

Why is he doing this?

Over the past few months, she'd devoted time and effort to forget time spent in that cabin -- the smell of burning logs, the clean, crisp scent of Nick's aftershave, and the instantaneous jolt she experienced whenever she gazed into his eyes. Returning to the cabin and being assaulted by those memories would be like running smack into a brick wall.

Shameless need curled deep inside her, however, chipping away at the protective barrier she'd built around her heart.

"You owe it to yourself, and to Nick, to face your feelings for one another," Ada said, cupping Cassi's cheek with her palm. "Whatever they may be," she added, and the protest died on Cassi's lips.

Chapter Thirty-Three

Nick's long, torturous wait ended when Cassi's Honda appeared through the falling snow. She stopped in front of the cabin. Considerable time passed before she opened the door and stepped out.

Heart hammering as if he'd run a marathon, Nick swung the cabin door wide.

Mere steps away from him, Cassi froze. A mantel of snow adorned her cascading hair. She grasped her coat lapels, pulled them close, and raised her luminous eyes to his.

If she walked out of his life forever, he would never forget her stunning beauty.

"Come inside, Cassi. We need to talk."

Nick closed the door with a soft click. He took a moment, hands pressed against the rough wood surface, before turning and moving toward her.

Cassi spun away from him, facing into the room. He placed his hands on her shoulders. "Let me take your coat."

Removing her gloves, she tucked them, along with her keys, into her pocket. He helped her shrug out of the heavy garment, then stepped away and hung it up.

On a table by the window sat the tiny tree he had decorated. She moved closer to it.

"It's real." She touched its feathery branches, making the tiny white lights dance.

Nick dropped his gaze to the penny medallion resting within the framework of her open collar. She shivered when his eyes moved lower, roaming in bold admiration, before returning to her face. "Why wouldn't I have a real tree?"

"I assumed something so... so *unstylish* wouldn't be to your taste."

He moved closer.

Squaring her shoulders, Cassi lifted her chin.

Unfazed by her challenge, he lifted the penny medallion, adjusted her collar, and repositioned the pendant on her skin.

"I don't know about the tree, but a brown velvet dress and sexy leather boots look very stylish to me." He angled his head and admired the hint of thigh exposed by a discrete slit in her skirt. "The whole package is definitely to my taste."

"Really?" Tears welled in Cassi's eyes, and she looked away. "Or am I just a convenience for when you come to Pine Bluffs on vacation, or for the holidays?" She bit off each word. "Your girlfriend in Philadelphia must resent the fact that you're here again, or is she going to join you, despite the distasteful lifestyle?"

"Cassi," Nick coaxed. "Look at me." Her patent, ramrod stiff posture contrasted starkly with the pain reflected in her eyes. "I should have known better. I screwed up that night. Things looked bad, and I let them spin out of control. Whatever was once between Michelle and me is over. It was that night."

He lifted his hand helplessly, and let it fall. "Later, when I saw you on the ground covered in blood, I almost lost it. I knew then that I'd fallen in love with you."

Cassi's mouth opened, then snapped shut.

Ahh. Now he had her attention. "When you refused to see me, I had no choice but to return to Philadelphia. I'd taken extra days off to make sure you'd recover, and my boss insisted I come back to work. He went ballistic when I marched into his office a week later and gave him my notice."

"You quit?" Cassi widened her eyes and searched his face. "And you... love me?

Hearing the catch in her voice, Nick moved in and pulled her into his arms. To his relief, she melted against him.

"Falling in love with you wasn't part of my plan. I came to Pine Bluffs for a vacation, intending to sort through my life and see why I felt as if something were missing." He caressed her hair and rested his cheek against the silken softness. "Then I met you, and things went haywire."

"Well." Cassi snuggled closer and fingered the lapel of his jacket. "I certainly didn't try to screw up your plan. I had enough problems of my own."

Blinking away moisture, she gave him a reprimanding frown. "Why didn't you tell me how you felt?"

"Because, honey," he rasped out, "I didn't know I'd fallen until I'd almost lost you, and then facing a future without you wasn't acceptable."

She cupped his face with gentle hands. "So now you're unemployed and living in your aunt and uncle's cabin."

"Not quite." He covered her hands with his, and smiled into her concerned, gorgeous eyes. "As of January first, I'm the new Chief of Police in Pine Bluffs. Uncle Tom is retiring, eagerly, I might add, and this humble abode is now mine."

She kissed him, and just like that his tilting universe settled. For now he'd come full circle, back to where he belonged. His pounding heart resettled, its beat strong and steady.

Fate had tipped the scale. Beginning with a fatal plane crash and ending with attempted murder. Like falling dominos, a series of seemingly unrelated events had occurred and ended -- thank God -- with Cassi tumbling into his arms.

He brushed his lips over hers. "A penny for your thoughts?"

"My thoughts?" Her mouth moved against his. "Why, Nick McGraw, I think I love you."

Nick steered them toward the crackling fire. A faint frown flitted across her brow. "Hey, brown eyes, then why the sad face?"

"Oh, Nick," she said, touching his gift as it sparkled in the firelight. "I didn't thank you for this. It's perfect, but I have nothing for you."

"Oh, honey." He pushed the collar of her velvet dress aside and inhaled the scent from her deliciously fragrant skin. Nibbling his way downward, he undid her buttons one by one. "I'm sure we can think of something."

Deadly Triad Book Two: Deadly Revenge

About Nancy Kay

Nancy Kay resides near Lake Erie in Western Pennsylvania with her husband, a former member of the Marines and the Pennsylvania State Police Department, thus providing valuable insight for her stories. At various times in her life she has worked in banking, as a veterinary assistant, and as an aerobics instructor. She pursues a healthy lifestyle and enjoys her part time job in an exclusive lingerie boutique. As a member of Romance Writers of America and three affiliated chapters, she keeps involved and informed while pursuing her writing career. Her stories are set in small towns and inland communities scattered along the shores of the Great Lakes amongst rolling grape vineyards and glorious sunsets. They focus on romance, intertwined with the love of hearth, home and family, yet are sprinkled with suspense, danger and intrigue.

Learn more about Nancy at **www.nancykayauthor.com**.